*Praise*

## KATE GALLOWAY

'A perfect heartwarming read full of secrets, tears and laughter all set in a glorious and dramatic location. An absolute delight!' *Clare Marchant*

'Hilarious. Wholesome. Wildly romantic.' *Laura Carter*

'Romantic, fresh and incredibly uplifting - Wild Swimming is a must-read.' *Claire McCauley*

'The sweetest, unputdownable rom com.' *Mandy Baggot*

'As invigorating as a plunge into a Highland loch and as heart-warming as a fireside cuddle, this unforgettable romance is the perfect escapist read.' *Jenni Keer*

'A ravishing, mist-filled sigh of a book. An ode to the Scottish Highlands and its breathtaking beauty, and a love letter in finding yourself. I adored it.' *Polly Crosby*

'If you're looking for adventure, WILD SWIMMING has it in spades — a heartfelt story of self-discovery, a swoon-worthy, sizzling unexpected connection, and stunning descriptions of Scotland. A fun, escapist read at its best.' *Claire Kershaw*

# Also by Kate Galloway

Plain Sailing

# Wild Swimming

Kate Galloway

WILD SWIMMING

Copyright © 2025 by Kate Galloway

Published worldwide by Firstlight Press

This edition published in 2025

Copyright © 2025 by Kate Galloway. The right of Kate Galloway to be identified as the author of this work has been asserted in accordance with the Copyright, Design and Patents Act 1988.

All rights reserved. No part of this book may be reproduced in any form or by any electronic or mechanical means, including information storage and retrieval systems, without written permission from the author, except for the use of brief quotations in a book review.

All characters and events in this book are entirely fictional. Any references to historical events, real people, or real locales are used fictitiously. Other names, characters, places, and incidents are the product of the author's imagination, and any resemblance to actual events or locales or persons, living or dead, is entirely coincidental.

Cover design by Summer Grove

Edited by Greenstone Literary Agency

***For my daughter,***

*You are my greatest story.*

*Your kindness, strength, and boundless imagination inspire me every day. May you always believe in the magic of love and the power of your own dreams.*

# Chapter One
## Day One

"Hi, I'm Fliss" I smile broadly, as though I haven't just lied to the three strangers with whom I'm destined to spend the next two weeks.

They smile back politely, and I have no idea if they've already done introductions, so I quickly take a seat next to a young, blonde woman in activewear whose attention is already fixed back on the phone gripped tightly in her hand.

A tannoy chimes an announcement over our heads. I listen carefully to the echoing voice calling for last boarders at gate eleven and wonder, not for the first time today, where I'll be by sundown.

Fliss. What made me say that? I haven't been called Fliss since I was in primary school. My brother, Frank, found the syllables of Felicity too difficult to get his mouth around and had gotten stuck at the first one.

Fliss? Probably the same need for anonymity that made me pick a rucksack that is almost the same height as I am, and walking boots, rather than my usual uniform of jeans and a Breton top, with added wheelie suitcase. This is a wellbeing *trek* after all, I can at least pretend I know what I'm doing. A secret holiday destination that was advertised by the friend of a friend whose company it is as '*a chance to connect with nature and yourselves*' with the added caveat that it's '*not for the fainthearted*'. I wonder if it's too late to swap for an all-inclusive in Spain with a pool bar and tanned locals. Either of those would work just as well for the purpose of fleeing the country to escape my looming birthday and a party my parents were desperate to organise for me. Who wants to celebrate turning thirty-five? Not me.

Looking at the other trekkers—gathered under the company sign by the seats outside M&S as instructed—I'm glad I haven't brought my old bright pink wheelie suitcase that I purchased deliberately so it would stand out at airport carousels. They have large rucksacks in front of them too, precariously leaning on their knees so they don't touch the person next to them. I wonder if they've also spent the days prior to departure worrying which rucksack to buy to look like they've been trekking the hidden wonders of the world all their life and not just the occasional dog walk with friends over some churned up muddy fields in Kent.

The email had said there would be four of us, so this is it. Here are the other fearless explorers who put their lives and holiday goals in the hands of *Hidden Holidays*, a company who provide luxury getaways designed to release its customers from their idèe fixe in magical natural surroundings.

It had sounded too good to be true. A much-needed getaway—even if I did only book it to escape my parents—*and* a chance to reconnect with myself that I can only afford because I have no dependents, an almost paid-off mortgage, and no real commitments except for my work at an investment bank. Actually, now I come to think of it, maybe they're the real reasons I am hiding behind a persona called Fliss.

Phone girl scoffs at something as she's scrolling, shaking her head in mirth, her tightly plaited French braids holding up her eyelids. I offer her a look of solidarity which is quite hard from this angle without it looking like I'm trying to catch a glimpse of her screen. The airport check-in area is surprisingly deserted and I hope that we're not about to be pretend kidnapped like Louis Theroux on his weird weekends' documentary. That would *not* be good for the wellbeing, no matter how exhilarating. At least we're in Gatwick, so my hopes are high for a long-haul flight with enough time to finish my book. Warm clothes and waterproofs were on the helpful list that was sent out with the email a few weeks ago, along with swimwear and thermals, so I've been thinking perhaps cryotherapy in Croatia or thalassotherapy in Sardinia. Though maybe those countries are hot in August too which would negate the need for thermals. England certainly is right now, my stylish topknot is at risk of wilting into a normal bun.

A young man rushes towards us, bringing with him a

cool waft of airport air and the energy of someone who loves adventure and excitement; either that or he's just downed five espressos. He's cute. And outdoorsy. And could be straight out of uni he's so youthful.

"Intrepid explorers," he says in a posh accent, clapping his hands together. "Welcome to Gatwick and to the first leg of your *Hidden Holidays* adventure. I am your group leader, James. I will be with you throughout your journey as a guide to what may seem like the impossible to start with, but you'll thank me for it when I drop you back here in two weeks' time."

Things are looking promising. The Instagram scroller next to me looks up from her screen, her attention fully grabbed by James' muscular arms making even a clip board look sexy. He's holding what looks like it could be our itinerary. I try to sneak a peek at the title, but he tilts the board out of my sightline with a side-eye and a flash of a smile.

"It's roll call time." He reads out the names of the others as they raise their hands in acknowledgement.

"Brianna Kirby." *Instagram scroller.*

"Maya Inkton." *She reminds me of those girls at festivals who still look good by the time the final day comes around; she has a proper rucksack and walking boots that look well worn.*

"Oliver Harris." *So far hidden behind the pop-up sign we were told to look out for, I've only just really noticed him, and he looks as uncomfortable as I feel.*

"And last but by no means least, Felicity Taylor?"

"Yep," I say, flinching at his use of my whole name. "But please, call me Fliss!"

## Wild Swimming

I hope he isn't going to swap out my rucksack for my pink wheeled suitcase or tell the rest of the gang that I can't actually sleep without an eye mask and ear plugs and the calming scent of a diffuser filling my bedroom with lavender. Those beauties I shall save for another day when we're fully engaged in whatever exotic adventure we're about to embark on. I can forgo the eye mask for a safari tent in South Africa.

James tucks the clipboard under his arm and claps again, clasping his hands together in glee.

Okay guys," he says, leaning in conspiratorially as we all quieten to hear where we will be jetting off to. *Switzerland. No, the Himalayas. Matchu Pitchu.* "Let's gather up our luggage and get on our way. If you'll all follow me to the boarding gate we can check in and get on our plane. We'll be in Inverness by lunchtime."

# Chapter Two

"Scotland?" Brianna the Instagram scroller splutters in a Welsh accent as beautiful as she is, her phone long forgotten as she drags her rucksack off the floor and throws it over her Fendi crop top and matching orange leggings. I'm not sure how she's taking all the weight on her shoulders, she's so petite. The rest of the group laugh awkwardly as they plod after our guide with their own rucksacks in tow.

But to be fair to her, it was exactly what was going through my head too.

*Scotland?*

I haven't paid over the odds for a secret holiday destination, curated by the very best for the very needy, to be hauled off to bloody Scotland. No. James, the guide, must be pulling our legs. I laugh as I throw my backpack over one shoulder, trying not to topple as my centre of gravity shifts with the weight of hundreds of pounds worth of new clothes bought especially for llama trekking in the Andes. Not Scotland.

Maya brushes past me, her own huge bag clipped and fastened securely around her white t-shirted chest that makes her tan look like she's flown straight from somewhere that's definitely not Scotland. Piles of curly, brown hair are wrapped up on the top of her head in a colourful scarf and her socks are rolled down to the tops of her walking boots with a casual ease that screams *I didn't just buy these*. Her mouth is set in a firm line as she races to catch up and walk with Brianna, probably because they're a similar young age and I look like I'm a tweed scarf away from a Barbour advert. Oliver slopes behind us, sighing loudly every so often, so I can't really get a proper look at him without being too obvious. Our guide strides ahead and I have to skip every so often to keep up with his long legs. This backpack is really quite heavy.

My eyes scan the boards above each of the check-in desks, hoping that James will lead us to the famous blue and white of British Airways or the swash of red of Emirates whose signs still flash with the hope of exotic destinations. But we keep walking, all the way past the queues of lucky people at these desks and down to the bright orange queue of our own. Inverness emblazoned in letter flaps above a woman who is checking boarding passes with a big smile on her face. I watch the letters, hoping that when James reaches them, they will flutter like they do in the movies and our true destination will be revealed. But they remain firmly resolute as we join the back of the queue.

## Wild Swimming

"I was kind of hoping for a different part of the world, at least," Brianna whispers back to me, flapping about in her handbag as she pulls out a leather travel pouch. She has a sing-song accent straight out of the Welsh hymn-books. "Still, you never know. Maybe they'll fly us on to Iceland when we get there. I've heard amazing things about their geothermal pools."

Hope springs eternal in my chest though the destination letters remain firmly stuck on Inverness as our group reaches the desk.

"I'm Bri, by the way." Brianna rolls the r around her mouth like a sweet. She holds out a perfectly manicured, super soft hand, and I shake it.

"Fliss," I say, sticking with it. "I have just renewed my passport, so I'd love for that eighty pounds to be money well spent."

"Where else can you fly from Inverness that you can't get to from Gatwick?" Bri asks, the contents of her handbag dropping to the floor as she tries to stuff everything back in, giggling loudly.

I'm sure we're both sensible enough to know that Gatwick and its hundreds of gates that lead anywhere from Timbuktu to Canberra, would offer more chance of a hidden getaway than Inverness.

"Maybe we're not flying onwards from Inverness, maybe it's a train or a boat." I say, hopefully.

"Or maybe we're actually just going to Scotland," Bri shrugs.

I make a non-committal noise because I've just met these people and don't want to be labelled as a moaner.

I'm not a moaner. I get on with things because what's the point in moaning? But really, Scotland?

James is at the front of the check-in desk now, leaning over the counter making the woman in orange laugh. He turns back to Maya who is waiting behind him, and ushers her forwards. I can hear the gentle Scottish lilt of the woman as she asks Maya to put her baggage on the scales and hope I haven't overpacked the woolly jumpers. I don't think I've got enough cash to pay for extortionate weight limit fees and my bank account is already in the red because of buying all the woolly jumpers in the first place.

Maya's bag must be filled with air because it's as light as a feather. Which makes up for Bri's hundred pound fine. James tuts loudly but his smile is kind.

"You might be wanting to offload some of that before the real fun starts," he half jokes. "Backache is a killer."

"Thank god the real fun hasn't started already," Bri half jokes back to him, pouting her very pink lips and fluttering what can't be real eyelashes.

James drops her a quick wink. He certainly knows how to diffuse the situation as Bri smiles coyly and steps aside to let me put my beast of a bag on the scales.

"Hi," the woman at the desk sings. "How're you doing today?"

"Excited, I think," I reply, as she watches the computer with knotted brows.

A label pops out of the printer and she sticks it around the handle at the top of my rucksack.

"Dead on the weight limit," she smiles.

"Someone *has* been doing their homework," James says, and he guides me by the shoulder out of the way so Oliver can check in.

I feel a buzz at being a teacher's pet when in actual fact I had totally forgotten to weigh my bag and it is pure fluke that I'm not flogging a kidney to pay for it. Bri whoops at my unplanned aptitude and gives a small round of applause as I step past James. I give a little bow and wonder if she's a cheerleader by trade or just dressed like one with the enthusiasm to match.

With us all checked in, our next stop is Wetherspoons. James gets in a round of drinks. I opt for a shandy, because eight in the morning is too early for full on alcohol, even if I am in need of it. Turns out I'm the only one who think this way. No-one ribs me for it though, we're not quite at that stage of friendship yet. Whether we'll be there in two weeks' time is anyone's guess.

"To the trip of a lifetime," James says, raising his own pint.

"Cheers," we say in unison, clinking our glasses against each other's.

A lull falls over the group as we sip. The adrenaline that was pumping through my body only minutes earlier has been diluted with tiredness at the thought of what I'm actually doing, and by the looks of the drooping shoulders amongst us, I feel I'm not alone. I can't believe I'm holidaying with a bunch of strangers. Never in my whole life would I imagine going on a *day* trip with a load of people I don't know, let alone two weeks in an unknown place on an adventure to *find myself*.

When my parents had descended on my house to inform me they'd booked a hall and were wondering what kind of catering and entertainment I'd like to celebrate my birthday, I'd had to think on the spot. I'd not celebrated my birthday in years, since I was a teen, I didn't really see the point anymore. So, I'd told them I'd already booked a holiday. Then when they asked if they could join me, I'd had to make up the expense and the secrecy and the possible trekking. I'd felt sick with guilt when Mum looked near to tears as she realised she wouldn't be spending my big day with me again. But they try, and fail, to make me celebrate every year, and I didn't know that thirty-five would be the year they *actually* try to plan something.

When Dad had asked to see the website of the company I was travelling with, so they could at least join me in spirit, I'd jumped on to Facebook and shown them the *Hidden Holidays* page. I'd remembered seeing the advert being bandied about by a loose acquaintance somewhere in the depths of one of my evening scrolls through social media. I wasn't even planning on booking anything, just hiding away from the world for a few weeks. Yet here I am. Sitting around a sticky table drinking to the health of three people I will get to know really well if the brochure is anything to go by. Four, really, if I include James. I look at him over the top of my glass as he chats across the table to Oliver. They both glance towards me as though they are drawn by the weight of my stare and I quickly cast my eyes down into my shandy.

"This holiday," James says, turning in his seat and addressing the whole table. "Is a chance to step out of your comfort zone. To push yourself. It's not necessarily an opportunity to do all the things you've ever wanted to do. It's more than that. And less."

I can't quite believe these motivational words are coming from one so young. It's like he's swallowed a self-help book.

"What I think the main purpose of this trip is," he adds, looking directly at me. " To face up to your fears."

Silence descends as we all look at each other not quite knowing what to say. I pick at the edge of the sticky table with a thumbnail as Oliver crosses and uncrosses his legs next to me, bashing my knees as he goes.

"Sorry," he mutters quietly and I'm about to say no problems when James lets out a huge guffaw.

"You guys will need to learn to lighten up a bit if this holiday is going to be any fun," he says, still laughing. "You've done the scariest part anyway. Look at you all; you're here, aren't you?"

We nod as a collective and a tannoy announcement has James chivvying us all from our drinks and out of the pub. My stomach is flipping with the butterflies that always appear as I board a plane. Nervous excitement. I think of my blood pressure and try to deep breathe as we walk up the ramp and step into plane. As we're flying with neither Emirates nor British Airways, it's a free-for-all with the seats once we're onboard. And to be honest,

I'm happy to find myself sitting next to a little old lady who promptly pulls out a copy of Take A Break once her seatbelt is tightly fastened. There's really only so much mingling I can do in one day. And I fear I may have already hit my threshold.

# Chapter Three

It's like stepping under a cold shower as we all traipse out of the airport and look expectantly at James for some answers. The biting wind that I thought was going to take down the plane as we landed is still whipping around my neck and I pull the collar of my wax jacket up around my ears.

There is nothing to see for miles. I thought Scotland was meant to be hilly. It's just an expanse of grey as far as my eyes can make out. As though the clouds have fallen from the sky and are hanging around near the featureless landscape to make them even less welcoming.

"Well," James says, still clapping his hands enthusiastically as four wet trekkers encroach on his personal space to hear him over the howling gales. "This is unusual, even for *Scotland* in the middle of August!"

He laughs but this time no-one—not even perpetually enthusiastic Bri—joins him. Our general malaise doesn't seem to bother him though, and I have to give him credit for that. Maybe there is something to be said for daily fresh air and outdoor exercise. I lug my rucksack onto my back and follow him as he takes us past the large grey building of the airport and into a carpark that looks like it's for trucks and vans only.

The rain has changed from a light drizzle to a full-on torrent and icy drips are now running down my back and plopping off my nose. I can barely feel my feet through my thick socks and I can't work out if it's the cold or if I've tied the laces of my stiff, new walking boots too tight. I wriggle my toes to make sure they're still there. There's no point trying to talk to anyone, most of us have our hoods up and tightened over our faces. Only Maya seems to be enjoying the downpour. Her skin looks luminescent as she tucks her scarf around her mouth and nose.

"I hope you've all been for a wee!" James says, as he slides open the side door of a Mercedes van with blacked out windows. "The next part of our trip is a three-hour drive."

I can hear a general murmur of discontent and I join in. I'm not sure I can do three hours whilst soaked to the skin squatting on my haunches in a cold damp van. So far, this trip has done nothing for my wellbeing except remind me of how good I have it at home.

I laugh to myself. *Maybe that's the whole point.*

Though when it's my turn to step up into the van I concede that perhaps I was a bit quick to judge. James takes my rucksack and gives me an arm to lean on, the heat radiating from the open door like a welcome hug. I resist the urge to squeeze James' arms muscles as I climb into the van, it's been a long five years since my one-time long-term boyfriend decided to move to Australia for some space—as though the other side of London wasn't quite far enough away to offer him adequate distance—but no matter how taut his muscles are, James is most probably on the wrong side of twenty-five for me.

There are four luxurious looking leather seats, Maya has taken one of the seats at the back of the bus and is staring intently at the door as I climb aboard. Bri is taking the seat over the gangway, rummaging once again through her bag to retrieve something from its depths. I throw my rucksack to the back of the bus with the others, then take a seat in front of Bri, sighing with relief as I stretch my legs right out in front of me, groaning as I make the most if it after being cooped up on the plane. The downside to having long legs and enjoying travelling.

The minibus fills quickly with Oliver taking the last empty seat. Maya leans around her chair to try and say hi, but he's avoiding all eye contact as he makes himself comfortable, his jaw set so hard he has the profile of a Superman poster, his Henry Cavill curls licking around his ears. He's handsome, in a clean-cut kind of way. I think it's the moodiness he's exuding that does it. I tilt my head to get a better look at him. My pulse flurries, my stomach restricting. I think he might actually be *very* handsome. James rolls the door shut and I remember where I am and stop staring.

So, here we are again. The four of us. There's a small screen behind the driver's headrest playing what looks like MTV if that's still going, and the automatic tint on the windows lifts slightly as the door clicks closed. This bus is higher tech than the plane was.

"Still Scotland?" I ask, turning my head and smiling at Bri.

"Looking likely." She grins back in between snapping some photos of the minibus and a few peace sign, tongue out selfies.

As James climbs into the driver's seat and slams his door closed, the bus quietens to a hush. He leans over the back of his chair to look at us all.

"Right gang," he says. "I hope you find yourselves comfortable in our luxury minibus. Like I said, we've got a three-hour journey to our first destination. No spoilers just yet. I promise I won't do any awkward icebreakers at all this trip, but I think these three hours give us a chance to get to know each other a bit better, don't you?"

"Isn't that what an icebreaker is?" Bri pipes up, laughing.

"If I don't mention the word icebreaker, it's not an icebreaker, okay?" James laughs too. "I just want a little intro story from each of you to help pass the time. Names again, where you're from, anything you'd like to share with us all. But, and this is quite a big *but*—no sniggers please—I don't want any of you to go into too much detail about your home life, your past, secrets you've got hiding in the closet, that kind of thing. Not just yet. This trip is about the here and now, and we actively discourage you from bring any kind of pre-conceptions with you. So that goes for disclosing too much too. This is a chance to reconnect with yourself and others, without the baggage that you normally carry! When we're further into our stay, when we know each other as *people* rather than judging each other on historical facts, then we will have the opportunity to be more open."

The bus is so silent I could have heard a pin drop. But inside I am having a little party all to myself because, if no-one is asking, then my secrets can stay tucked away neatly inside me. No one really needs to know the reason I'm running away for my birthday.

"*Right,*" James says, oblivious or ignoring the trepidation his words have just caused. "Let's get on our way. Oh, and I was just joking about the loo, if any of you do need to go, please just shout. I don't know about you, but I have drunk enough coffee to have my insides churning like a beatbox."

He turns back around and switches on the engine with the push of a button.

"I wondered what it was that gave him the energy of an excitable chipmunk," Bri says over the loud rumbling of the diesel engine, leaning her head through the gap between my seat and the window of the minibus. "I thought a wellbeing holiday would mean no caffeine, just organic yak milk and some green stuff. Still, I won't turn down anything he's offering, just saying."

"If I was five years younger, I would wholeheartedly agree with you." I laugh. Bri studies my face astutely, nodding slowly as she does so. "Plus, manhunting is not on my itinerary this fortnight. Nope, just some well-deserved me time amongst the gorgeous surroundings of Scotland."

"Me too." She grins even harder, her milky cheeks flushing ever so slightly, as we both look out the window at the non-view.

Settling back into our seats, we start on our journey, the building falls away behind us and we're soon surrounded by green scrub and purple moss. Still no signs of any hills or mountains though. I catch sight of a road sign advertising the Scottish Highlands and I nudge Bri's leg to point it out.

"Yep?" Bri says, sticking her bottom lip out. "Absolutely without doubt, still Scotland."

If it wasn't so grey out, and if the rain wasn't insistent enough to cover most of the windows with a constant fine spray, it might look quite beautiful. In a moody, literary veil that needs a backing track of Enya.

"Right," James shouts from the driver's seat. "Who's going to go first?"

He is greeted by deathly silence.

"Oliver?" he says, boldly. "You've been quite quiet, fancy telling us a bit about yourself?"

I glance another look at the man sitting over the gangway from me. Heat rising in my chest making me shuffle in my seat, not sure what to do with my arms. He's staring out of the window; his hair looks as though it's a few months late for a cut which doesn't match with his new looking clothes and boots. Maybe his holiday shopping is as telling as my own. He looks away from the vista and at James in the rear-view mirror. His jaw is so clenched I'm surprised I can't hear the grinding of his teeth over the thumping of tyres on tarmac.

"No thanks," he says gruffly, and I'm thrown by his rudeness as he goes back to staring out of the window.

Handsome or not, there's no need for a lack of manners.

"I'll go first," Bri pipes up behind me, dragging herself up with the headrest of my chair to wave at James over my seat.

I feel an affinity to her as she has swooped in and diffused what could have been a difficult situation. I turn back to look at her as she leans out into the aisle to get a better view of the bus.

"I'm Brianna, call me Bri, like the cheese. I'm from Tenby in Wales and I am an influencer," she says, then looks at me. "For those of you millennials who are a bit over the hill for that, it means I get given loads of free stuff that I post about on Instagram and then get paid for it."

James laughs and I raise an eyebrow at Bri and relax back against the window so I can look out at the others.

"So," Bri continues. "You'll have to excuse me snapping away while we're trekking, my followers are all hankering after some adventure. Though, hashtag, who wants to see that?"

She points out of the window at the drizzle and we all laugh.

"You didn't pay for your holiday?" Maya scoffs in a low-pitched voice.

"I *did* pay for this holiday as a treat to myself for a big achievement," Bri says, shrugging. "But I normally don't pay for anything if I can help it. Food, alcohol, clothes, beauty products. Someone sent me a dog kennel once and I don't even have a dog."

"I wish people would send me products for free," I say, tucking one leg up underneath me. "I pay a fortune for moisturiser to make me look like I'm still in my twenties."

Bri studies me closely.

"I wouldn't bother," she says, not unkindly. I can't tell if she means I don't need it, or it's too late. "I will take a group photo on this amazing minibus if that's okay with everyone. When we get off though, I need you in it too, James, gotta sell this thing somehow."

"Thank you, Bri," James says, winking at her in the mirror. "I think!"

Their flirty banter lifts the spirit of the minibus as we all live vicariously through these attractive people whose hormones are so full of vitality they're floating around the air like oxygen.

James clears his throat.

"Who's next?" he says, and my insides turn to ice as he looks at me in the mirror again.

I shake my head ever so slightly and he nods his eyes boring into mine.

"Okay, okay," I concede. "I'm Fliss, originally from Kent, now residing in Camberwell. I'm here because I wanted to escape away for my big birthday this week."

"Forty?" Bri asks and I reach back and hit her on the leg as she laughs.

"Shut up," I say. "Thirty-five actually."

"Embrace your birthday, Fliss," James says. "Every new year is filled with many amazing experiences."

I have to suppress rolling my eyes.

"Tell me you won't be shit scared of your life passing you by when you turn thirty-five and then it's just a slippery slope all the way to forty, James," I say to his reflection.

"Give me ten years and I'll let you know," he says, winking.

I'm glad to pass the baton on to someone else as Maya raises her hand and gets the attention of the whole bus. This way I don't have to think about why I'm doing this wellbeing trek alone for my birthday, rather than spending it with loved ones at a scarily large party back at home. It's just two weeks. I can get through this if I take it one day at a time.

## Chapter Four

"Maya," James says, his eyes back on the road now. "Is it your turn? What can you tell us about yourself and why you're here?"

"No, not my turn" Maya says, shaking her head. "But I'm busting for a wee, can we pull over for a quick minute?"

James laughs, and when I check my phone, I'm surprised to see that we've been driving for over an hour. With the rain still thrumming at the windows, and the conversation flowing despite Oliver's bad start, I'd barely noticed the time pass. James is obviously good at this. I take a moment to look properly out of the window and notice that the landscape is more undulating than it was when we left the airport. There are even a few proper hills. A single row of tall conifers line either side of the road. They stand side by side, guarding us like sentinels above the cracked granite. A buzz of excitement crackles in my stomach, dormant since I found out our destination was Scotland. It *is* beautiful, even with a sideshow of drizzle.

"Okay," James says. "You have two options. I can pull over and we can all check out the view on the opposite side of the bus, or there's a Little Chef about half an hour away."

"Here please," Maya says, sitting forwards in her chair. "My Mooncup is pressing on my bladder and I don't think I can wait."

She laughs the laugh of a forty a day smoker, though I can tell by her lack of wrinkles and glowing skin that she doesn't have the habit.

"In fact," she continues. "I think that about sums me up. I'm here for adventure and I'm very open with my views."

"Roger that," James says, unfazed by Maya's openness about both her peeing abilities and her sanitary wear.

Bri squeaks behind me. "Mooncup?! Oh, bloody hell."

She could be balking at the choice of product or the fact Maya has just blurted out an intimate detail in a van full of strangers and it hits me just how close we will all be by the end of these two weeks, whether we like it or not. I can barely talk to my *best friends* about my periods and going to the toilet is something I can only do at home… alone. The happy buzz is turning into a *shit what have I done* buzz.

Maya jumps out of the van and hot foots it behind a tree, whipping her knickers down before she's rounded the trunk. I turn quickly to look at the opposite side of the bus to give her some privacy, catching Oliver's eye as I do. His face gives away no emotion as he looks away resolutely. As his head turns to look out over the valley, I see the tips of his ears turn red. I'm glad I'm not the only one who is fazed by bodily functions.

Maya is still adjusting her long skirt as she makes her way back onto the minibus, I catch a glimpse of her tanned, toned legs and her large silky knickers as she pulls the material back down, and so does the rest of the gang. Oliver scowls as Maya blows him a kiss and steps over my strewn legs back to her seat.

"Thanks, guys," she says, releasing her hair from the top of her head and running her hands through it as it cascades in soft, highlighted, brown curls down her back. "Onward, ho."

James gets the minibus back on the empty road as we sit chattering quietly.

"What do you think we'll be sleeping in?" I turn and ask Bri. "The webpage said adventure and sleeping under the stars, but I don't know, given the weather."

"Oh tents, definitely tents," Bri says, grabbing a bag of Maltesers she must have stashed earlier in her seat pocket and ripping them open. She offers me the bag which I gratefully dig into. "I bloody hope they'll be teepees or shepherd's huts though, you know? Glamping, not camping. That's all the rage these days isn't it? Camping for the weak, which I definitely fall under when it comes to outdoorsy stuff. I had a guy try to offer me a complimentary night in his new Air B&B caravan once, I turned it down though 'cos it was an old dilapidated touring caravan in his back garden in the middle of Newport and the only facilities were in his house. I didn't want to be traipsing in for a pee in the middle of the night and find out he's an axe murderer or kidnapper with a fetish for rubber and hoses."

"Might have ended up a fun night," Maya pipes up loudly from across the aisle.

She's taken her shoes off and has her feet crossed underneath her. Her skirt spills over her legs. Bri leans over and offers her the bag of chocolate, chattering away.

"True," Bri agrees. "It has been such a long time since I've had any action; rubber and hoses would be quite fun."

"My ex was a complete prude," Maya says with an edge to her voice. "Never mind the S&M, I offered him the chance of a threesome once and you would have thought I'd have asked him to perform an exorcism on a goat."

Bri laughs along with Maya.

"Is that why he's your ex?" They burst into more laughter.

I'm totally in Maya's ex's gang on this one. The idea of a threesome, even when I was in the prime of my twenties, fills me with horror. Why would I want to add an extra body into the mix when one person seeing me naked is enough, let alone fuelling my flames of jealousy with another naked woman having fun with my man. Nope. No thank you very much. Not for me.

I keep my mouth shut and my eyes firmly fixed on

Oliver's red ear tips until the conversation hushes back down to a quiet lull, interrupted occasionally with the crunch of a Malteser and the giggle of Bri as she scrolls her phone.

The hills are encroaching more now, their faces still green with moss and scrub. A body of water big enough to be a proper loch appears on the left-hand side of the mini-bus, I watch the water, dark and flat, little white tips punctuating the surface in random ripples.

"That, my friends," pipes up James from the front of the van. "Is the Atlantic Ocean. Which means we have only thirty minutes until we reach our first destination."

A rush of excitement floods the van as we all crane our necks to look at the ocean. We must have driven right across the country. And by my reckoning, thank you GCSE geography, we're on the west coast of the Scottish Highlands.

The shore becomes more craggy; white stones mix with sand where the sea falls back from the road. Occasionally I wonder if we're going to end up in the water as the waves lick the sides of the tarmac, the spray misting my window. But my trust in James as a tour guide keeps me from jumping over to the safe side of the minibus and sitting in Oliver's lap.

The sea terrifies me. Its power and unpredictability make my skin pop up with goosebumps whenever I'm near it.

*What if a freak wave drags me in? What if I'm caught in a rip tide and can't swim back to shore? What if I am dragged down to the dark, murky, depths and die down there? What if? What if?*

Not quite the cheery feeling I'd like to associate with the warm, turquoise Med or the salty Aegean. But this Ocean to my left is exactly what I picture in my mind when I'm caught in the waves and sinking.

I focus on my hands in front of me as I feel the familiar sensation of panic rising in my chest; my nails bitten to the quick, the fine downy hair on the backs of my wrists, the blue veins running to my fingers giving them movement and life. I count my breaths in my head. In and out, in and out, filling my lungs with air, not water. The conversations around me melting into echoing voices that I can't quite reach. But my chest relaxes before it's too wound up, the well-practised techniques coming to my rescue once again.

It's not normally the sea that sets me off, I respect it more than fear it. And now is *definitely* not the time for that to escalate. A wellbeing trip that needs a swimsuit is suddenly taking on a whole new meaning. Not spa treatments and jet-filled pools, but large bodies of open water and the Atlantic Ocean.

"Ladies and Gentlemen." James' voice startles me. "Welcome, finally, to your hidden holiday."

He turns off the highway onto the gravel drive of a large stately home built in the darkest of grey granite. It's huge. And a sign, almost as big as my smile, announces the building as Glasmakirk Hotel and Spa.

## Chapter Five

Glasmakirk Hotel and Spa looks like something out of Downton Abbey, there are more turrets than I can shake a stick at. Grey granite blocks fit together like a Minecraft castle, wings spiralling out from a central keep with four pointy hats that fly a flag for passing motorists and paying guests.

We bundle out of the minibus, glad to stretch our legs and it doesn't look like the rain is bothering anyone anymore. I know I'm certainly not feeling it, though the temperature has dropped a few degrees and I'm glad of my extra fleece. James rubs my shoulder as he passes in front of me and heads for the door hidden deep inside an ornate stone archway. I expect a loud boom as he knocks but am slightly disappointed that the door slides open with a twentieth-century update that nobody needs.

"This way folks," he shouts.

Bri catches up with me, bouncing on the balls of her trainer clad feet.

"Isn't this amazing?" she gasps, catching her breath. "This is more like it."

"It's certainly something," I agree, not wanting to divulge the trifling discomfort I'm now feeling.

It *is* something. It's the most beautiful place I've ever laid eyes on, with views on one side out over the Atlantic and on the other on the purple moss-covered hills. It's a castle. Rapunzel could pop her head out of the tallest turret, and I don't think I'd be surprised. From the neat uniform of the staff who welcome us through the doors to the gentle aroma of relaxation, I can tell this place is luxurious and definitely worth the money spent through *Hidden Holidays*. It's going to be wonderful for my wellbeing, I am already feeling a few stone lighter at the thought someone else will be cooking my meals and doing my housework. Yet—and I don't say this out loud because I don't want to sound ungrateful—it's *too* luxurious. How can I reconnect with myself through nature better in a castle with a spa, than the local Champneys clinic down the road from my workplace? Maybe they'll wrap us in seaweed collected from the beach in the back garden (is it called a garden when it's a castle?) and have local eagles peck the dry bits of skin from between our toes. But it will still be a spa. I wonder if maybe it's a health retreat and we won't be fed solid food for the whole time we're here, and I'm grateful for the handful of Maltesers I scoffed on the long drive.

James is at the check in desk, leaning on the grand wooden counter that could double as a church altar. There are stone steps leading up from either side, circling back around, and joining at the top where I assume the bedrooms start. A small unobtrusive sign points to the spa whose own door is hidden behind a huge fig leaf tree. If I was looking for a wellbeing holiday that meant I could relax for two weeks and be pampered, then this absolutely ticks all those boxes. But something doesn't feel quite right.

I'm handed a key with a large leather fob. Room number thirty-three. On direction of the receptionist, we all skip up to the first floor with as much light-footedness as four people carrying their body weight in thermals can muster. Our footsteps clack on the stairs then swish on the thin woven rugs scattered at the top. Maya has broken out from the group and is walking on her own, her head turning back every few seconds to check we're still here. Bri skips breezily down the dark corridor and I take a couple of little quick steps to catch up with Oliver. He's taller up close than I thought he would be, broad too, though the way he holds himself makes me think he'd rather take up less space.

"What room are you?" I ask, my interest in him peaking and I want to get a chance to speak to him before we all disappear into our rooms.

Oliver turns to look at me, glancing in the direction of the two other girls out of the corner of brooding, dark brown eyes as he does so. He shifts his bags and holds up his fob.

"Thirty-four," he says, poker-faced.

"Ooo neighbours," I say, trying but failing to lighten the mood.

Oliver, still stony faced, nods and speeds up away from me.

*Rude!*

There's so much dark wood that, even though it's daytime, the corridors are lit with numerous chandeliers so we don't trip over the suits of armour or miss the beady eyes of the stags' heads staring at us. James speeds past us all so we follow him through another thick wooden door into a hallway much like the one we've just left.

"This is our wing," James says, coming to a halt at the first door. There's an iron thirty fixed onto the wood. "This one is me; your rooms are all on this corridor, just match up your key with the number. I don't know why I just said that, you're all adults who can count! Anyway. Head on in and get freshened up. There are Jack and Jill bathrooms in between each room, but don't worry, you can lock both doors so there are no weird meetings in the middle of the night."

He winks at Bri who giggles into her chest. Oliver shakes his head and starts up the corridor.

"Feel free to have a look around the place. There's a pool on the ground floor and a library somewhere. I'm pretty sure the Glasmakirk ghost only shows herself when it's dark so you're safe for the meantime. Please can we all meet in the restaurant, I've a table booked for eight pm; haggis is on the menu." And with that he disappears into his room.

Bri is next, her room neighbouring James', and the smile on her face as she skips in the door is contagious.

Which is good, seeing as I'm stuck between Maya and Oliver who have been less than chipper what with Maya's side-eye glances and Oliver's stony silence. But maybe we're all just a little tired and a bit deflated.

Inside my room, I throw my bag on my four-poster bed and head to the window to check out the view. The grey Atlantic Ocean stretches for as far as I can see, blending in seamlessly on the line of the horizon with the grey mist of the sky. Turning back, the bedroom is just as I expected, dark wood, ornate, elaborate, but comfortable and cosy too. The bed is covered in a rich, red bedspread and there is a matching footstool at the end. I could be in a period drama and I love it. The door to the bathroom is ajar and I poke my head around to the claw footed bath and separate shower. Oliver's face greets me as he does the same from his bedroom.

*Crap!*

"Sorry," he says, pushing his door closed with a loud bang.

I wonder why someone who has spent a small fortune on a holiday to get away and find himself, is being so dour. But I don't want to bring down my jubilation with Oliver's issues, so I head into the bathroom for a quick wee, making sure I turn on the tap to block out the tinkling sound of water on porcelain, and check out the freebies littering the sink. There is posh looking soap and shower gel and bubble bath. I make a note to leave enough time tonight to soak in the huge tub and I can feel my shoulders relaxing already.

Back in my room, I check my phone again for the

time, there's a few hours until we have to meet for dinner. My mum has sent me a message hoping that I'm not too cold and miserable in a tent, or too hot and relaxed on a beach. I don't reply just yet. I'm not sure how to word the fact I'm still in the country in a hotel and spa whilst justifying my expenditure and absence from their much-wanted party. Grabbing my backpack, I throw on some of the jogging bottoms and a t-shirt I had packed for sleeping in and slip into my trainers to take a look around the hotel. May as well make the most of the time before dinner to see where I'll be spending the next few weeks.

The corridor is empty as I make my way back to the reception. It crosses my mind that maybe I should have knocked for the others to see if they wanted to come exploring, but I figure that we have the rest of the time together and I really just need some space. I've had to grow used to being alone and now I like it. So, throwing myself into a group holiday wasn't really what I wanted to do for my birthday, but given the limited time I had to find a legitimate excuse for not being at home for a big party, I'll just have to make the most of it.

A man with a white dickie bow and gloves tips his head at me as I reach the bottom of the stairs. I give him a smile and follow the intricately woven rugs laid over the stone floor towards the back of the hotel. The spa gives off the scent of eucalyptus as I pass the closed door. It's a scent not unfamiliar to me seeing as I use spa-ing as a verb more often than I use running. I look forward to checking it out later in the week. Further on through the vast hotel the ceiling height rises to multi-story car park

## Wild Swimming

level, though it's dotted with more chandeliers and ornate carvings and not humming strip lights. I'm starting to wonder if we're the only guests here. I haven't seen another soul since we walked through the front door, save for the staff. Another ballroom opens up and I pick the first door I come to, hoping I can find my way back when my stomach starts growling.

I can see daylight flooding in at the end of this corridor and walk towards it, finding myself in a large orangery. Plants grow like triffids, butterflies flit about around my head. I walk around the pathway and find a small iron bench with a view through the glass towards the ocean. As I sit, I feel my scar stretch across my ribs, aching with the movement after sitting for so long today already. I resist the urge to scratch it, the constant reminder of what happened to me, and focus on the sea instead. Here, where I'm enclosed safely in glass, I can enjoy it for what it is. Even as our lives come to an abrupt halt, the seas will carry on moving. They were here long before we arrived, and they will be here long after we have all departed. It's mesmerising as the waves pound over themselves rhythmically, I can almost hear it if I listen closely. But perhaps that's the blood pounding in my ears at the thought of what kind of dinner conversations will pop up this evening, and how much of myself I will be willing to share with my fellow trekkers. Once again I'm grateful for James' insistence that we remain focussed on the here and now.

Stretching my feet out I wonder at the four people who I have been thrown together with and am thankful that the hotel is big enough to keep my space. Yes, my family and work colleagues may tell me regularly that I need to be more sociable, but they're not here, are they? And little white lies won't hurt them.

*Of course I joined in. Yes we were a great bunch of friends by the end of the two weeks, how could we not be thrown together like that. Etc etc.*

If I can make it through the holiday without having to get into a deep and meaningful then I will be happy. And I can head home with a reasonable excuse of being too tired for socialising when I get back too. Win win, really. I'm not unsociable by nature, not at all. But people like to ask questions, and sometimes the answers aren't what they want to hear. I've tried being sociable because I love the stories people tell and the friendships that live through them, but it's not for me. Not anymore.

I think maybe a castle is the best place for me. Who needs wellbeing when there's the opportunity for withdrawal?

## Chapter Six

By the time dinner comes around, I'm famished and ready to mingle for the sake of my stomach. Thankfully, as the food is to die for. Our table is big enough to seat the King's consort for a traditional banquet, with the five of us taking up not even a tiny fraction of it. James is at the head. Maya and me on one side, Oliver and Bri on the other. Dishes of hearty stews and mash and vegetables and lots of deep-fried offerings were emptied first onto our plates and then into our stomachs. I have to surreptitiously undo the top button of the jeans I had changed into after my exploration. Maya sucks away at some ribs and the clatter of cutlery has quietened from the ravenous noise we were making when the food was placed in front of us.

I feel like maybe James is preparing for a speech. He's been shifting around in his seat for the last few bites of his haggis. It's unnerving me because I know that feeling so well. The anxiety riddled fidgeting. But what's James got to be anxious about?

Waiters appear as if by magic as the last one of our party puts down their knife and fork. Main course dishes whisked away and replaced by trifles and panne cottas, cheeses and crackers, and our wine glasses haven't reached the bottoms once over the last hour or so.

As everyone is tucking into their choice of pudding and I'm wondering if I can just grab the big bowl of trifle and claim it as my own before anyone else takes any, James stands from his chair and starts tapping his glass with a teaspoon like we're at a wedding and he's the best man.

"So," he starts as our chatter quietens. "What do you all think of the hotel so far?"

"It's perfect, an absolute total dream," Bri says, raising her wine glass in a toast. "I can't wait to check out the spa. When can we go?"

"All in good time, Bri," James says, looking around the table. "Any other feedback for *Hidden Holidays* about the Glasmakirk Hotel and Spa?"

Maya stops midbite, her camembert covered rye toast still held aloft.

"I'm so glad I'm here," she says, looking across the table to where Oliver is poking his crème brûlée with his spoon. "It's decadent. Like this cheese. The library has a first UK edition copy of one of my favourite Agatha Christie novels, I am impressed. Though I hope that's not a sign of things to come, is it?"

James leans over his plate, both hands on the table.

## Wild Swimming

The candle illuminating his face flickering ominously. "Kill you off one by one Christie style?" he asks.

We all fall quiet, waiting for his answer which is taking an awkwardly long time to arrive. James slams his hands down in one quick, loud movement and laughs as we all jump.

"No of course not," he says, relaxing back into his chair. "Half our income is repeat guests, I'd be shooting *myself* in the foot, let alone you guys."

"My shower was like a waterfall," Bri adds, as we all quiet to a lull. "I'm definitely going to do an Insta story in there. Don't worry Maya, I'll make sure it's empty first."

Bri giggles but Maya looks a little non-plussed. I wonder if she's a bit tired of Bri's welcome, but persistent enthusiasm.

"You should take some videos of the staff," Maya says eventually, drawing her words out languorously as she stretches her arms across the table to prong another block of Camembert with her fork. "They're all attractive enough to entice even the shyest of travellers. Wouldn't you say, Oliver?"

Through Bri's surprisingly dirty laughter, Oliver remains stony faced and staring at his pudding. Maya smirks and spreads her cheese onto a cracker. From his behaviour so far, I don't think Oliver will give his own verdict on the *Hidden Holidays* venue de jour so I bite the bullet and go next.

"This place is amazing," I start and James nods enthusiastically at me. "But it doesn't feel quite right."

All eyes on me now and I can tell what they're thinking. *Look at that poor rich girl in her Toast cashmere and NYMD jeans, even this place doesn't live up to her expectations.* Which couldn't be further from the truth of the full-on bankruptcy I will be facing when I get home and open my credit card bill full of holiday gear.

"Don't get me wrong." I direct this at Maya whose scowl could give her a headache. "It's the nicest hotel I've *ever* been in, the nicest *place* I've ever been in quite possibly. It's just not what I imagined I'd be doing when I signed up to a secret wellbeing holiday that advertised itself as *not for the fainthearted.* Was that bit just aimed at the initial disappointment of not flying to the Himalayas?"

That gets a giggle and I feel a warm rush of proudness at my ability to speak my mind, perhaps there is something to be said for being amongst strangers.

"You're very astute, Felicity," James says, adding to my warmth.

"Please, it's Fliss," I remind him, keen to keep up this persona as I'm growing to like her.

"Fliss," he continues. "Every time I fly a new group of people up to Inverness, I can sense their hopes of a five-star luxury spa-safari fading into the grey sky. I know what you mean."

"It's not that I don't like Scotland," I say hurriedly, not wanting to give people the wrong impression. "I love it, it's beautiful, but staying in a gazzilion star hotel just doesn't seem *out there* enough for what your website was offering. No matter how decadent the hotel."

"And we want to make your birthday one to remember, right?" James asks.

"We all wanted a memorable time here, James," Oliver pipes up from his pudding.

*Oh, he does speak,* I think, his stare is pulling at me, but I resist looking over.

"Of course you do, Oliver," James smiles, undeterred. "And this is why I want you all to think long and hard about the offer I am about to put on the table."

You could hear a pin drop. Even the wait staff seemed to have stopped moving for James' big announcement. They must be used to his melodramatic show by now and know when to start holding their breath.

"Spit it out, James," Maya interrupts the muteness. "I want to eat this bloody cracker."

James laughs, though there is an edge to his voice.

"You're a tough crowd, I'll give you that," he continues. "Ok, this hotel provides a safe space, a retreat for those who would like to stay here for the rest of the trip. Because we are a secret holiday provider, we have learnt over the years that not everyone is cut out for the type of wellbeing services we offer."

*Oh god, is it going to be some kind of sexual orgy or cuddle party or some other kind of wellbeing that I am quite content not being involved with? I think I'll stick with the safe space if so.*

"We have the most amazing place on our doorstep here. The Scottish Highlands. Home to some of the most magical scenery you will ever clap your eyes on. This trek is not only about discovering this scenery and being amongst it stripped back of electronics and wifi, but also about discovering *yourself*, stripped back of electronics and wifi."

"How am I supposed to update my followers if I've got no phone?" Bri asks.

"You update them when you're back," James presses on.

"I don't really know how to compute that," she adds, trying to be funny but her smiling façade is slipping ever so slightly.

"Fair enough," James says, shrugging. "You can always stay here and send lots of photos of the spa. Besides, you can't really tell your followers what you'll be doing on a huge platform anyway, it'll spoil the surprise for the guests of years to come."

Bri mutters under her breath and pulls out her phone, keeping it hidden under the table but it's making her face glow. My interest has peaked at what James is about to announce.

"And as Fliss here so eloquently put it, Glasmakirk is not *out there* enough for a Hidden holiday. I want you to feel that Scottish wind through your hair, to see the sun as it's rising and setting, to feel that primal instinct rearing its head when you're looking out over landscapes that most of us can only dream about.

"So, for those of you who are up for *real* adventure, I am offering the chance for wild camping at four of the most magical hidden swimming locations around the Scottish Highlands and Isles. We leave tomorrow."

The silence returns. Nobody says a word, not even James, though the smile hasn't once left his lips. He's lulled us into a false sense of security after a rocky start and has now just ripped that out from under us. I don't

## Wild Swimming

know about anyone else around this table, but my well-being has been on a rollercoaster and is now feeling like a sick child who's had too much candy floss. Maya's hand is still hovering near her mouth, her Camembert long forgotten. Only Oliver has a wry smile on his face.

"That's certainly not what I was expecting," I say breaking the silence, ignoring the thrilling sense of doom at the thought of wild swimming in the ocean that's crashing at the rocks below the hotel.

# Chapter Seven
### Day Two

I sneak out of my room before the sun has risen the next morning. My head thumping with last night's left-over gin and cocktail hangover. Who knew that an alcoholic drink made with Irn Bru could taste so amazing? With my towel and robe hanging over my arm, I walk swiftly through the maze of corridors and down the stairs. The ever-present receptionist points in the direction of the pool and I follow her red talons around behind the stone stairs, the familiar scent of chlorine leading me the rest of the way.

The water feels cool and refreshing, and I have the Olympic sized pool to myself, so I make the most of it. Plunging into the water and cutting through it with a speed that would have taken me places had I not stopped practising, I feel a sense of calm descend. I'd taken up swimming as a child to get out of a house full of anxiety. But as an adult, by then already escaped, I found myself going less and less often to the pool. Then my six am swim had turned into a six am pre-work slump that I could only claw myself out of with three espressos and a cigarette.

It always takes me by surprise how much I miss the water when I'm in it now. The occasional trip to the local pool, the holidays abroad with the choice of three large pools, Centre Parcs even. No matter the pool, when I sink my shoulders beneath the water, I feel free and safe and wonder why on earth I gave up something that I loved so much. I start swimming gently across the length of the pool to warm up my dormant muscles.

As I swim, I take the time to think over James' offer. I wasn't the only one stumped when he'd thrown it in the mix at the dinner table last night. Maya never did get around to finishing her Camembert, it had wilted there on her plate until we all disbanded for the bar and drank until wild camping was as fuzzy as the peaches in our kombucha.

I had wanted something more than a spa hotel, I'd said that right there at the table, with all my new friends as witnesses. But wild camping in Scotland; swimming in the ocean. Can I really do that? I slice through the water now, feeling my lungs burn in a way they haven't for years. I'm fit. I'm still young. I don't doubt my physical ability to sleep under the stars and poke a toe into freezing water. But mentally? I don't know if I can handle a wellbeing trek that's going to reduce me to a primal mess before my stove kettle has whistled for morning coffee. There's too much hidden deep within, clawing to get out of me.

## Wild Swimming

I power through to the edge of the pool, my lungs screaming at me to stop. As I haul my upper body out of the water to have a breather, I come face to face with a pair of very male feet. Not unattractive by any shape of the imagination; just a bit hairy, on the human side of Hobbit though, thankfully. My eyes drift upwards to find they're attached to Oliver who is standing in his shorts watching me intently. I sink slightly back into the water, treading there to stay afloat, waiting to see if he will say anything. My pulse flutters, quickened by his presence.

"You're fast." He sits down on the edge, dangling his feet in the water beside me.

"Thanks," I say, still puffing with my general lack of swimming practice and the shock in which he appeared when he was the last person I had expected.

Oliver moves his feet up and down under the surface which causes me to bob slightly in the water. He hasn't taken his eyes off me. I'm very aware of myself under the water, the lack of make-up, the swimsuit clinging to my body. He watches me carefully, steadily, confident as anything, but the gentle flush rising on his neck is a sure sign giveaway that he's not as comfortable as he's making out. I pull myself out of the water and sit next to him on the side of the pool, away from his scrutiny, but glad of my swimsuit covering my scar so there's no awkward questions.

"I thought I'd better get some swimming practice in," he says, studying his thumbnails now. "Seeing as it's been years since I was last in the water and we're about to be thrown to the sharks, possibly quite literally. I got up early so I'd have the pool to myself. That worked well didn't it?"

His laugh is quick and sharp, almost as though he didn't mean to let it out. He moves almost imperceptibly a few inches away from me.

"Swimmers always train early doors," I say, shrugging. "You'd need to be here at lunchtime to avoid us."

"So, you're a swimmer then? A *real* one."

I shake my head, watching my toes make patterns in the water. Oliver is quiet beside me. I can feel the movement of his breathing and a tug of tension starting to grow between us, pulling at me like a rubber band. I look at him, he has a small scar on his ear, just above the lobe, not quite high enough to be hidden by his hair.

"I used to be," I say, feeling a bit like an imposter now I've said it. "And actually, it's lovely being back in the pool. I've missed it."

"What happened?"

"Life," I snort, trying to joke, but it comes out like the sad adage that it really is.

"Yeah," Oliver sighs. "I know what you mean."

We sit for a moment in another blanket of silence. Until Oliver slaps his hands against the rough wet tiles and slides into the water.

"Feel free to hang around if you fancy watching an aquatic version of the hippo dance from Fantasia," he says, as he pushes off with his feet from the edge and glides very unhippo like on his back to the middle of the pool.

It's the most I've heard Oliver speak since I walked

into that room in Gatwick airport twenty-four hours ago. He's got a Northern lilt to his voice, almost Lake District, but it sounds as though it's been gradually pushed out by the dropped Ts of urbanisation. I wonder what has happened in his life that makes him sigh as much as he has been.

"Your stroke looks alright to me," I shout over the loud splashing as Oliver turns over and front crawls to the other side. "It's certainly unique."

He splashes his way back to me and leans his arms on the edge. Little droplets of water pool at the end of his long lashes and drip into the curve of his cupid's bow.

"I'm hoping the swimming will take place in a flowing river or the sea, to make up for the fact that half the water will be lost with my generous arm muscles."

He flexes a surprisingly large gun and we both laugh as his head disappears under the water with the effort. Popping up seconds later looking sheepish and coughing with the mouthful of chlorinated water he's just swallowed.

"Maybe you should do a few more lengths, just for a bit more practice. Don't want to be sinking into the great depths of the Atlantic." I raise my eyebrows and shrug a shoulder.

He glances at me incredulously. "Nope. No. I definitely don't want to be doing that."

"Just a joke, Oliver," I say, swallowing hard as his hand brushes past my leg to grab the lip of the wall.

"Uh huh," he nods, pushing back off the tiles with his

feet. "But you're right. I don't want to be sinking in the kind of water I can't see to the bottom of..."

His words teeter out as his lips pull into a grimace and I know exactly how he feels. He flips over to his front, sending torrents of water over the flush sides of the pool to the little white drains running along the tiles as he pushes himself through the water. I lower myself back in and start doing my own lengths. Just a few more and then I'll go and get ready for breakfast. We pass each other in the middle of the pool. Oliver swimming one way, me the other. He looks over to me and smiles, waving an arm and pretending to sink. The look he is going for is spoilt slightly by his fingers gripping his nose shut.

I grab Oliver's shoulder and haul him upwards, trying to assimilate the idea that I will be wild camping with this man, as well as others, and that means essentially squatting over a hole in the ground while they all toast marshmallows and sing Kumbaya My Lord only a few feet away. The door to the pool opens, bringing with it the swimming costume clad body of Maya. Oliver wipes his face down with his hand and catches sight of the other woman. I drop my arm and he turns and swims to the other side of the pool, as though we've been caught out.

"Oh," Maya says in mock shock. "I hope I didn't interrupt anything I shouldn't have?"

I laugh and swim over to the side of the pool.

"Nope," I say, getting out and picking my towel up from the lounger. "Just a little morning swim to get the blood flowing."

I wipe my face and hope it covers the blush creeping

onto my cheeks. There's no logical reason for me to be blushing, but I'm doing it anyway.

"We haven't even started our adventure yet and here you are getting friendly with the men. Is that why you're really here?" Maya adds, grinning like a hyena.

"No," I stutter, wrapping my towel around my body as a shield. "Of course not, we were just swimming."

I look to Oliver to back me up but he's head down in the water, powering through, oblivious to my embarrassment. So, I say goodbye and start back to the changing rooms before my face combusts with heat.

## Chapter Eight

"I'm so proud that we have the full monty trekking with us this expedition," James says as we stand like school kids about to embark on their first residential trip without their parents. "I hope you're all ready for an adventure."

The minibus is loaded with our paired down rucksacks and James has promised that there will be tents up and ready for us when we arrive at our destination. I feel as though there's a gaggle of elves going forth and securing us a good nights' sleep, when in actual fact it's probably locals who can throw up a tent on minimum wage. I'm a little surprised all four of us have decided that the hotel was far too luxurious and have opted for the full experience, especially if it does come with the prospect of added frostbite. I wondered if Bri might stay behind in the lap of luxury and Instagram the castle and spa; but she's here, rucksacked and booted.

Oliver was still swimming when I got back to my room so I'd stood under the molten lava, rainfall shower head for an age because I had an inkling it would be the last time my bones would feel warm for the next few weeks. As we had all sat around the breakfast table and eaten our body weight in pain au chocolate there had been an air of trepidation sitting heavily amongst us, like the aroma of coffee, only sweatier.

I wonder if, like me, the other three paying guests were afraid to stay at the hotel for fear of being ridiculed by the staff for not being brave enough to wild camp in the Highlands. But I'd googled what wild camping actually meant and I don't think the staff would feel any disdain towards people who like creature comforts. I am sorely glad to hear we will have tents, some wild campers go so far as to sleep under the actual stars. Literally, not even figuratively. I need something to protect me from the northerly winds and the sleet that has decided to grace the skies this morning.

*It's August for goodness sake.*

We clamber into the warm minibus before we get too damp and set off on the journey to the first 'secret but magical' location. As the hotel disappears behind the back of the minibus, I wonder again at what on earth I am doing here and why I'm not sipping on a Pina Colada served by a shirtless waiter with a six pack and a twinkle in his eye.

Bri looks a bit lost without her phone glued to her hand, she bites her bottom lip and stares at the rain. She looks younger, but despite this, she seems to have already formed friendships in the short space of time we've been away. I marvel at her easy way with others, not remembering a time myself when opening up to strangers was ever that straightforward. Even at first school my parents drummed it into me that I needed to make some friends that weren't my twin brother, but I didn't quite get how. Frank and I were like one, we didn't need to make an effort with each other because it came so naturally. Back then, I was so used to knowing what Frank was thinking without even asking him, his friendship was easy to me. So, to please my parents, I tried too hard and scared people off with my insistence that they play with me. I followed one poor girl around like a little lost dog until she had to get the teacher to stage some sort of anti-stalking intervention with glue and glitter.

Now I'm going to be shoved into close proximity with these four strangers and I can't rely on Frank anymore. I have to deal with it, because there's no turning back now. Just two weeks, I remind myself, as I crane my neck to see the last of the flags visible from the Glasmakirk Hotel and Spa, waving in solitude as the bus descends down into a valley and the outlook of the Highlands finally comes into view.


"Right," James yells to the back of the minibus as he turns off the endless windy road and into what looks like a forest and cuts the engine. "We're here. Before we get out I just want to make clear now that we all have to look out for each other these next two weeks. *Really* look out for each other, be allies, be kinfolk, be family, because there may be some nights where a superficial friendship just won't cut it."

I look at Bri sitting next to me on the bus and we give each other a half smile-half grimace. I, for one, do not want to know why some nights call for risk assessing a camping buddy.

"I hope no one here snores," Bri laughs, nervously. "Because tent walls won't be keeping that at bay."

And with that simple retort I know that for the next two weeks I shall not be sleeping a wink.

We clamber out the van as enthusiastically as we clambered in. But as I haul my rucksack over my shoulders, I start to notice the little things around me. The tinkling of a nearby stream that sounds as clear as a spoon on a crystal glass, the sun finally pouring through the tall pine trees that are surrounding us radiating the woody, lemony scent of camphor that prickles my nose, the loose chatter of the birds all around me like a happy laughter. I stretch my shoulders out and lean my head back so the sun filters down over my eyelids, turning them pink.

"Okay gang, has everyone got everything from the bus?" James asks, bringing my eyes back to earth and I have to blink a few times to shake the fuzziness. "Then follow me."

We traipse after the tour lead, following James along the surprisingly dusty floor of the forest. Bri skips slightly to catch up and walk beside him, her bright active wear visible clearly through the trees and the thick undergrowth. Maya drops back and walks beside Oliver whose face is once again turned down and steely, closed off to those around him. *Maybe it's nature he doesn't like!* I haven't had a chance to speak to him again this morning, but we shared a glance at the breakfast table that nearly made me inhale my cinnamon swirl.

The trail leads past more pine trees; upright soldiers reaching far up into the sky but with branches low enough to make climbing them a possibility. There's the odd tree dotted here and there that looks more like a craggy old man with a walking stick, but for the most part, the forest is uniform in height. Thankfully the heavy foliage isn't too thick for the light to filter through, the rain gentler now, so fine it's almost non-existent.

I step gently over roots as the path comes to single file. James in front, closely followed by Bri, who is demonstrating her birdsong knowledge with loud, variable, squawks; then Maya. Oliver has slowed down and is now keeping up the rear. Not looking at any of us as he goes. He seems more reticent than even I am about being sociable.

Just as Bri starts cawing what sounds like it could be the vocals of Foghorn Leghorn, the trees open up onto a body of water so twinkly I think we must have walked through the wardrobe doors to Narnia. The loch is long and thin, flanked on the opposite side by steep craggy mountains. I walk towards the water's edge to take in more of the panorama across the way; the top of the loch is dotted with a patchwork of miniature islands scattered with trees, the bottom of the loch stretches farther than I can see. All around the banks where we're standing, the tall pines stretch upwards, sentinels guarding the water. There isn't another soul in sight, the water itself as still and clean as glass that hasn't been damaged by years of dishwasher soap.

A collective sigh rings out amongst the group. James looks like the cat who got the cream, his thumbs tucked into the straps of his all-worn rucksack like a landowner surveying his quarry. And quite rightly; though he may not own this land, James has done a great job in turning the trepidation of his trekkers into a bunch of slack jawed wonders. Even Oliver has lost the tight grip on his grinding teeth, his eyes wide with emotion. A large-winged bird swoops down over the water, grabbing a fish in its talons and flying away, and Bri lets out a foghorn squawk again as we all laugh.

"Did you have that osprey primed and ready for its cue?" she asks James as she pokes the edge of the loch with the toe of her walking boot sending ripples out over the surface. "This place is amazing."

"Isn't it just?" James replies starting to walk around the water's edge towards the top of the loch and towards a large rock sticking out of it like a molar. "And the birds are dime a dozen round here so don't go leaving any food out overnight or they'll be flying off with your tent in tow."

We watch the giant bird hold tightly to the wriggling fish as it soars over the water and disappears behind the rock face on the other side of the loch. There is no doubt in my mind that whatever bird it was could lift a flimsy tent and I thank myself for the extra breakfast pastries

I've been eating, because there's no way it would get me off the floor.

"Talking of tents," James continues waving an arm in the direction of the scattering of islands at the north end of the loch. "If you'll follow me for one last time today, I'll lead you all to your homes for the next two nights and the second trek leader who has erected them."

He starts to walk then turns back to face us all.

"Perhaps 'homes' is pushing it a bit!" he says and starts back on his way, chuckling under his breath.

# Chapter Nine

They're up! The tents are up and waiting for us as we round the top of the loch. After what feels like a whole day slogging over the rough terrain I'm surprised to see it's only been eighty minutes since we left the minibus; and ten of those were spent standing around as Bri undid the thick laces of her walking boot to tip out a sharp stone that had jumped in while we were making our way over a rocky bit of shore edge.

There are six tents. Green. Basic. The type I imagine Bear Grylls to whip up in seconds whilst chewing on a snake's innards and fighting off a stampede of buffalo. They're facing the water, a semi-circle of sorts, with a campfire blazing out the front and a copper kettle hanging over it. I feel like an Amazon, and a bubble of excitement pops in my stomach sending goose bumps rippling down my arms. The sun has come out from behind the rain clouds properly now, beaming down at us all with warm rays as though James has planned this too.

It highlights the tips of the lush grass sprouting behind the campsite and sends the shingle beach into an array of oranges and reds. James drops his rucksack outside the first tent we come to.

"Here we are," he says, opening his arms wide and gesturing to the sandy shingle beach, where the water laps gently at the shore. "Loch Rosingar, once home to a Seventh-Century Irish monk brethren who used to use each of those small islands as individual dwellings. Our first stop on the wild camping trek."

His eyes are sparkling, the same green as the clear water with the reflection of the trees in all their splendour. Though the terrain where we are all standing now —where the tents have been erected—is flat, the mountain rising on our left has a sort of terrifyingly savage outlook, with its sharp slate face.

"That's Cheldiac," James says, noticing me staring at the grey facade. "Thirty-Two hundred feet of stone and slate. Impenetrable from all angles. Just how I like them."

The group wonders slowly down to the water's edge. I hang back, savouring the quiet. The beach is dotted with large rocks, and Bri stumbles as she goes. Oliver reaches out almost instinctively and grabs her arm to stop her hitting the deck. Quick as a flash Maya is there by her other elbow. They've both obviously settled into this *all for one* camp attitude already.

I drop my own rucksack with the bundle by the fire and follow the rest of the group down to the loch. As I edge nearer the water, I can see how clean and clear it actually is. Crystal all the way down to the creamy shingle underneath. Tiny fishes dart around strands of water lobelia, hiding beneath the single white flowers as Bri dips a toe of her boot into the water. It ripples around her foot and undulates over the smooth pebbles on the shore.

"I don't know about you guys," Maya says, breaking the silence that has descended over us. "And this seems to be a running theme, but I need to go for a pee, and I'm guessing that the facilities are less than opulent here in the wild."

She turns back to James who is unzipping his tent, his backside sticking up in the air.

"James," she shouts and her voice echoes around the water. "Where's the lavvy?"

James straightens up and smiles.

"I was wondering when this would come up," he says, hauling out a large, and what looks like, very heavy rucksack from inside. "If everyone could grab one and remember whose is whose."

He tips the bag and shakes it a bit and six smaller canvas bags fall out. They're cream and from the looks of how cream they still are, they're brand new. A small *Hidden Holidays* logo is emblazoned on the bottom left-hand corner in bright red. Oliver picks them all up to hand out. I swap my thanks for a bag and peer inside. There's biodegradable tissue, dog poo bags, hand gel, hand wipes, and a rainbow-coloured trowel that I don't think I'll be using for planting Petunia anytime soon.

"Oh, dear Lord," Bri says, half-jokingly as she pulls out her own luminous green trowel.

Maya hops from foot to foot.

"I'm a pro at outdoor toileting, and I know a Poo Pack when I see one. Can I dash off now while you're explaining to the others?" She looks like she's going to outdoor toilet on the spot, so James sends her on her way with a reminder to keep at least 50 meters away from the path and nowhere near any water. Maya throws her thumb up in acknowledgement and runs into the trees. I had deliberately not had an extra coffee this morning and have been rationing my water because I can barely toilet when there's someone else in the house, let alone out in the woods where anyone might walk by and see my naked rear end.

"Come and sit, I think the kettle is almost ready," James says, indicating the logs that have been placed as seats around the outside of the fire. "A conversation like this calls for vodka mostly, but our alcohol is limited to practically zero because it's so heavy and getting drunk on your first night wild camping is not a good idea. So, who's up for a cuppa?"

We all take a seat on the logs, peering into our bags. I raise my hand, warily. If I sip my tea very slowly, I could maybe cry out some tears to dehydrate myself again. James gets some metal mugs out of the hiking bag and drops a teabag into each one. Filling them with water, he stirs in some powdered milk and hands me my mug, I have a feeling my tears may be easier to come by than I first thought as I take a sip and savour the relief of a hot drink.

With us all ensconced around the blazing fire, tea in hand, James starts talking.

## Wild Swimming

"Wild camping toileting 101," he starts. "As you will have heard me saying to Maya just then; when you go, and it's *when* not *if* for those of you hoping you'll be able to sit on the porcelain throne anytime soon, make sure you're at least fifty meters away from any paths and don't go near any water. Especially running water as they will be our source of drinking water, and I don't know about you, but I'm not into water sports or drinking urine for health benefits. And don't get me started on the other…"

I look again at my tea, the murky grey colour less appealing as the conversation goes on, and place my cup on the grass beside me.

"The shovel is there for pooing, dig at least six inches, you'll all know what that is by now," he winks at Bri who looks as though she can't decide between gagging or grinning. "And if you need to use paper, bag it in the nappy sacks and bring it back with you. Same goes with the wet wipes. We'll dispose of all bags when we pass a bin."

*Oh God*, I think, at the thought of all of my carefully contained fears spilling over at the idea of carrying soiled toilet tissue in my rucksack. I shuffle on my log, my arms and legs feeling like they're in the way, too long, too heavy. I hear Oliver clear his throat and wonder if he's feeling as uncomfortable about this as I am.

"The main takeaway from wild camping is…" James pauses for effect. "Leave no trace."

*Leave no trace as I scurry back to the airport and fly to an all-inclusive?*

"And don't eat curry," he adds, jokingly, which sends Bri into a high-pitched squeal of disgusted laughter, though it could be crying given the look on her face. "And don't leave it to the last minute, because who knows how long it'll take you to find somewhere suitable."

He stands up, his jumper riding up and flashing me a glimpse of his toned stomach which is almost enough to make up for the fact I know I will be leaving the Scottish Highlands with a UTI.

Maya picks this moment to arrive back from the woods, sighing in relief and stripping her own jumper off her back. Her tanned skin glows from under her vest top, but I'm shivering at the thought of stripping away any of my layers.

"It's getting warm," she says, and Oliver casts her a raised eyebrow, turning slightly away from her as she sits practically on top of him on the empty space on his log.

"Okay, gang," James keeps talking. "We have an hour or so until lunchtime, why don't you make yourselves at home in your tents. And take a mosey around the Loch."

I look over at the sixth tent, wondering if that's a hospital tent for all those afflicted with extreme self-doubt and want to offer myself up for it right now.

"No flies on you, yet again, Fliss," James says, clocking where I'm looking.

"Not yet, give me a few days with no running water and I'll be their best friend," I joke.

He laughs. "Like I said back at the hotel, we have another trek leader who sets up the tents and starts the fires for our first location. He'll stay with us now for the rest of the trip. I can't look after you all on my own. He's been with us for as long as I have, though he's not quite as knowledgeable, or handsome!"

Bri sniggers and James flashed her a wonky smile.

"He's probably out picking stuff for supper, he's good like that. A real forager as he's pretty much a local boy now. But I'll sure he'll be back…"

"Right about now," a voice from the trees announces his arrival and James jumps from his seat and rushes to the edge of the woods where he gathers the newly arrived tour guide in his arms.

*Oh shit*, I think as I spot the recognisable man-bun of a guy who grew up two street away from me. A guy who knows more about me than I care to imagine. A guy who is a liability when it comes to keeping my well-built facade away from the rest of the trekkers.

*Of all the places in all the world.*

I swallow my fear, I should have known not to panic book something through the company of a man I went to school with. I just didn't think he would have hired his old playground buddies to work for him. I forget sometimes that normal people keep in touch with old school friends, normal people don't have reasons not to.

## Chapter Ten

"Gang meet Sam," James says, his arm around Sam's shoulders like an old buddy.

I slink to the back of the group, my head down, my stomach churning. How did I come all the way to the other end of the bloody country and end up with Sam here? Two weeks away from everyone who knows me, a chance to recharge and refresh on a holiday I wasn't even going to book, yet now I'm going to have to hope Sam doesn't remember too much about me and my family and give away my tightly held secrets. I haven't seen him since he left Kent and I was about thirteen, maybe he won't recognise me. I know that's probably not at all plausible, seeing as I recognised him from the back of his head, but there's no harm in hoping.

Sam looks just like I remember him, to be honest. His tall, willowy figure has filled out a bit with the ravages of age, and his hair has retreated slightly towards his ears, but his scruffy ponytail and huge smile look just as they did twenty-two years ago. I hope my changes are less subtle and he doesn't recognise me anymore than Maya or Bri.

"Felicity Taylor as I live and breathe." Sam pushes past the group and stands looking at me, his two front teeth still as gappy as ever, his scruffy boyish charm just as sweet. "Is that you?"

"What a surprise," Maya mutters under her breath.

She looks put out and I notice a little frown creep on Oliver's face. But it's soon eclipsed by Sam as he gathers me up in a huge bear hug, my arms stuck by my side. Despite my initial reaction and the icy dread flowing all the way to my toes, it's actually lovely to see Sam again.

I mumble a few words into his duffel coat.

"What?" he holds me out at arm's length, his eyes scanning my face. I can feel the stares of the others on me and I force a smile the way someone being greeted like an old friend probably should. "What was that? Oh, Felicity you look like a sight for sore eyes."

"Sam," I cry back, knowing that my voice sounds all wrong. "It *is* me. God, look at *you* though, how are you? What are you doing *here*, of all places? How small is the world?"

*Deflect. Deflect. Deflect.*

Sam throws his head back in a laugh. James can sense the others trying to leave in that way people do when they're not included in a conversation and he pats Sam on the shoulder and heads off with Bri who is churning out question after question as she skips along beside him to keep up.

Sam and I are left alone at the edge of the forest. I wrap my arms around myself, pulling my coat over my neck and burrowing my chin into the zipped-up collar. Sam starts walking towards the water and I follow.

"I knew it was only a matter of time before I saw someone I knew!" he says, picking up a stone and skimming it along the calm water. It bounces three times before plopping under. I think of the advert, and all of a sudden wish I'd just Googled somewhere to travel to instead. Sam doesn't recognise the discomfort in me and continues talking, the smile on his face so open and welcoming, I feel sad that I can't reciprocate. "This is where my parents brought me when we left Kent. I stayed and finished school then I wanted to travel for a bit before settling down to the grind of work. Turns out I have never really known the grind of the nine to five. I loved travelling so much I have never stopped."

"Wow," I say, genuinely interested in what he has to say now, and not just because it means not divulging anything about myself. "What did you do?"

We walk along the water's edge, the stones crunching under our feet.

"Worked a bit here and there to pay for it. Factory work. Fruit picking. Teaching English. I loved it so much. The freedom, you know?"

I don't know. I've never known that kind of freedom but listening to how Sam's voice sounds like he's still there on those citrus farms twisting lemons from their stalks makes me yearn for a moment away from memories and real life.

"Then I came back to Scotland and started working with *Hidden Holidays*, it's perfect for me. I get to conquer the wilderness every single day! What about you, Felicity?" he asks, as we round the top end of the loch and are greeted by the side of Cheldiac in all its jagged glory.

It looks as ragged as I feel. Insurmountable. Bleak. Not as wonderful as it had looked with the sun beaming fiercely on it earlier. Not as wonderful as it had looked before Sam arrived. I take a deep breath.

"Oh, you know, went to Canterbury Uni. Moved to London. Got a job in finance." I am trying to stay as neutral as I can. "But my story is boring. Tell me more about what you got up to when you weren't working. What made you continue traveling?"

"Surfing mostly. The waves were amazing in Hawaii and Oz, you don't get waves like that in Scotland, or Kent! I'd surf as much as I could. And I loved the hiking, especially in New Zealand's Middle Earth." He smiles but my skin prickles as I know what's coming. "That reminds me, how's your family? Your brother?"

A cold sweat forms on my back, tickling me. I start to shake my head in reply but am saved by Oliver as he runs up towards us holding out a net and shouting something about searching for cockles for supper. Embracing the chance to escape from any further questions, I greet Oliver a little over-enthusiastically.

"Oliver," I squeal, grabbing his arm. "I'd love to find

your cockles, show me the way! Bye Sam, great to see you again, catch up later."

The words come out too quickly, tumbling over each other. Oliver looks taken aback, peeling his arm from my tight grip he half smiles and leads the way across the shore and back to the tents. James is giving Bri a little private tuition about what a good cockle looks like, his eyes twinkling and his face almost smiling. Bri looks up at me and moves slightly closer to the tour guide, grinning.

"Right gang," James says as we all gather around. "We need something for dinner tonight. I've got some noodles to rehydrate, but we need an accompaniment. Cockles take a while to soak out the sand and grit, so if we can pick a good load now then we can cook them up for supper later. We can also collect sorrel and I noticed some chanterelles on the hike up here from the van. I'll get those though; I don't want anyone poisoning the rest of the group with Angel's Wings. I had enough toxic brain injury on the last trip to last me a lifetime."

I scrunch my face up as James takes a moments silence. No mushrooms for me tonight.

"Nice one," Bri pipes up, forcing a nervous laugh out with her words.

James doesn't say anything, so we all stand for a moment in an awkward silence.

"He tells that joke every trip," Sam whispers in my ear, making me jump as I hadn't heard him coming.

I catch Maya's eye as she watches Sam lean into me. She'd make a good poker player. It's weird, the group dynamic; as though we all know we've got to get along with no graces and judgement. There will be no room for bashfulness when we're three days into a trip with no running water. It's too early, we haven't quite worked out how to do that yet. No-one has been willing to take that giant leap into express friendship. Maya has come close a couple of times with her easiness around Bri, but she's obviously got the confidence that goes with hoiking her knickers down in front of a bus full of strangers or announcing she's off to toilet like the bears. The rest of us mortals just need to let go, and I normally have to down at least five vodkas for that to happen, and even then, I'm still guarded. And now, with Sam here, I can't afford to *let go* in a way I may have done had I not known anyone because he'll know I'm lying. It's like when I interviewed for my job, a little white lie here, a half-truth there. It wasn't as though I had been lying about my quantitative acumen or my first-class maths degree, but I had stretched the truth about how aggressively hungry I could be for the right company stocks.

Everyone does it, don't they? Big up the bits where truthfully they're lacking. That was what I was going to do here, just to get me through the weeks. But now I can't even do that!

"James, you need to change up your repertoire, mate," Sam says. "No-one will eat the dinner if you're banging on about deadly mushrooms."

James has a wicked smile on his face. "But my jokes are hilarious."

"Maybe if you haven't heard them a million times before," Sam replies, and James throws him the evil eye.

"If Sam will stop ruining my fun, we'll continue," James carries on, sticking his tongue out at his friend. "So who's up for digging for cockles?"

Bri picks up a trowel by James' feet.

"Thanks, Bri," James says, winking at her. "If one other person could grab the spare trowel, you and Bri can go to the water's edge around on the side of the Loch where it's sandy not stony," he says, holding out the trowel which I run over to take before Sam can ask me any more questions. "Look for either the pattern of the cockle in the sand, or an indent, which is a sure sign there's some yummy shellfish hidden just underneath. Fill this and then head back over."

He hands me a tea towel and I grab it and follow Bri as she starts walking slowly over towards where the mud takes over from the shingle at the edge of the Loch.

"Any idea what a cockle actually looks like?" I ask her as she pokes at the mud with the toe of her walking boot, her face scrunched up in a grimace. "I've only ever eaten lobster and oysters. I've not got a clue what we're looking for."

Bri raises an eyebrow at me.

"Posh," she says as a kind of statement with no inflection or question at all in her voice.

I want to argue that my family grew up in a council house on the outskirts of Tunbridge. That I am so far removed from posh that I could have ended up as destitute had I not thrown myself into schoolwork and uni work and then actual work. That it's not my fault my job pays well, even if I add up all the hours I work in a week and it equals more than my team's combined age—almost. That I only work that many hours in a week because it means I don't have to focus on my *actual* life.

What I actually say is.

"We're on a secret wellbeing holiday that costs a lot more than I've ever forked out for a holiday before, aren't we *all* posh?"

## Chapter Eleven

Bri digs down into the sandy mud with the trowel, squatting close to the ground, the mud is squelchy enough to sink under our feet. She's holding the trowel right at the tip, her hands staying well away from the mud. I frantically try to think of something to say to make up for my posh comment, but nothing is forthcoming.

"Look!" Bri exclaims poking harder with the trowel. "Look! Here!"

She scoops with the tool and lifts out a mud encased shell that looks like the type I used to make necklaces with for Mother's Day at first school. It's small and bumpy with furrows in uniform lines, and I like how neat it is. Bri holds it out to me on the end of the trowel and I take it, swirling it in a few inches of water to clear off the dark sand. I offer it back and Bri takes it with her nails, her face squirming.

"Perfect," James says casting a shadow over us as we

squat at the water and scaring us both half to death. "Now tap it and see if it closes. If it does put it on the towel, if not, throw it away. No-one wants the squits when they're doing it in the woods. When you're done, lift the corners of the towel and dunk in the water to rinse the sand off."

He heads back to where I can see Oliver and Maya trying to catch something in a net together. She has a hold of the long handle, struggling to hoik it out of the loch, laughing. An easy, carefree laugh, despite her shorts being soaked through with the water. Oliver is distant, holding the net at the very end which is about as much use as me helping from here. I feel a stab of jealousy, which I try to ignore because it's a ridiculous notion in more ways than one. I turn my attention back to Bri and the cockle she's now pounding with the trowel.

"Jeez," I laugh. "If that doesn't send it flying back to the safety of its home then I don't know what will."

Bri laughs and we both stare at the shell as it lays on a rock, willing it to close.

"I don't want the runs," she says by way of explanation. "I had them once on a holiday in Ibiza. Ruined the whole trip."

She flinches as the cockles closes and we both let out a laugh.

"This isn't quite what I was expecting," she says, throwing the cockle on the towel and picking up her trowel. I join her in the hunt for more food. "I thought a wellbeing trek, even one designed for the adventurous, would be somewhere hot and with a buffet of freshly caught crab or lobster. Caught by someone else, mind. This feels more like brownie camp, and I hated them when I was younger because I'm not built for the real outdoors. Running is as extreme as I get!"

I glance a look at the young woman as she chews on the end of one of her tight, French plaits.

"I don't know what to think," I say as neutrally as possible as I haven't decided quite who I want to be this holiday yet. "But isn't fresh air and lots of fresh food supposed to be good for our skin? Maybe we'll go home shining beacons of how wild camping is the new spa holiday."

"I think I'll just go home a shining beacon because my nose is so cold I'll look like Rudolph. That's if it hasn't fallen off with frostbite, then I'll just look like Voldemort."

I go to reply but am momentarily excited with myself as I spot a familiar shell under the piece of shore I'm digging in. I fish it out with my fingers and wash it off. The shell is already closed so I throw it on the towel. The sense of achievement has done wonders for my confidence, and it's only one cockle.

"Maybe Voldemort won't be such a bad look, smell's overrated anyway, especially with the squits," I say, laughing. "As long as you can keep your fingers and toes, I'm sure you'll be fine."

Later, when the sun has set and we're gathered for dinner, the smell from the large pot bubbling away over the fire proves me wrong. The smell is definitely not overrated, and it sets my stomach off on a rumble that could trigger a rock fall if I'm not careful. I press my hand to quieten my stomach through my layers of clothing and throw an awkward smile to the rest of the group sitting around the fire. James throws a couple of packs of dried noodles into the pot and stirs it with a stick that he must have cut from a tree when he was off foraging for mushrooms.

The sun has set behind the mountain, or Munro as the Scots say, and the air has a nip to it that still manages to penetrate through all five layers of clothes and my coat. I wrap my arms around myself and jiggle my legs on the balls of my feet. Half to warm up, half to stave off the need to go for a wee. The darker it gets, the more likely I am to sting myself on a nettle or get a tick stuck somewhere no-one has ventured for a *very* long time.

"I guess this is cheat's wild camping," Maya says as Sam hands out a metal bowl to each of us. "I mean, wouldn't normal wild camping mean eating out of our hands with only a sharp stick to chop things up with? Sleeping under the stars with only the wind between our bodies?"

She looks around at us all, the sense of calm radiating off her makes my cheeks flush with the idea that this shouldn't feel so hard if it's a cheat's version. Oliver must be feeling the same as his face is almost inside-out with the scowl.

James laughs and starts ladling what looks like a noodly version of bouillabaisse into our bowls. I have a favourite restaurant just down the road from where I work, they serve me up dinner when I work late, which is at least three times a week. I'd pay a small fortune for what James has just plonked indelicately in front of me.

"We have locally sourced cockles, freshly picked samphire and mushrooms, and Aldi's finest quick noodles," James says, giving it the Chef's Kiss. "And this is wild camping with a twist, Maya, my woman. We like to keep it erring on the side of luxurious."

James sits down with his own bowl and we all tuck into what has to be the most delicious thing I've had in my mouth in ages. *Sorry favourite restaurant.*

"We each make our own judgements, Maya," James continues, wiping his chin with his hand. "And who are we to take away any of the experiences that we will all get out of this adventure? Sometimes our limits are lower than we imagined, and I don't want to push anyone into the guilt of feeling they're cheating by saying what they're experiencing isn't authentic. We will make of this what our own conscious thoughts and feelings make of this. No judgement. No minimising of anyone's experience."

Maya looks suitably chastised, but no-one really pays any attention as they all look as famished as I have realised I am.

"Right, sorry James," Maya says churlishly, slurping from her spoon, her eyebrows raising when she tastes the broth whisking the look clean off her face.

"See," James says, smiling. "*We* made this. All of us. And that's pretty incredible for six people who had never met before we came on this trip. We're a team now, and we will be the best and most open and caring team there is for the next two weeks."

He addresses the rest of us now and not just Maya. Bri looks at him with wide come-to-bed eyes.

"And, in being a team, we join together as one to know each other's wildest fears and secret dreams. You can't be thrown into a situation like this and not learn more about the person sat next to you than perhaps you know your friends at home. Here we are vulnerable. Here we are free of all the constraints we have back with our families, our jobs, our mortgages. We can just be ourselves. Like I said right at the start. This trip is to get over our fears."

Everyone is nodding intently. But my appetite has vanished into the dark, night sky and I'm thankful that the light being shone by the fire is already red and flickering, just like my face is right now.

*I don't come away to open up and be myself. I come away to hide.*

"And to help us on our way to being open and honest with each other," James continues. "Before we retire for the night, we're all going to strip down to our skins and run into the Loch."

And I want the ground to swallow me whole and spit me out when the trek is over and I'm happily ensconced at my desk at work, fighting it out with a broker over the value of shares from a company that has already gone under. Where at least I can pretend to be the person I've carefully constructed over years of practice.

## Chapter Twelve

After hitting us with that delight, James gets up and drags over the huge duffle bag. It looks slightly lighter now we've emptied it of the poo packs. He unzips it and shows us what looks like a load of dressing gowns that are neatly folded into the top. The kind of dressing gowns that my dad used to wear and probably still does. Towelling ones, not like the big fluffy monstrosity that I have hanging on the back of my bedroom door that I find hard to take off once I've snuggled into it.

"Okay," James starts, sitting back down on the log. "The first rule of wild swimming is to never try to impress. It's too cold here for any of that. Only stay in for a few minutes to start with. We may be in the height of summer, which you can tell by the blizzards of midges trying to feast on you at any given moment, but Scotland's waters are like an ice bath and can be dangerous if you spend too long in them. Just be sensible and you'll be fine."

"That's why we're stripping off to swim then, is it?" Bri laughs.

"It's actually quicker to get warm if you're naked when you get out. And we'll all be keeping our hats on, modesty and all that." James lifts one of the robes. "And of course, a luxury holiday is nothing without the best of the best. And these, my friends, are *the best* in dry robes. Take one, pass the bag around."

I feel like I'm missing something when everyone starts to murmur excitedly. But when I'm handed the duffle, I pull out a robe as instructed. It's long, it'll reach past my feet which makes a change for me and my lengthy legs. The inside is the softest towelling I've ever felt and the outside of it is waterproof. I think I might start wearing it to work on mornings when the sun hasn't bothered to get up before me. I hold it up to my shoulders, catching Oliver doing similar. One eyebrow lifts, his eyes pass up and down my dry robe and a cheeky smile appears on his lips. I shake my head, rolling my eyes, giving off a cool exterior whilst inside my dinner is having a party with the hormones that have just flooded my system.

"There are neoprene gloves and boots for you all too," James adds, focusing me back on the task in hand. "I can't have any punters losing phalanges, not on my watch. Let's take half an hour down time, and I'll see you all back here at eight for a race to the water."

Bri grabs Maya's hand and drags her to their tents, comparing their robes and booties, though Maya keeps turning back to me, and I wonder if she's going to ask me to join them. By the time they're both zipped away in

Bri's tent I wonder no more. James nods his head in the direction of the woods to Sam and they scurry off leaving Oliver and me alone by the campfire. He picks up a stick and starts to poke the red-hot logs. Little puffs of blackened wood float from the flames, up into the air and away on the slight breeze. The fire reflects itself off Oliver's hands, flickering across his strong knuckles and tightly gripped fingers.

"Do you fancy a shot of something?" he asks, checking around to make sure no-one can hear him breaking the rules. "I think I'm going to need one for this evening's frivolities."

I catch his eye. His gaze is steady and there is no hint of his habitual grouchiness. I swallow as a smile tugs at the corner of his lips.

"I'd kill for a minibar or some pool entertainment to be honest," I say, running a hand through my knotty hair. "So, I'm more than up for a shot or five. Do you know where James keeps his stash of juniper berry vodka, or whatever the hell he's got hidden away for when he knows we can all be trusted not to get so drunk we wander off in the middle of the night and come a-cropper with some nettles."

"Come with me," he says, getting up off his log with a groan.

I follow suit, my old joints moaning at the cold and damp, geed on only by the thought of some warming liquor and Oliver's hands. His tent is next to Sam's, he squats to unzip the door and shuffles in, poking his disembodied head out moments later with an unmistakable tall, thin, green bottle of Absinthe.

"Oh, Oliver, I could kiss you," I say without thinking, squatting down to his eye level.

I wobble a bit as my balance tips forward and my face looms precariously close to his. His eyes widen and he moves his own face back inside his tent. *Too much?* I didn't mean it, though, did I? But only a second later he's lifting the door flaps and offering me a seat in his tiny one-man tent.

I get on my hands and knees and crawl in beside him. It's cosy. A bit too cosy, but once I've unlaced my huge walking boots and popped them just outside the tent flap, it's easier to manoeuvre. I fold Oliver's sleeping bag and use it as a cushion, crossing my legs under me as Oliver does the same on his new dry robe. We're close. The sides of the tent pushing us both into the small space in the middle. I can smell the wool from his jumper and the freshness from the bag of toiletries he has packed neatly in one corner. He unscrews the cap and offers me the bottle.

"So, is this pilfered or smuggled?" I ask, sniffing the luminous green liquid and wincing.

"Technically neither as I wasn't told not to bring it. Just an innocent addition to my already weighty rucksack," he says, totally deadpan, nodding at me to drink. "I had to leave all my books at the hotel, and that was hardship enough, so no-one is parting me from this bottle."

I snigger and steel myself. Sipping the smallest

amount, the tang of not-quite liquorice hits my tongue as it shrivels with not only the alcohol content but also the bitterness.

"Jeez," I say, puffing out air as my eyes start to water.

"I know," Oliver says, taking the bottle from me and subjecting his own taste buds to a quick death. "I'd have preferred to be a gentleman and offer you a nice glass of wine or at least a sugar cube with your drink—isn't that what you're supposed to do with absinthe?"

He shudders all the way down to his toes and laughs.

"This is the first time I've ever sampled the green stuff," I admit, shrugging and taking back the bottle, this time going for a slightly larger swig. "I always err on the side of caution, especially when something is advertised as an hallucinogenic that could kill me. That's reason enough to steer well clear."

He lifts an eyebrow again. His teasing smile is back. "Yet here you are drinking it! What's changed your mind?"

"Having to skinny dip with a bunch of strangers. I'd rather die."

Oliver chokes on his mouthful.

"Honestly though," I continue. "I can't think of any way in which I am going to get my kit off in front of everyone without being completely hammered. I don't have a young person's body like Bri or Maya, and I don't work out like you obviously do."

Oliver looks down at the floor of the tent, it's too dark to see properly but I think he might be blushing.

"My job is very demanding," he says. "I work out to take my mind off it. It's not a vanity thing."

"What is it you do?"

"Oh god, it's too boring to talk about, and I don't think we're allowed to anyway." He takes another swig from the bottle.

"Okay, fair enough," I say, and I know he's holding out on me but I'm not exactly one to talk here. "Whatever it is, I'm sure it's ten times better than sitting at a desk getting a fat arse all day like me."

"Your arse looks perfectly fine to me," he replies, the absinthe obviously taking hold of his senses already.

I grab the bottle and have another turn, my eyes on his as I do. It could just be the darkness of the tent, but Oliver's eyes look like they're wholly pupils, black gold. The tension mounting in the tiny tent is turning the air to a thick smog. Unless it's just me. Can one person make it feel like there's electricity running through the air? Maybe it's just because we're surrounded by so much nylon.

I giggle at the situation and Oliver cocks his head in question, his eyes holding mine for just a fraction too long. I zip my lips shut with my fingers and wonder if perhaps I'm a little tipsy too. I take another swig, just to make sure.

I want to ask why he's been such a grump since Heathrow. I want to know his secrets. But even with the fuzzy edge of drunkenness I know that's not a good idea. Oliver would have offered them up by now if he was going to share. I have another swig and wonder what it would be like to kiss him right now instead, his full lips are very tempting. But, I remind myself, there are my usual casual flings where I can escape as soon as they're over; and this, a casual fling where I will be trapped with the other person, unable to flee in the morning with everything I arrived with except my dignity. Not a good idea. No matter how much my body is trying to argue with me right now. Besides, he's not exactly a barrel of laughs himself, no matter how attractive he's looking in the light of the tent. I pack the idea of Oliver firmly away in one of my many boxes never to be opened, and hand him back the bottle.

"Let's go now," Oliver says, his face creased into his chest as though he's trying to suppress a giggle.

"Oh my god, yes!" I cry, ideas of kissing him long gone, replaced by excitement that someone else wants to escape back home as much as I do. "Do you know how we can get back to the airport though? Have you ever hitchhiked? Show me your thumbs, I bet you have the perfect thumbs for cadging a lift off a stranger."

Oliver holds his thumbs out in front of his face, studying them closely, balancing the bottle of Absinthe between his thighs. I look at the bottle and wonder if I can shape-shift into glass without him noticing. His eyes change focus from his outstretched thumbs to my face and a laugh explodes from his mouth.

"Oh Fliss," he sniggers under his breath. "You're really funny, do you know that."

I laugh, though I don't know what I'm laughing at quite yet.

"You've got your Jedi robe here, let's just do it!" he adds, and I realise he doesn't mean go home, he means go into the loch. Just the two of us. Swimming. Right now!

I'm not sure I've consumed enough alcohol to dip my toes in the icy water yet, let alone strip off and immerse my whole body in it. Though when I look at the bottle, I'm surprised to see a lot of the absinthe has disappeared.

"Come on. I'll turn around while you get changed, you can do the same," he says, his heady excitement is catching, either that or the alcohol is loosening my inhibitions.

It's relatively dark in here even with the fire still burning brightly through the tent flaps. But there's a bloody great maglite out there between here and the water, just waiting to illuminate all my wobbly bits. Keeping my scar hidden is a sobering enough thought to make me second-guess my whole trip, especially with Sam out there with his questions about my family and his intimate knowledge of my unscarred torso from long summer afternoons down by the river before bashfulness was a part of my repertoire.

"I don't know…" I start, but Oliver is already making like a contortionist and trying to face the wall of the tent.

"It'll be fun," he says, snorting with laughter as his foot gets caught on his elbow. "And I could use a bit of fun right now."

I wonder why Oliver is in need of cheering up, grabbing the bottle by the neck and swigging some more Dutch courage. With a few bumped elbows and a few more swigs of Absinthe we're dry robe-suited and neoprene-booted and ready to swim in water that, now we're out of the tent, looks like black tar.

Oliver pulls me along, keeping a firm grip of my hand as we edge towards the water, spluttering our giggles the way that drunk people do best.

"Hey," I hear James shouting from the edge of the forest. I squeal and laugh and grab at Oliver's other hand as we speed up a bit. "Stop."

James shouts louder, as Oliver and I are practically running to the shore. I drop Oliver's hands now, grab my robe and pull it tighter around my body, no longer wanting to get naked. The cold has sobered me up. It's too much. Too scary. I'm not brave enough when push comes to shove. But Oliver is off, his robe dropped by the edge of the water, and I watch his rather lovely bottom run out into the loch as he screams at the drop in temperature that I can feel through my boots where I've stopped at the water's edge.

"What are you doing?" James cries as he reaches me where I'm standing feeling guilty at being drunk, *and* guilty at my lack of camaraderie with Oliver. This one is very much a lose lose situation.

I step back out of the water as my toes feel like they've already dropped off. Oliver whoops as he splashes about in the shallows, fuelled by more than just the absinthe because the look on his face, highlighted by the Maglight James is shining right at him, is pure exhilaration. James is muttering under his breath about there *always being one* and he looks to me and scowls.

"Well, I suppose," James shrugs, checking his watch. "If you can't beat them."

And he strips out of his own long waterproof robe and steps tentatively into the water, his own backside taut with what I think is the cold, but it could just be good genes.

There's a high-pitched whooping noise from behind me as Bri makes her way towards the water, her own gown flapping open showing a tiny, toned body. Maya jogs past me without a robe at all, her breasts bouncing joyously as her eyes scan the water. I don't know where to look. Sam is nowhere to be seen yet, so now would be my perfect opportunity to strip off and join the gang in the loch. They're all too busy squealing at how cold it is and splashing each other to even care about what I'm up to. But I'm rooted to the spot.

*I can't join them now.*

It's too late, I have faltered just a second too long. Though really, deep down, I always knew I wouldn't be getting in the water with nothing to hide myself behind; in more ways than one. I pull my gown closer around me, rescue my clothes from Oliver's tent, and slink back to my own in the hope that I won't be missed.

# Chapter Thirteen
## Day Three

I'm woken what feels like moments later by the smell of bacon. Lifting off my silken eye mask I'm shocked by the light streaming in through the walls of my tent indicating that it is, in fact, morning. I roll my head around on my neck and stretch my shoulders out. I've slept so well that I've not even moved through the night and have now got a living rigor that I need to shake myself out of. And a raging need for a wee and a drink, in that order.

    Sitting up, my head throbs and the memory of sharing a bottle of illicit substance with Oliver returns and almost vomits right out of me. I close my eyes for a second to stop the tent spinning around me, then realise just how desperate I am for a wee, James' words of *not leaving it to the last-minute* echoing in my head alongside the thrumming hangover pain.

    I throw on some socks and my walking boots, tucking the laces in around my ankles so I don't have to spend an age doing them up. There's no time for niceties as I pass

James and Sam at the fire with a frying pan larger than my head full of sizzling bacon and eggs, so I duck my head down and wave my trowel at them as an excuse.

I make it within an inch of my teeth. The spot of land looked perfect when I approached it at breakneck speed. Away from the path, away from any running water, away from our campsite. It's only when I'm pulling up my cashmere long johns and pyjama trousers that I notice Oliver walking behind me, his own trowel glistening in his hand.

"Morning," he says, grinning, looking pointedly at the sky through the mass of trees. "Beautiful day isn't it? You missed a great swim last night, where did you go, you deserted me to take the wrath of James on my own. He properly laid into me when we got out of the water, I felt terrible, and I don't think it was just the absinthe. He did go and find you, to make sure you were okay and not face down in the loch somewhere, but he said you were snoring by the time he unzipped your tent."

I can see he's pulling my leg, but shame curdles in my stomach because everything he's saying is true. I pull my coat around me, glad that I'm not carrying a bag with soiled loo paper because there's only so much heat my face can take before my whole head combusts, and I'm pretty sure I'm at the peak of safety levels now.

"I've got to get back," I say, and speed up back to the camp, trying to ignore Oliver as he calls after me.

I throw myself back in my tent and grab my hand gel, squirting too much over my hands and ending up a sopping mess. Tears sting my eyes, though it could be the strength of the alcohol that I'm trying and failing to mop up with my flannel trousers. There are more voices outside now, I can hear the girls up and about, laughing and crunching on the shingle shore. The smell of bacon is stronger, and they must have started eating because a lull falls over the chatter.

I feel like a failure. A fraud. Tears are coming down my cheeks and I can't wipe them away for fear of irreversible damage from the hand gel. So I sit on my sleeping bag with my shoes still on my feet, cold seeping in through the flap in the tent that I haven't zipped back up, and a dampness creeping through my bones. Even my hair feels wet, though it's not raining, and I didn't dare to go swimming.

The unzipped flap of my tent blows in the breeze and gives me a view of Sam, James, Oliver, Bri, and Maya all wrapped up in their thickest clothes sitting round a fire that is somehow still going. James is wiping egg from his chin with his sleeve, Maya has her pillow of long hair wrapped around a colourful band piled on the top of her head sitting crossed legged on the floor, and Bri looks like she's stepped out of a Sweaty Betty catalogue with not a care in the world. And Oliver? What was I thinking getting drunk with him last night? I was carried away by a man who showed me a little attention. And yes, it may help greatly that he's attractive and mysterious and almost at one with the landscape, like a rugged lumberjack. But I can't get involved with someone, not here, not when I'm going to be stuck with for them for the next two weeks.

I'm an idiot.

"Felicity?" Sam's cheeky smile pokes through the gap in my tent, his ponytail hangs by his shoulder like the racoon tail on Davy Crockett's hat. "Do you want to come and join us for brekkie?"

He takes one look at my face and can obviously tell I'm sat here crying like a baby.

"Are you okay?" he whispers so he doesn't let on to the others that I can't cope. "Is there anything you want to talk about?"

And for an Earth stopping split second I search his face, wondering if he knows all about what has happened with me and Frank and is waiting for a good moment to tell me what he really thinks. But his eyes look kind so I just shake my head furiously and bite my lip so hard it makes me wince.

"Just a bit cold, that's all," I say, quelling the panic rising in me.

"Come on out and sit by the fire and warm up. I'll make you a roll with extra bacon." Sam winks, then retracts his head.

The thought of going out there and joining the others makes my stomach turn, but I need to eat, and I can't exactly avoid them until we fly home. I strip out of my pyjamas, trying to fold them and leave them neatly on my pillow as I was taught from a young age, but it's harder to do in a tent made for a Leprechaun than a three-bed semi in Kent. I try to pull my sleeping bag out from underneath me so I can straighten it out and have some semblance of order, but the material is filled with so much duck down that I'm sliding around on my backside and getting nowhere.

I can feel the panic tumbling over in me like a tide, now, because of the lack of control I have over my environment; the one thing I thought I could rely on to keep me calm when I realised we'd be camping in Scotland. *Not now, not here.* I lie back down and close my eyes, breathing in and out as my psychotherapist taught me to, so the panic can't get its claws into me and drag me under. The frequency that this strangle hold of panic seems to be happening on this trip is enough to bring on another bout of tight chest. The numbers I'm trying to count to are getting all mixed up in my head with the intrusive thoughts of how useless counting to ten is anyway.

*Come on, Felicity Taylor. Focus.*

I make a concerted effort to unclench my jaw and relax my hands. To bring myself back to the tent, even though I don't want to be here. The soft material under my fingers, the sounds of the birds soaring in the sky, the sleeping bag that was causing so much stress soft under my back. They're all grounding me, telling me that I *am* okay, that I will *be* okay. A wash of relief spreads through my body and warms my stomach, which I know is starting to eat itself with hangover and hunger. I sit up and rub my hands over my face to clear my thoughts, feeling the rough skin from lack of moisturiser and remember too late about the potent hand gel. Luckily, most of it has sunk in already and I'm just left with a slightly greasy forehead emitting an obnoxious smell.

Pulling on a thick jumper and a pair of fleece-lined water-proof trousers over my long johns, I take a deep breath and wriggle out of my tent, trying to ignore the screaming voice in my head telling me I need to straighten out my sleeping bag now I'm not sitting on it.

"Fliss," Bri cries from her perch on the log, wiping grease from her chin with the back of her hand. "Where have you been? Didn't think you could get jet lag from England to Scotland."

I pull a smile on my face and go and join her, cursing myself for not at least having a mint to take away the smell radiating from my mouth. It's toxic enough to strip a rodent of fur.

"Morning, gang," I say. "Sorry about last night, I think maybe a cockle too many for me."

It's a good enough excuse, I have no-one else to blame other than myself.

"You missed a great swim," James says, as Sam hands me a roll filled with so much bacon that my smile turns real.

"It was the *best* thing I've done all year," Maya pipes up, not even trying to hide the fact she's got a mouthful of bap. "I'm still feeling it now."

"I dipped my toes in," I try to joke. "And I still *can't* feel them now."

A small ripple of polite laughter flits around the group of campers and, as I take a huge bite of delicious bacon roll so I don't need to speak again, I count down in my head just how many days I have left to endure.

## Chapter Fourteen

"Okay, gang," James says as he pops the last bit of his breakfast in his mouth. "We've got a treat lined up for you today."

"Oh, that's my cue." Sam jumps up from his log and heads off in the direction of the woods, waving as he goes.

"Can we get undressed for this one, too?" Maya asks, her eyes darting to Oliver.

"Nope, swimsuits and booties for this one, please," James answers. "And maybe a sweater too as the air has a bit of a chill to it. Probably a hat."

Bri laughs.

"So fully dressed then?" Her own eyes twinkle as she speaks.

"Let's go with swimwear underneath with extra warm on top, though you will hopefully be staying out of the water." James has a cheeky grin on his face, he hauls himself up off the logs stretching up to the sky. "So off you pop and get changed, meet by the water's edge in fifteen."

We all disband, slowly, as though stuck to our own logs with moss. I think it's more likely our creaky bones from sleeping in a tent with only a sleeping bag between us and the cold, hard, highland floor.

"Fliss," James comes up behind me as I'm making my escape. "Do you have a minute?"

My now full stomach drops to my toes, but I nod in what I hope is an encouraging way. He indicates towards Loch Rosingar with a flick of his head and I follow him to the water's edge as we head towards the mountain face of Cheldiac. We walk for a moment in silence, just the crunching of the shingle underfoot and the soft lapping of the water. The air is crisp and clean, each breath a lungful of pure restorative oxygen and I can see for a moment how James manages to conjure up motivational quotes as though they're second nature to him. In the right frame of mind, this Loch could do the same for anyone.

We reach the edge of the Loch where the water meets the mountain, and the noise of the waves is louder here.

"Why is the water acting like the sea today?" I ask, stopping by the great wall of slate that makes up the side of Cheldiac. "Look, it's like it's tidal."

I point to where it's lapping against the great husk of wall where it sinks under the water

James takes a seat on a large slab of granite that protrudes over the water from the base of the looming rock. He pats the space next to him and I perch as close to the edge as I can.

"It *is* tidal," he says, throwing a small stone into the dark water. It must be deep here, there's no sign of the shingle underneath, just a black stretch of water lapping against the sheer mountain drop. I pull my legs up as a barrier and wrap my arms around my knees to hold them there. "All bodies of water are attracted to the gravitational pull of the moon."

I can feel his eyes on me, but I focus on the inky black water.

"This loch is one of the larger ones, so the tides are noticeable, you'll see in the next one we visit that it's much smaller and less… wavey."

A giggle bubbles up in me despite myself.

"Wavey?" I ask, an eyebrow raised. "Is that the technical term?"

James screws up his own face, his pout turning into a smile.

"There we go," he says, his face softening. "A smile."

He drops his chin, his eyes meet mine, staring up at me through his thick eyebrows. Something tugs at my stomach; I think it might be fear that James has spoken to Sam about me and can now see right through my eyes and into my broken soul. I pull my gaze away and look again at the water. Magnetised by the pull and push of it against the rock face.

"Is everything okay with you, Fliss?" he asks me, crossing his legs under him. "Only, I've noticed you've been a bit withdrawn since yesterday and I wanted to check in with you. It can be tough, when we first arrive, and you realise what the next ten or so days entail."

He picks at a bit of rock by his side and I keep quiet, scrambling for words that mean I can go and hide back in my tent.

"I really want all my guests to get out of this what they can," he says, and I can feel him looking at me again. "And to do that you really have to want to join in. Otherwise, you'll miss out, and I don't think you're here to miss out, are you? You said, back in the hotel, that you wanted more than a five-star spa. Here it is, right here in front of you, and you don't seem to want to let it in."

*Is he going to give me a way out? A helicopter back to Kent perhaps? Can helicopters fly all the way to Kent from here?*

"We're in wilderness that can change at the drop of a hat," he continues. "And because of that we need to look out for each other. We need to know we can depend on you, Fliss. Because anything can happen. Even though I *am* the best tour guide this side of that mountain."

I sneak a look at James. The cheeky grin on his face tells me what I already guessed.

"I just…" I start, but I don't know what to say to him.

*I just what? I'm just worried that swimming is going to give me hypothermia and I'll end up in hospital. I'm worried that people will think I'm boring. I'm worried about going to the fucking toilet when there are other people around. I'm worried that after last night people will forget I'm here and that maybe that is for the best. I'm worried, because that is what I do and who I am. And I have a very good reason for being like this.*

"I'm fine," I say eventually. "I am just a bit tired that's

all. I'm sure I'll be up for a paddle later on today. And I promise to join in. I can be a team player when I need to be. And I can see that this trip has team player written all over it!"

He studies my forced smile for a moment, and I can see it written all over *his* face that he doesn't believe a word of what I just said, and I'll give him credit for that. He places a hand on my knee, the warmth of it seeping through my layers of waterproof polyester and soft, thin long johns.

"Maybe lay off the Absinthe then," he says, smiling softly and scrabbling to his feet. "See you later, Fliss."

He jumps down onto the shingle and throws me a look.

"I'm always here for you, you know Fliss. Just don't tell the others." And with a wink he's striding back down the beach towards the campsite.

I shake my head, laughing, and let go of my legs, my hands aching with the strength it took to hold them against me. I let them drop over the edge, where I'm sure they're far enough away from the lapping water. My right knee is still warm where James had laid his hand. He's kind, he has our best interests at heart, and I feel guilty at my lack of participation last night. But his words *have* helped me, and I need to tell him that when I next see him.

I stretch out onto the sun-warmed slab of rock, leaning back on my elbows and close my eyes for a moment's peace. The sun stains the inside of my eyelids the colour of pink roses. The water sloshes about rhythmically beneath my feet and it's all I can do to stay awake. Fear of slipping from the rock after nodding off, sinking into the dark depth of the water, is enough to keep me awake. The sun is warm on my face and I notice that my jaw isn't as clenched as normal.

*This is okay*, I think, adjusting my legs so my heavy untied boots aren't at risk of falling from my feet.

I lay for a moment. Taking in the noises of nature around me, the smells of air so fresh it whips right up my nose and into my brain, and I make a vow right here and now to join in with these people as much as I possibly can. That might at least make the days go by quicker, and that's no bad thing.

Back at my tent, I'm already cursing my newfound fortitude for being a team player as I struggle out of my underwear and into my swim wear. I'd deliberately bought one of those all-in-one tankini things when I'd splashed out on new clothes which I thought might take a dip in the lakes of the Himalayas. It's got shorts and sleeves and looks like it could pass for a wetsuit. Though it's a Boden one so I think it looks stylish as well as covering up all the extra bits of skin I don't want on show. Thankfully, it's not normally at the forefront of my mind anymore, but my scar has been so tight with the cold weather that I've been forced to think about it since we arrived. I dread to think what the freezing temperature of the Loch will do to it. Shrivel it up so much my ribs will be sucked in and I'll look like I'm straight from the pages

## Wild Swimming

of a Victorian period novel with ribs misshapen from corset use. Urban myth or not, I do *not* want to look like that.

I unzip my tent and throw on a hat, a long sleeved thermal, and a jumper for good measure. My booties back on my feet after their little dip last night, it's just my legs left to fend off the cold.

Maya and Bri are already at the water's edge. Maya is doing some form of yoga, standing on one leg with her arms stretched up to the sunshine. Bri is standing in the water with bootie clad feet, her arms wrapped around her body. I decide to go and join them, the panic rising in me at the horrible thought they might reject me, but I'm already walking in their direction and I can't do a U-turn now. It's like the school playground all over again; red hot fear stabbing in my chest. At least back then I had Frank to rely on, always there for me whether or not the girls in the playground called me weird and sent me flying. No chance of that kind of moral support these days.

"Hey, Fliss," Bri says, her ponytail swishing as she turns to me. "Nice to see you. What do you think our surprise is, I can't quite work out why we need swimmers *and* warm clothes?"

I breathe normally, the fear dissipating at her friendly smile.

"No idea," I reply, my voice still a little shaky. "Maybe some form of log rolling?"

Maya looks at me curiously.

"I think it's going to be a team building exercise," she

says, her nose wrinkling in disgust. "Maybe they decided we need to bond more."

I wrap my arms around my body, though I'm sure Maya isn't directing her disdain purely at me.

"Will you actually get in the water today, do you think?" she asks me. "I saw you swimming back at the hotel with Oliver, you looked pretty at home there."

"I can see to the bottom of a pool," I say. "And they tend to be heated to a temperature that won't make my extremities fall off."

Maya snorts. "I don't think James would let us swim in water that will give us frostbite," she says, smiling acerbically.

"Oh no," Bri adds, quick to defend the young tour guide. "He's definitely making sure we're safe."

A small ripple runs over her skin, enough to make her shoulders shake as she bites down a smile that is spreading over her face.

"I'm sure he is," I reply.

"So, you'll come in the water then?" Maya slips an arm through mine and squeezes hard enough that I can't break free.

Luckily I'm saved from having to answer Maya's question by James' booming voice.

"Right then," he says, clapping his hands together, and I can tell he's been back on the coffee; never mind the wildlife, James' caffeine habit is another reason the fire can never go out. "If you're all ready, please follow me."

# Chapter Fifteen

Maya drops my arm and starts skipping after James as he walks around the edge of the water of Loch Rosingar.

"Can I just take a moment to apologise?" Oliver says, catching up to me, a hand on my arm throwing me off guard. "I shouldn't have gotten you drunk last night. I wanted to drown my own sorrows and ended up almost drowning myself. There was no need to drag you down with me."

He looks at me with his huge brown eyes and I feel my stomach turn over itself like the small waves at my feet. I falter, my foot hitting a boulder that I didn't see because my eyes were too busy looking at Oliver. His hands shoot out and grab me by the shoulders before my face has a chance to hit the boulder too.

"Whoopsie, thanks," I say, trying to remember to breathe as Oliver pulls me back upright, his hands lingering as I turn to face him. "And please don't apologise."

Oliver looks at me, his eyes searching my face, eventually landing on my lips and staying there for a moment longer than they need to. I feel like my heart is about to burst free of my chest as his mouth parts slightly, his two front teeth perfect in their imperfection. I draw my bottom lip into my mouth to give myself something to do as Oliver looks back up into my eyes.

"Okay," he says, his voice croaky. "But, just so you know, I won't do it again."

"Oh," I exhale. "Right. Okay then."

The joyous screams of Bri and Maya interrupt my train of thought, which is just as well as I was about to tell Oliver he's welcome to get me drunk every night if he'd like to, but that feels slightly desperate now we're not staring into each other's eyes.

*He's just said he won't do it again, leave it at that Felicity.*

Oliver mutters another apology under his breath as he races off past me to join the others. They're in a clearing, a small alcove through the trees where the loch ripples up against the sandy bank in regular waves. James is in the water, all the way up to his waist, flicking fingers of spray at the girls and making them laugh, their joy obvious. But my eyes are drawn to Sam, where he waits by the edge with three large, bright yellow, inflatable boats and a handful of paddles.

"Dinghies?" I say, heading over to check out how sturdy they look.

"Dinghies?" Sam says shocked, handing me one of the paddles. "Felicity, love, these are your finest Scottish inflatable *kayaks*."

## Wild Swimming

I look down into the murky depths of the two-seater inflatable. The insides are grey and there's a small puddle of water at the base, not to mentions the seats are already covered in splotches of watery mud.

"It says *made in Taiwan*," I kid, as Sam throws an arm around my shoulder and laughs from his belly.

Maya glances over, her eyebrow raised.

"Right gang," James shouts from the water. "Time to pair up and pick a boat."

Quick as a flash Maya has her arm through Oliver's, grinning like the cat that got the cream.

*That's her game? She fancies him too. Well, that makes sense.*

Oliver lets himself be led over to the kayaks by Maya and they grab a paddle each and start to drag the inflatable boat to the edge of the loch.

"You and me then, hey?" Bri says, staring at the two kayaks left and biting her lip. "I don't have the best sea legs, just to warn you."

"That's okay, Bri," I say. "I don't think it'll be too choppy out there."

She doesn't look too sure, but we go and grab an end of a sunshine yellow kayak each and start to haul its surprising weight to the water. James holds it steady as we clamber in, Bri grabs the back seat and is holding on so tightly her knuckles are as white as the little frothy peaks of water tumbling over the rocks beside us. I steady myself with my paddle, leaning on it and stepping into the front of the kayak. It wobbles with my weight, and I wobble too, praying with all my might that I don't keel over before I've sat down. My balance is normally pretty good, but the movement of the boat is making it hard to stay upright. Eventually, with a little help from James, I'm sitting comfortably, and our boat is bobbing calmly on the water.

Oliver and Maya are already rocking gently on the water out near the middle of the loch. Maya has her feet propped up on the back of Oliver's seat, while he paddles furiously in our direction. I can hear his deep voice as it travels over the water, and he does not sound happy. Mind, I wouldn't be either if I was having to do all the work.

I lift my paddle in the air like a sword.

"Tally ho," I squeal as water drips all over me from the flat end. "Off we go."

Bri shouts in laughter as James pushes our kayak out into deeper water and we sway side to side with the movement.

"I'll paddle on my left," Bri shouts as we try to work out who should be paddling on which side.

"I think that's my left too," I shout back, my stomach pinched with laughter. "So, I'll go right."

I've no idea why we're shouting to each other, I'm almost sitting in Bri's lap, but we do anyway. As we start twisting in circles around to the left, I glance a look over my shoulder.

"Bri," I say, tears of hysteria rolling down my cheeks. "That's not your left."

Bri can't get any words out she's laughing so much. Our boat starts to bob further out from the shore towards where Maya and Oliver are floating calmly now Oliver has stopped paddling. I see him look over at the commotion, a smile fleetingly on his face whipped away quickly by Maya poking him in the back with her paddle and saying something I can't hear over Bri's honking like a seal.

We're gaining on their boat with surprising speed, so I try to get my paddle to move us away. It's not kayak bumper cars we're playing. But my paddle only serves to spin us around again, so now we're heading to Oliver straight on. I can see the trepidation on his face as we start to loom ever closer, but I can't do anything about it because my insides have cramped up with the hilarity and Bri is less than uselessly lying back on the shelf of the kayak because she can barely breathe anymore.

Oliver's apprehension soon fades to a smile and he shrugs helplessly at me as our boats bash into one another. Bri screams and laughs with a splutter, her legs shoot out and push at the back of my inflatable seat, her paddle splashes into the loch. I grab the sides of the kayak, fear gripping me now at the thought of falling in the freezing water. Oliver must see something in my face.

"You're okay," he mouths across the water to me just as Sam and James row up beside us and grab hold of the edge of my kayak.

"Well," Sam says, handing Bri back her paddle before it floats away. "From that display, I'm assuming none of you have ever kayaked before?"

It's too much. We all crack up again. A great release of tension of all the stress and apprehension from the start of a trek that had turned out so differently to how we all imagined. Though I'm sure the rest of the gang released a lot of pent-up emotion last night with their swim, I'm glad I can join them now. My shoulders release a little from where they've been resting up by my earlobes.

"We're going to have a race," James adds when our mania has calmed to a lull full of sniffing and sighing. "At least, that was the plan, but if rowing in a straight line is going to be a problem then maybe we need to rethink."

Bri flips her paddle over behind me, spraying my bare neck with icy drops of water. I flinch and shake them off as best I can, thankful for my hat, even though it's making my hair itch now I'm warming up.

"It's okay," she says, coughing. "I've worked out which is my left now, so we'll be fine. Bring it on!"

Oliver chuckles and Maya is at his back with the poky end of her paddle again. He sits upright and gets ready for battle.

"Once around Loch Rosingar," Sam shouts as our two kayaks are splashing to get into position. "First ones back wins the packet of Skittles I found in the glove box of the van."

"Ooo, I love Skittles," Bri shouts, pumping her paddle on the water. "Fliss, we have to do this. You go right. I'll stay left."

"Wait," I yell as James starts the count down. "Bri, you weren't left to start with, do you mean you'll stay right?"

"Just paddle!" she yells as James shouts *GO!*

We all start to paddle frantically, sending more water

up in the air than behind us. Neither of the racing kayaks are moving very fast, and we're so close to each other that I can almost smell the cologne from Oliver's clothes which is very distracting, and I wonder for a moment if he's doing it deliberately. And when he and Maya race off ahead of our kayak I fear I might be right.

"Paddle!" Bri is shouting, her Welsh accent spreading out the letters beautifully. "Fliss, paddle!"

"I *am* paddling," I squeak, as my paddle finally finds purchase in the water rather than skimming off the top.

The kayak lurches forwards and we are off on our way. James and Sam's own kayak floats gently in the water and with an ease that seems unfair, starts to follow the race.

"Make sure the flat bit hits at this angle," I say, tilting my head back so Bri can hear me, as I hit the water again and push the kayak forwards.

"Right 'o," Bri says, and she must have been watching as we start to move smoothly and glide rather than judder over the glassy surface of the loch.

It doesn't take us long to get into the swing of it, and soon we're gaining ground on Oliver and Maya. Bri starts yelling *pull* every time she rows, like a novice coxswain who doesn't know the terminology but has all the enthusiasm. It is helping our teamwork though, and Maya glances back and screams something at Oliver. Though from where I'm sitting, he still looks like he's doing all the legwork, well, arm work.

Loch Rosingar is huge. By the time we've reached the far end and are trying to negotiate the deep curve to bring us back up, my arms are aching, and my stomach muscles have forgotten what relaxed feels like. I feel invigorated, and from the sounds of the chanting behind me, Bri is the same. The small islands dotted in the loch are resplendent at this end, just big enough for a single bird's nest or a resting seal, they're like a giant's steppingstone over the water. Oliver's kayak is heading straight towards one of the larger ones, his strong arms powering their kayak pretty fast though the water, despite the distance they've already covered. Maya's own oar is hitting the water every five or six of Oliver's strokes. I can just imagine the muscles in his back and shoulders are screaming as much as mine are, or maybe not, maybe he's actually quite fit. I smile at the thought of them, memories of his naked rear still fresh in my mind from last night, and I'm glad no one can see me fawning over a man I barely know.

"Pull, Fliss, pull!" Bri shouts, and I try to get back into the rhythm after being momentarily distracted by an attractive man. "I want those bloody Skittles."

Oliver pulls out around the plinth-like rock and we're not too far behind them now. He's losing strength, I can see his shoulders slump a little as he starts to row up the other side of the loch. In order to get ahead and go around their boat, Bri and I are going to have to do some smart thinking that I'm not sure either of us are up to right now. So, while we're gaining ground we're heading for another collision.

"You row harder, let's cut them up on the inside," I yell, as the back of Maya's head come into sharp focus.

Maya must hear me as her head spins in our direction. Her eyes are narrow and the look she gives me makes me want to get out and give her the bag of Skittles myself. I didn't realise quite how competitive she is. But then again, why would I? I've known her less than seventy-two hours.

"I don't know what that means, but I'm hitting it as hard as I can," Bri pants.

I lift my paddle out of the water and we turn towards the centre of the loch. As I start to row again, my bum muscles now joining in with the screaming, our kayak glides alongside the opposition and Oliver looks over at us. I feel hot and sweaty under my hat, and self-consciously I don't want to look back at him, but he flicks me with water from his oar with a side smile and a cheeky grin.

"This is war," I yell, smiling back, and rowing as hard as I can to take our kayak's nose slightly in front of theirs.

"Prepare to be defeated," he yells back over, flicking me with water again.

The action slows their boat enough for Bri and I to gain the upper hand. Maya is shouting angrily at her partner to stop messing about and start rowing again. I don't look back, my own sense of competitiveness streaking through now we're actually ahead.

It's only as Bri and I are swerving around another small island that I hear a loud splash behind us. We both stop rowing, our breathing ragged, the sound of a whistle piercing through the silence that has enveloped us now that we're still. Behind us, the opposition kayak is bobbing on the water as Sam and James row towards it. Maya sits serenely in her seat and Oliver's head bobs up and down in the water beside her.

"Remind me never to get between Maya and her sweets!" Bri says, as we all sit around the fire spooning what tastes like delicious, freshly caught monkfish into our mouths.

Oliver is wrapped in enough layers to look like a Michelin man and is hugging his arms to his body.

"It was an accident," Maya says, sweetly. "I didn't mean to tip him overboard; I was simply trying to get him to focus on the task ahead and not the enemy."

James laughs and pokes at the fire with a blackened stick.

"The enemy?" he asks, grinning, lifting a full kettle onto the flames.

"Well, you know, the other boat," Maya says, side-eyeing me.

I think I may have been right in thinking Maya has a soft spot for Oliver. I'm just glad it was him she tipped into the water, and not me.

"Share these amongst you," Sam says, handing me a grab bag of rainbow-coloured sweets. "Just don't kill each other in the process."

I rip the bag open and take a handful, savouring the sugariness even though it's not been that long since we left the hotel. The hit is almost immediate, which shows me just how reliant I normally am on sugar to get me through the day, and how much my body has been craving it.

"Enjoy," James says, crunching an apple. "And try to swim later, or jog around the loch to ease your muscles a bit, or you'll all be feeling them in the morning, and we have a long day of walking tomorrow."

I sip at the cup of coffee handed to me, looking over at Oliver as I do. He's deep in thought, somewhere miles away from Loch Rosingar and Cheldiac, and for a flash of a second I'm glad I'm *not*.

## Chapter Sixteen
### Day Four

"Is everybody ready?" James bellows over the torrent of rain drowning out even the loudest seagulls today. He's standing on the trunk of a fallen tree, surveying his trekkers.

We all nod as a crack of thunder rumbles overhead. Frank loved a storm when he was little, used to run outside in them and see how many seconds he could count between lightning and thunder. He'd shout up at me hiding in my bedroom when the storm was on its way off. I could do with him here now, because that clap of thunder sounded loud enough to shake the earth. I look to James to gauge if I need to be concerned, but his face is ever the excited chipmunk. We're leaving Loch Rosingar today and heading off to pastures new. Despite the fun I had yesterday, I can't say I'm sad. The loch this morning looked foreboding, the rain cutting through the normally glassy surface like needles. My skin feels permanently damp, and even my bones are shivering. I wonder what the chances are for another five-star hotel with spa at the next location, but I know the answer before I've even thought of the question.

"Sam will be taking down the campsite and driving to the next location so he can drop back the kayaks and greet us with a fire and a cuppa," James says, pointing to a very sodden but happy looking Sam.

Sam gives a salute and sets about undoing the tents. Or whatever it's called when a tent is unpinned from the floor and collapses under the weight of the rainwater collecting on the roof. We turn back to James.

"This is one of the longest treks of the trip," he says, from his position on the tree. "It'll be nightfall by the time we reach our destination. There's a lot of tricky terrain, so I hope you're all wearing your boots with two pairs of socks, and have a spare pair in case of hidden streams or bogs?"

Everyone nods again. I have on two pairs of good quality, thick, fair isle socks that are made of bamboo and cost me an arm and a leg. I just hope they don't cost me my feet too because the salesman who sold them to me reiterated the need for plasters, despite having the best walking socks, quite a few times as we were heading towards the till.

"Make sure you've got plenty of water in your bottles, though we can restock on the way; there are lots of streams with fresh, clean, cool drinkable water. And I've got a bevvy of snacks in here. Plus some wild rice and my camping stove." He pats his own laden rucksack. "So if everyone's been for a toilet stop, then let's head off."

That was one thing I had done. First light this morning. I woke early and walked as far as I could without getting lost. I was back by six and ready for breakfast of fresh kippers and mushrooms. No-one batted an eyelid at my being ready for breakfast early this morning, and I feel as though I'm slowly being enveloped into the folds of this small, and ever-present community.

We start off back through the woods, following James. Bri and Maya seem to be forming a proper bond and they quick step behind James, laughing at something unheard. I'm behind them, and Oliver is bringing up the rear.

Maybe I should slow down, fall into step with Oliver and start up a conversation. But ever since he fell out of the kayak yesterday, his mood has sunk back as low as the temperature of the loch. Then the path narrows before I've made my decision, making it for me. So, the two of us carry on in silence.

The trees fold in over the top of us as we walk further into the forest; blocking out any sun that may have appeared, but also a lot of the rainfall too. The noise the rain makes as it patters on the leaves above is wonderful, like the tropical shower in the Centre Parcs Spa, just colder and less luxurious. It's rocky underfoot and I have to really concentrate so I don't slip over and twist my ankle, even though my brain is screaming at me to fall over and twist my ankle. Notions of rescue, and early release, and warm beds, and solitude are all flashing like welcome beacons; maybe I'll wait until we're nearer a road at least.

The further we walk the harder it is getting, and I think we might be on a slight incline as the drops of rain that *are* penetrating the foliage are running down the rocky path past me towards Oliver. I sneak a glance behind me, he's concentrating on his own feet so doesn't see. He looks miles away, figuratively; he's only a few steps literally. But he's calm, his face relaxed and deep in what looks like positive thoughts. It's the first time I've seen him totally serene and it's a look that suits him. I feel like I, on the other hand, look like I'm trying to work out my tax return without a calculator.

There's a lot of uneven terrain over the next few miles, we're up and down over tree roots, circling around large boulders, stepping over mini streams, and squelching through mud covered puddles. Though it's the height of summer, the forest floor is slippery with damp fallen pine needles. I'm aching. My lungs are screaming for a rest, my mouth for a cup of tea.

*Not for the faint hearted?*

What was I thinking? This is like a spot in SAS: Who Dares Wins, only I can't take off my armband and be rescued anytime I like. We're all walking in silence now, though if anyone spoke to me at the moment, I'd struggle to get out any words to reply. I didn't realise how unfit I had become. I used to be able to walk without breaking out in a sheen of terror sweat. Now I haven't even made it five miles and I'm already dead inside. I really do miss the energy that being fit gives me, that buzz of adrenaline I used to have when I'd leave the pool and cycle to work. I make a mental note to try my hardest to restart my early morning swim. If I make it home; the jury is still out on that one.

"Shhh," James hisses, startling me, his arms flaying out by his sides to halt us all in our tracks. "Everyone quiet and get down."

*Oh god, what's happening?*

I don't even think about what I'm doing, I just reach around behind me and grab hold of Oliver's arm, gripping it tightly, squeezing my eyes shut to the horror ahead. The adrenaline rush has my heart beating hard in my chest but the longer my eyes are squeezed shut, the dafter I feel at my breakneck overreaction. Oliver squats down at James' command and I follow his lead, ignoring the pain in my poor legs as the blood that had been pumping rapidly with all the walking is now trapped under my bent knees and filling up my calves.

I bury my head in Oliver's duffle jacket to hide my embarrassment, only slightly distracted by how nice he smells and how protective his arm feels through the many layers.

"Fliss," he whispers. "That was quite something, everything okay in there?"

"All good. All good. Just caught me off guard," I whisper back, trying not to laugh.

"You're not kidding," he says, his voice full of fun.

"What were you expecting? A T-rex? Deliverance-esque Hillbillies with no teeth?"

I feel Oliver's body shaking next to me, a muffled snort escaping him. I peel an eye open and realise how close my face is to his. And he's biting his lips to stop a laugh, his face puce.

"Look," he says, nodding towards where James is now crouching on all fours, Bri and Maya giggling at the sight of his backside stuck right in their faces.

I take in the sight myself as my heart rate slows a little.

"No," Oliver whispers, seeing that my line of sight is looking straight at James' muscular buttocks. "Look."

He uses his free arm to move my head in the direction of two giant stags through the trees. I gasp. They're beautiful. They can obviously sense us as they're standing stock still, like a shot from a postcard. Their heavily antlered heads both looking in our direction. Huge pools of black eyes check us out, as though ready to strike, their breath clouding around their muzzles. One of them snorts, the noise surprisingly loud amongst the trees. He moves a hoof and my nerves return at the thought of a stag stampede which could be as fatal as a pair of gap-toothed mountain men with a banjo. I squeeze Oliver's arm again, tucking myself in behind his body this time. He shakes his head, laughing quietly.

"They're not going to come after you," he whispers right into my ear, my skin prickling with a different kind of sensation this time. "They're just checking us out, wondering if we're a danger to them. If we all keep still and quiet, they'll soon leave us alone."

"And if I accidentally move because my legs feel like jelly?" I hiss.

"They'll charge you, probably squash you into the rocks underfoot," he whispers. "Maybe prong you with their razor-sharp antlers depending on how quickly you can get out of their way."

I tense.

"I'm joking," Oliver whispers again. "They'll flee. They're only brutal with each other, and that's only when it's mating season. Uh oh, I hope you're not giving off any pheromones."

Now I don't know if he's still teasing or not, but I metaphorically cross my fingers and toes as the more I squeeze Oliver's arm, the more my pheromones will be oozing freely from my pores. I ignore him instead, and focus back on the huge, majestic—if slightly scary up close—creatures. The noise of a bird taking flight above us spooks the stags into action. With a jolt of their feet and a snort of their muzzles they're galloping through the forest with a thunder of hooves. It's humbling. We all listen in silence until the stags are out of earshot and James gives a laughing whoop.

"Wow," he says to the group, jumping up from his position on all fours as though his legs can handle the lack of blood that have turned mine to jelly. "That was a sight and a half. Amazing. What did you guys think of that then, hey?"

"That was pure magic, thank you, James," says Bri as

she brushes her knees clean of dirt and rearranges her hair in her woolly hat. "Though they would have gotten me a lot of insta likes if I had been allowed my phone with me."

James laughs and Bri pushes his arm and pouts at him.

"But I bet it was better to view through your eyes than through a phone camera?" he says, steadying himself on Bri's arm.

She gives him a small nod, the pout dropping from her lips as they draw into a smile that is as real as the stags had been.

"One hundred percent," she says, quietly.

"I saw a pair of red stags just like that when I was travelling, except their antlers were a totally different shape." Maya interrupts their moment. "It makes me feel so alive being that close to such wonderful animals."

"You're an adventurer then, Maya?" James asks, hoiking his rucksack higher on his back. "You like to travel."

"I do," she says, pulling up her walking socks then rolling them down to the tips of her battered boots. "It's in my blood."

Oliver lets out a snicker which he quickly disguises as a cough.

"Deliverance?" he says, thankfully still whispering, helping me to my feet and singing the famous banjo song under his breath.

"I used to like horror movies when I was younger," I say, shrugging and blushing in equal amounts. "I can't watch them anymore, though. They're too creepy for me."

"Really?" Oliver says, the smile dropping from his lips. He watches me for a moment, his face serious, his eyes dark, and my chest constricts enough to stop any more words escaping. "Is there anything you're not scared of, Fliss?"

## Chapter Seventeen

We walk on, I think about what Oliver has said, how I reacted instinctively to what I presumed was danger. And how Oliver hadn't made me feel silly about it, not really. Was this how it was supposed to feel? Not panicky and anxiety inducing, but manageable? The thought rocks me but I don't have time to dwell on it as James thrusts a canvas bag under my nose and gathers Oliver and me into his arms.

"You two." He grins, taking me by surprise as I'd been daydreaming about danger. "You're on blackberry duty. No prizes for guessing which bushes you'll find them on, so get to work."

I look over at Maya and Bri who have their own canvas bag and are trudging along looking up at the trees. I wonder what they've been asked to forage for.

"You hold the bag open for me, Fliss," Oliver says, nodding in the direction of a rather resplendent looking bramble bush. "I'll go in for the kill. Wish me luck."

He sets off, over a fallen tree that's rotting into the mulch of the forest floor. I follow, treading in his steps, watching the ease at which he traipses off the beaten track to our goal.

The bush is dense with blackberries and thick with thorns, butterflies flit silently between the vines, and the ambrosial scent of fruit is rich and sweet. Oliver reaches out and puts a hand on my arm, stopping me in my tracks, and nods to the ground where a small cluster of furry looking purple flowers spring through the earth.

"Watch your step," he says, his fingers gently tightening around my arm. "They look like they've had a tough life already, let's not squash them."

"Oh, sorry," I whisper, looking at how pretty the petals look surrounded by the mulch and moss.

"Fliss." Oliver looks at me now, dropping his hand from my arm and blinking slowly. His eyes darken. "Don't be sorry. I was just pointing them out."

His voice is only just a little above a whisper too, so I lean in, trying hard to hear him over the exuberant bird song. He smells of oranges and woodsmoke and something else that makes my face heat. A single bird begins to sing, louder than the rest, a clear warble that pitches through the sound of my heart beating in my ears and I have Oliver's full attention now. It's slightly disconcerting, as though he is taking in every detail of me in minutiae, and I peel my eyes away before my chest restricts any further.

"It's good to watch out for things that can't watch out

for themselves." Oliver clears his throat and steps around the flowers to the blackberry bush.

I hum a reply and fold open the canvas bag with shaking hands.

---

"We're almost there," James says, battling though a thick bramble bush we've not unladed of berries. "This is a little more overgrown than the last time I came this way, watch yourselves."

After our encounter with the local wildlife and our respective foraging trips, James had found us a spot by a brook to stop for some lunch. It had been pretty dry underfoot as the tree cover above was so thick that not even the gnats could get through. I had stripped off a few layers and gladly accepted a cuppa once James had the fire going. We had all refilled our water bottles and eaten the sweet, clean tasting early chestnuts that Bri and Maya had found, topped off with a feast of thick, juicy blackberries that stained our fingers a deep purple. The scenery of babbling brook and the conifers had made it easy to switch off and zone out and really make the most of not walking. When we set off again, through the thicket to our destination, the muscles that yesterday I had forgotten even existed had started to complain a little louder.

Oliver moves in front of me quickly, holding the brambles back with his own body so I can pass unscathed. There's a loud scratching noise as he pulls away from the bush himself, followed by a few choice swear words. I duck back around and mouth *sorry* at him, but he smiles a lopsided smile at me. *It's okay.* Despite the grand gesture, Oliver looks a little green around the gills. We all do. The spring in Bri's step had bounced off about a mile ago, and even Maya, outdoor queen herself, isn't looking as sprightly as she was when we left Loch Rosingar. Her dragging feet scuffing on every rock reminds me of when I was little. Frank and I used to drag our feet deliberately and loudly with our Clarkes school shoes just to get a rise out of our poor mum.

I wonder what mum would think if she could see me now. Probably *check yourself all over for ticks or you'll get lyme disease.* I laugh out loud as I imagine her jumping around me with the Deet-filled insect repellent, spraying so much that *I* can't breathe let alone the midges and gnats.

James looks back from the head of the trek and raises his eyebrows at me over the heads of the girls.

"Nice to hear you laughing, Fliss," he says, going back to bashing down the brambles blocking our path.

"I think it might be hysteria, James," I shout back, more giggles exploding from my mouth. "There's nothing remotely funny about my whole body right now. I feel like a blancmange."

"What the feck's a blancmange when it's at home?" Bri pipes up, her own voice ragged with heavy breathing.

"It's a seventies desert with no backbone." I laugh, though it hurts. "A jelly made with creamy stuff."

Bri lets out a snort. "Yep, that sounds like my legs feel right now too."

"We're nearly there," James shouts. "Just through here."

And he must be telling the truth this time, unlike the last fifty times he's said it to gee us all along. The brambles make way to a path. The trees are thinning too. Their huge trunks not so tightly packed together. The rain is pattering down through the gaps, and I've never been quite so happy to get wet now the storm has passed.

Everyone's steps quicken and green-looking Oliver grabs my hand to pull me out of the tree line. I can hear the ooos and ahhhs and wish that my legs would play ball. Never mind blancmange, my legs feel liquid at the feel of my hand in Oliver's, the warmth of his skin, the very slight roughness of his palm, the notion that he's chosen to look out for me, just like he had done with the furry purple flowers. It makes me smile even though there's not an ounce of energy left in my body. I grip tightly and hold on until I can step out of the forest and give my own explosion of wonder at our next camp stop. Only, when I get there, I can't utter a word.

"Welcome to Inverleck River," James says, grinning.

It's so breathtaking that I'm momentarily left with zero percent oxygen in my lungs. My eyes prick with tears, but I bat them off as exhaustion. About a foot from the tree line I've just escaped from, is a low, wide, fast moving river. The width of the M25, though so shallow I can see the greys and yellows and reds of the riverbed all the way across. The stones sit higher than the water line in some points so little waves cascade over them in tiny waterfalls that the fish are loving. Behind the river, the stark mountains of the last camping place have fallen away to undulating hills of purple moss. Here and there small groups of sheep dot the landscape. Even the rain can't take away the beauty of the colours and the way it lifts my spirits like the first sight of Liberty when I step off the tube at Oxford Circus.

Oliver gives my hand a little squeeze before he drops it and joins the group walking upstream towards the campsite. Sam is there already, stoking the fire and hopefully boiling some water for tea. There's a bundle of parcels on the fire, wrapped in charred leaves, and as I get closer the smell is enough to reignite the muscle memory in my legs.

"I caught us some brown trout," Sam says, turning the parcels with a large stick and blackening the other side. "Tents are all up but try to resist sitting down in them yet as you'll never make it out again."

He's erected the tents in two groups of three this time. Back from the water on a patch of mossy ground and facing each other like houses on a street. I spot mine, right in the middle of the row facing Inverleck river, and I want to go and climb in and sleep. The day of walking has left me feeling exhausted and very much in need of rest. But as I trudge one foot in front of the other towards the camp site, I realise it's not the same kind of exhausted I feel after a day at work or a long conversation with my parents trying to avoid talking about the elephant in the room of our relationship, it's an exhilarating exhaustion that makes me feel proud of what I've achieved. The gratification does nothing to take away the screaming pain in my thighs though.

"You're pitched in the middle," James says, sidling up next to me and squeezing my upper arm. "In between Sam and me, actually. We wanted to make sure you're okay this time."

I nod, grateful that they're so thoughtful as trek leaders, but again wondering if Sam knows more about my past than he's letting on. And, if he's told James, then it's no wonder they want to make sure I'm okay; to gather round me like my parents used to before I moved out to escape their suffocation. I search his face for pity, reflexively reaching up and scratching at my scar through my jumper. But James is off, dropping his backpack by the fire and giving Sam a fist bump. So I take myself a little downstream for a chance to be alone.

The others are all stripping out of their coats and heavy boots down by the water's edge, the ripe camembert smell of feet wafts downstream towards me, putting me off one of my favourite foods quite possibly for life. They're chattering away, seemingly not minding the smell, or the sight of feet that have shrivelled and puckered with a day stuck in walking boots. I can feel where the skin has ripped off my heels with the lack of plasters under my walking socks. I don't want anyone to see what a noob I am, so I sit down at the bank downstream, slightly apart from the rest of them, and start unlacing my own boots.

What feels like five hours later my feet are free, and they look like giant boiled hams with a caramel glaze all over. I roll up my trousers as far as they'll go up my swollen calves and step tentatively over the stones to the river. Luckily, I'm still downstream from the rest of the gang, so when bits of my feet start falling off into the water—which is more than likely— they won't end up paddling in it. The stones underfoot are rounded with years of being caressed by the river, so they're comfortable to walk on. Either that or my feet have been worn away by miles of walking and no longer have nerve endings.

I see Oliver heading in my direction and step from the stones into the water so I'm deep enough to hide my hams. It's freezing, but it's a welcome feeling.

"Hi," he says, looking pointedly at the water as he steps in to join me. "Look how much the water is magnifying your feet?"

He chuckles and I blush right down to my already pink toes because it's not an illusion from the water that makes my feet look like they belong to Pennywise. Luckily my embarrassment is soon focused on something else entirely as Oliver starts up again humming the infamous banjo duel under his breath

I reach over and smack him gently on the arm, laughing.

"It was a split-second reaction, some would say my fight or flight response is tip top. If there had been a danger out there I would have been safe, while you lot would have been gonners," I say, as he closes the gap between us. "It's not my fault I always think the worst, but thanks for not telling anyone about it."

"No worries," he says, looking down at the water. "And if that's your normal reaction to a possible danger, then I'm sticking by your side. You've got a survival instinct that I want to be a party to."

I laugh. *If only he knew.*

Turning my head, listening to the tinkling of the water underfoot and the soaring birds above us, I look up at Bri and Maya, who have now been joined in the water by Sam and James. Maya is looking in my direction, studying me a little too hard. I feel my face flush and wrap my arms around myself.

"It's a deal," I say, looking away from Maya's gaze and into the eyes of the man standing next to me. My stomach contracts a little at the lock of hair tickling his lashes. "I shall protect you from the imminent danger of giant stags, T-rexes, murderous sheep and ..."

I giggle at the idea of me saving Oliver from anything other than rapidly sinking shares.

Oliver cocks his head. "Banjo-wielding yokels?"

He winks at me, lifting his feet out of the water one by one and shivering slightly.

"Very funny," I smile, as my own body shakes with the cold.

Oliver wraps an arm around my shoulder and squeezes me into him.

"Come on," he says as we reach the edge of the river and he drops his arm away. "There's a fire lit, let *me* protect *you* from a touch of frostbite."

I watch him as he walks back towards the others, trying not to smile at how he's making me feel. Because, like the birds gliding effortlessly overhead, swooping and soaring in the blue skies, I'm starting to feel a sense of freedom.

# Chapter Eighteen
## Day Five

I wake the next morning, feeling energised. I slept like the dead, which is something that I haven't done since forever, yet that's twice now on this trip. The fish Sam had caught and cooked was delicious with more wild rice and some samphire that he'd picked on a forage through the forest before we'd all arrived.

As everyone had settled down for the evening around the campfire, I'd made my excuses and retreated to my tent so I could toilet and change before anyone else could accidentally catch a glimpse of a half-naked me. But I'd been asleep before my head had hit the almost pillow of my sleeping bag. Not even the vivid dream of banjo wielding bears frolicking in the river were enough to stir me from the position I had fallen asleep in.

As I blink the sleep away and try to move, my whole body screams in protest. The overworked muscles of my legs, my neck, my arms. Even my little fingers are getting in on the action as they're covered in midge bites. I must have missed them when I was spraying the repellent. I didn't know the little buggers were so shifty.

"Urgh," I groan, sitting up in my sleeping bag and hearing the clicks of my bones realigning.

I shuffle towards the zip, pulling it down a fraction and brace myself for the onslaught of icy rain drops thundering through the gap. But I'm pleasantly surprised by a bright blue sky and sunlight hurting my eyes instead. The noise I assumed was the rain is actually the river rushing over the stones. As quietly as I can, I pull the zip down as far as it will go, though with just the gentle rustle of the river water and the warble of bird song, the grating noise of my zip echoes off the trees like a chainsaw. Pausing for a moment to see if I have woken anyone else up, then happy that I'm still alone, I climb out of my sleeping bag and tent and stretch up to the bright sky.

It's warm. Like, London type of warm where I can walk to work with no coat on. I quickly slip a jumper and my unlaced walking boots on over my long johns and head off into the forest to wee. I don't understand those people who can wake up and not want to wee immediately. And I haven't even had children yet. Imagine what I'll be like afterwards? If I have any. Which isn't looking likely as I don't even have a whiff of a man to lend a hand there and I'm not getting any younger. Though maybe that's not a bad thing, I can barely look after myself, let alone a smaller, helpless version of me.

I ignore the pit of doom beginning to sit in my stomach and try to focus on the here and now. As I always do. No point worrying about a future that hasn't happened or a past that has.

All finished, I walk back to the campsite along the river, splashing water over my face and neck to try and feel more human after not showering for nearly four days. I watch the kingfishers darting into the water and carrying off prey that is twice their size. There are clutches of midges in pockets all along the water, like little vampires ready to cling on and drain me of all my blood. I avoid them because I need all my blood right now to heal my broken muscles, plus I don't want to be scratching like an alley-cat with fleas for the rest of this trip.

As I'm approaching the still quiet camp site, I catch a glimpse of a bright red jacket through the trees. I pause, not wanting whoever it is to think I'm spying on them. I can't quite see who it is as their hood is covering part of their face. Then she turns towards me and lifts her hand in a little wave.

"Fliss," yells Maya, changing direction and heading towards me. "You're up early!"

I nod, not wanting to tell her that my bladder always wakes me up whether I like it or not.

"Isn't it a beautiful day?" she adds, cupping her own hands in the crystal clear water and lifting it up to her face. "Bracing shower, you should try it."

She laughs again, hollow and stuttered. Her long brown hair ends dangling in the water as she washes.

"I have done," I say quickly, thrown by her comment.

"Kind of! Just psyching myself up to be fully immersed in it."

She flicks beads of freezing cold water at me, smiling sweetly before she runs her wet hands through her hair and drags it up into a messy top knot.

"Walk with me?" she asks, her tanned cheeks pink with the coldness, her eyes sparkling bright.

"Um, of course," I say, pulling my jumper sleeves down over my hands which are feeling a bit chilly now I've stopped walking.

I'm surprised when we turn around and head downstream. I thought she meant walk back to the camp with her, not walk, walk! Still, the sun is warming, and I'm better with one on one than large groups, and I've not really had the opportunity to chat properly with Maya yet.

"How're you *really* getting on?" Maya asks, her stride is fast and I'm finding it difficult to keep up with my boots undone.

"Yeah," I gasp, stepping quickly to try and close the ground she is making ahead of me. "I'm not bad. Getting on okay, I think."

It's a blatant lie but she's so far in front of me that there's no way she can see my face to give it away.

"Yeah," she mirrors. "You seem to be."

There's something in her voice, but I think I must be imagining it because of the blood pumping around my unfit body and muffling my ears.

"Do I?" I try to make a joke of it.

Maya stops abruptly. I try to hold in my aching lungs

and breath like a normal person out for a stroll, but I can feel the blood pulsing up to my eyeballs with the effort.

"Yes,' she says, her eyes running up and down my body. I feel embarrassed to be out now in just long johns baggy at the knees and a jumper that barely covers my backside. "I was worried about you to start with. But I'm pretty sure I don't need to be any more."

She gives me another saccharine smile and hugs me without getting too close.

"Thank you," I splutter, almost as a question as I can't work out if she's being genuinely nice. "I'm trying."

"I think I'm going to run back. You know where you are to get to the campsite, don't you?" she asks, not waiting for an answer before her and her taut behind are jogging effortlessly back the way we have just walked.

Inverleck river flows gently beside me, so I tread carefully into the water and stop for a moment to let my lungs fill properly with air. Sitting down on a large boulder splitting the water in two, I think about what Maya has just said. I'm glad I seem to have gotten my shit together, even if it is all just a ruse. Though I can't work out which part of my hiding away in my tent made her think she didn't need to worry about me anymore. I still haven't really been a team player and I haven't joined in any of the swims. She's outdoorsy, fun, and attractive and I'm wearing underwear out for a walk.

A loud squawking from the forest makes my insides jump, and I stand, feeling a bit shivery, and make my way out of the water to start to head back to camp. Luckily, I can just follow the river, and I know which way to go because of the flow of water, because without it I'd be stumped. Maya wouldn't have known that though, surely she wouldn't have left me out here if I couldn't get back myself. Not alone. To be eaten by the grizzly bears and the wolves.

The rest of the campers are up and milling around by the time I reach the campsite. The fire is roaring, and Sam is frying up something that smells delicious though it looks a bit like cat sick. I try to scuttle past them all and back into my tent, aware that I'm not quite dressed yet. I should at least try to get some proper trousers on before I sit down on the cold logs for breakfast.

"You're up and about early," James says as I move past him like a crab, to the tent. How on earth he still looks so fresh faced and smells like an aftershave advert I have no idea. "That's good to see."

"Yes," Maya pipes up with a smile from beside the fire where she sits with the others. "We went for a lovely little stroll and chat, didn't we Fliss?"

She glances around at the rest of the group as she talks, as though she's waiting for praise for helping out the loner.

"We did," I say, my smile slipping slightly smile. "It was beautiful when I woke, and I didn't want to waste the sunshine."

"Good," James says, clapping his hands together. "So, you'll be up for a swim later then? And some star gazing tonight?"

"Star gazing?" I ask, my empty stomach gurgling at

the smell of the food and the thought of watching the stars.

"It's a beautiful day for it. It's normally one of the highlights of the trip as the Scottish night sky is a sight to behold."

He does a little spin on the grass and heads over to the fire. I huddle my arms around myself and dash back to my tent, wondering if there is any way I can get out of this evening's activities without having to tell them why.

## Chapter Nineteen

I haven't been in my tent for long, before Sam comes along and knocks at the door with his voice.

"Knock, knock. Are you decent?" His accent has a very slight Scottish lilt now, but he's immediately recognisable as the Sam I grew up with.

I wait, hesitating for a moment, wondering what excuse I can use to fend him off, but I'm caught so off guard that I can't think of one.

"Yeah, I guess," I splutter, pulling on my socks and poking my head out the tent flap.

Sam's there, waiting patiently with his hands shoved into the pockets of his utility shorts, whistling a tune I haven't heard since I was in primary school when the boys would dance along with their short-legged version of the *running man*.

"Breakfast is almost served," he says, tightening his ponytail. "I wondered, seeing as you were up and about and eager this morning, if you fancied helping me fill some more water containers for the camp?"

I hurriedly search his face to try and feel a sense of hidden motive. But his tanned, laughter creased eyes hold nothing but a smile. And, really, I have no excuse to say no.

"Okay," I nod, a tightening around my stomach making my neck heat. "Let me just grab my boots."

They're sitting at the door to my tent, waiting neatly for me. About a foot away from where Sam is standing, so I can't escape back inside even to catch my thoughts and try to remember what I've already told him about myself, and what was going on at home when Sam's parents relocated their whole family life and plonked it down here in Scotland.

My fingers fumble as I tie my laces up tightly this time, and Sam holds out a hand to help propel me up from the grass. The smell of breakfast floats all around the tents on the soft breeze now, and the campers are drifting towards the fire and the huge frying pan. A circle of birds is forming way up in the sky above the makeshift stove, large black dots against the startling blue.

"It's like a budget Hitchcock film. What's got their attention?" I look over at the pan and try to determine what might have enticed the birds with its delicious scent.

"Dehydrated scrambled eggs?" Sam laughs. "Smells better than it looks!"

"I didn't want to say," I reply, grimacing. "So, are they liable to be as ferocious?"

Sam looks at me quizzically. "Oh, the birds?" He

shakes his head. "They won't attack humans. They'll wait and scavenge for leftovers which is why we tidy away as soon as we're finished."

I nod and make a non-committal humming noise. The weight of Sam's hand on my shoulder is enough to stop me walking on past the fire, I turn to look at him, wondering what he's doing.

"Felicity," he says, smiling, his brow wrinkled, "those birds are not going to pass up scrambled eggs for alive, unwashed human."

He stoops to pick up an empty, large, white water container from the pile of equipment beside the campfire. Handing it to me, he grabs another two for himself. Seeing us from where he's sitting on the other side of the flickering fire, Oliver raises his eyebrows and gives me a small nod. I hold up my container as a battle salute and chase after Sam.

"Fill it with gin!" Oliver yells across the flames.

"Did you learn nothing after stripping naked in a tent with a stranger after your last lush binge?" Maya chips in, flashing her white smile, as she takes a seat on the floor opposite Oliver and crosses her legs over themselves as though she's about to do some yoga. She's very bendy.

Oliver shrugs and leans his head down on his hands, resting his elbows on his knees. He's lost to the fire, staring at the flickering and seems to be a million miles away. I wonder if he's conjuring up some more Absinthe in his mind or regretting our last escapade. Sam gives me no time to ponder though.

"Ready, Felicity?" he says, and we start towards the river.

We head upstream, towards the purple mossy hills. The sun is brilliant above our heads, and even though we've only walked a few yards, I can feel a prickle of heat forming on my back. It's lovely. I stop for a moment and turn my head towards the sun, closing my eyes and enjoying the heat. The air even smells warm, a soft peatyness to it that goes with the sponginess of the ground underfoot.

"Are we at risk of being sucked into a peat bog around here?" I ask Sam, opening my eyes and seeing he's pulled ahead of me as I've been enjoying the warmth. I skip a few steps to catch up.

"What's that?" he says, turning around and stopping when he sees me trying to keep up. "Sorry, am I going too fast? It's my long legs!"

I can't help but chuckle, his legs are the same length as mine.

"No," I say, wiping a line of sweat from my upper lip with the back of my sleeve. "I stopped, but when I smelt the richness of the air and felt how squishy it is underfoot, I was wondering if we're at risk of, like, peat bogs around here. I don't want to lose a shoe, or my life."

I laugh again.

"A peat bog?" Sam laughs too. He drops both of his containers and stretches to the sky with his arms before turning to me. "You've got more chance of being eaten by the birds than being sucked into a peat bog. Where's your adventurous side? Do you remember the time you, me, and Frank rode our bikes all the way out to that farm when we were little? You were through the gate before we'd even jumped off our bikes."

I know exactly where Sam is going with this and I'm wracking my brains to try and think of a way to deflect.

"And there was this giant stack of hay bales," he continues, his eyes looking over my shoulder to the memory. "You scrambled up them like a monkey while Frank and I were shouting at you to get down because if you'd have slipped and fallen off, or lost footing and slid down the middle of them, we'd have been going home without you. But you stood at the top with your arms out and whooped at how high you were."

I lift up my water bottle so it's covering my chest and wrap my arms around it. I do remember that day as vividly as though it was yesterday. But a lot has changed since then.

"That was a long time ago," I try to joke. "Back when I was carefree and unburdened by what could actually happen if I fall through the middle of a stack of hay bales. I could have suffocated!"

Sam goes to speak but I butt in, lifting my container again and nodding to the river.

"We should get these filled before our breakfast burns." I step a little closer to the water. "Are we far enough away from the site to fill here?"

Sam shakes his head slowly, rolling his eyes and collecting his containers from where he dropped them.

"There's a place just a little further upstream with a

rock that acts as a jetty," he says, waking on again. "It's a good spot to collect water."

I follow behind, sighing with relief that he's not pushing the conversation any further. I don't want to keep thinking about back in the day. A huge, white bird swoops down beside me and picks something out of the water, flapping hard to lift itself again. I duck out of its way as water sprays from its wing tips onto my face. Only when I know it's not going to take off with me in it's great talons too, I try to enjoy the sight instead. I wish I could tell Sam why I worry about everything that could possibly go wrong, but we have so much shared history that isn't even an option. I study the back of his head as he strides in front of me, wondering if he already knows anyway.

"Do you come here every trip?" I ask, trying to think of something to break the string of tension building between us.

Sam glances back at me over his shoulder. "Is that the camping version of *do you come here often?*" He laughs.

"Oh, erm, I didn't mean it like that," I stutter out my words. "Sorry, I don't really like you in that way. You're too much like a brother to me."

Could this get anymore awkward? And I definitely don't need another brother. A particularly squelchy muddy spot has me almost wishing it would gather me up and suck me down.

"Relax, Felicity," he says, glancing back at me again. "I'm pulling your leg, besides I've a lovely lady waiting for me back at home."

I skip to catch up and walk beside him. "Tell me

more," I say, interested in who has stolen the heart of my childhood friend.

"She's called Morag," he says, the twinkle sparkling in his eye like the sun reflecting off the water we have stopped at. "She's a local girl, a vet, she's the best thing ever, and one of the main reasons I stopped travelling around the world. I'd love to introduce her to you one day. And Frank, he'd love her, I'm sure."

If he speaks this easily about Frank, he really doesn't know what happened. My stomach cramps up again and I try to stretch out a smile. Walking to the water's edge and onto the large boulder that Sam had mentioned earlier, I pinch some colour back into my cheeks before he notices. The boulder juts right out over the river, the water passing around it in small currents that look like miniature surf waves, translucent all the way to the bottom. I feel Sam next to me before I see him. He puts a hand on my arm, squeezing gently through my jumper.

"Let's get these filled up and head back," he says, his eyes glancing back and forth between mine, digging. I look away before he finds what he's digging for and step a little closer to the edge.

The rock curves downwards before it falls to the water, and I step again, wanting to see the best place to fill my container so we can get back to the group. And, as I step, I hear Sam behind me.

"Careful," he says. "The edge gets very slippery."

But I'm already sliding into the water before he can finish his sentence. It's not deep, but it's freezing. And as I'm sitting on my backside in the middle of the river, Sam and I watch my water container float happily away back towards the camp. I look quickly over at him, and he looks back at me, and for a split second I think he's going to shout at me for being so careless, story of my life. But he doesn't. And when his face breaks into a smile I cannot help but laugh until I'm clutching at my sides with the effort and my cheeks are wet with tears as well as river water.

## Chapter Twenty

"Has everybody got a mug?" Sam asks, later that evening, as he drags his sleeping bag in one hand and a mug full of creamy hot chocolate in the other and sidles in between me and Bri in the deliberately large space I'd left so I wouldn't have to engage in conversation.

A murmur of thanks and contented noises spreads around the group. I grip my metal mug in my gloved hands and blow gently on the dark drink, steam billowing around my mouth and over the sleeping bag I'm snuggled up inside.

I still remember vividly the night my Mum woke Frank and me up, throwing the covers off me and exposing my My Little Pony pyjamas. Frank had moaned about the cold, but we'd grabbed each other's hands and followed Mum out into our small weedy garden. Dad had been camped there already, mug in hand, binoculars at the ready and I wondered if we had been called to look at some sort of rare bird.

"Aurora Borealis," Dad had said, pointing to the sky.

"Blesh you," Frank had replied, and we'd bent over in fits of giggles. He was good like that; he could always make me laugh.

Dad had sighed, quietly tired of ten-year-old twins who should really be in bed.

"Your mum thought it might be a once in a lifetime opportunity for you to see her," Dad said, patiently, still pointing at the sky.

Mum had laid out a blanket next to Dad's chair and the three of us laid down on it, staring at the cloud covered night. I huddled my dressing gown around me, ignoring my cold feet because this was the most exciting night I'd ever had and I wasn't about to ruin it by going to get my socks.

"It's called the Northern Lights," Mum had said, an arm around both me and my brother. "It is very rarely seen this far south, but there's a chance it will be visible tonight and I wanted you both to see it. Especially you, Frank, we all know how obsessed with the sky you are, with storms and stars and anything galactic."

"What does it look like?" Frank had asked her.

"Like the inside of a pearl," Mum had replied. "Or the reflection of a rainbow."

"Wow," I had said, stifling a yawn.

"Or at least it will do," Dad had added. "If these bloody clouds go away."

We'd all laughed. Then laid in silence. Then, one by one, fallen asleep. We never did see The Northern Lights that night.

## Wild Swimming

The next day, as we'd changed into our school uniform, Frank and I had made a pact to watch the Northern Lights together at some point in our lives. Just so Mum could get her wish.

Sam whispers something to Bri and brings me back from our small Kent garden to the large expanse of Scottish night sky. We're all lying up on the top of the mossy, purple hill. It was taller than it looked from afar, but the incline was slow and steady, so I enjoyed the walk despite having trekked through the river to get here. I stayed upright this time, my boots holding off the water as it was so shallow, and I found my thoughts drifting to a kind of meditative state as I'd plodded up the hill. I thought about striking up a conversation with Oliver as he strode ahead of me, but I was so enjoying the peace I decided not to. It's hard enough to think about being at one with the wilderness to find myself, without the distraction of him.

I sip at my cocoa, feeling the warm liquid trickling all the way down my throat to my stomach. It may have been warm in the sun earlier, thankfully, as I had a number of items of clothes to dry off, but now the sun has set it's absolutely freezing. The bits of skin that I still have exposed are reduced down to my nose, eyes, and lips. The steam from the hot drink is making a little pool of condensation gather at the tip of my nose, ready to freeze solid into a stalactite, or mite, I never know which is which.

The rest of the group had walked upstream after breakfast and found a large, deep inlet to swim in. I heard their squeals and splashes from where I'd stayed sitting by the fire to try and warm up and dry off. I had been planning on going swimming, I was going to bite the bullet and actually get in, but after my unplanned dip in the water I lost my appetite for it. My core temperature had probably been as low as it should have been and there had been no point going back in when I'd have spent the time worrying about hypothermia anyway.

After we'd all warmed up and dried off in the sunshine, James had made the announcement that we would be sleeping under the stars tonight as the forecast was so clear. And we had left after supper, before the sun set, making a slow afternoon walk across the valley then up the Marylin to our final destination. I had been listening in to Sam explain to Maya and Bri that a hill of a height less than two thousand feet is called a Marylin in Scotland, just as the highest are called Munroes or Bens. It had been a fascinating insight into a country that I'm learning to love through its beauty, but perhaps not its weather.

James has a large pop-up grate type thing that he's promised to put over the flames when we're all tucked up and ready to face skywards. It won't kill the fire completely, but it will dim the warm light enough to make the sky luminous.

A little creeping excitement is bubbling away in my stomach and I feel guilty and happy all at once that I will get to enjoy this when Frank isn't here. I try to remind myself that it's just stars. And no Northern Lights will be flashing through the sky at one hundred million miles an

## Wild Swimming

hour so I'm not technically breaking our pact. For all I know, he's probably seen the Northern Lights now anyway. An anger threatens to sneak in amongst the excitement and I bite it back, shoving it down to the pit of my stomach.

"Are you enjoying your trip so far, Felicity?" Sam asks, sipping his own chocolate and looking far warmer than the rest of us. His blood must have thickened with the weather since he moved up here.

"I am," I say, feeling that for once I'm not having to lie. "Scotland is such a beautiful country, especially this far north. I can see why your parents wanted to move here from Tonbridge."

"Yeah," Sam says. "It is. Though I didn't feel like this when they announced it at fourteen."

I laugh. "No, I bet you didn't."

"Imagine the upheaval. I hated my parents for a good few months. I thought my life was pretty much over. Considering my whole life revolved around playing footy in the park with my best mates and trying to look cool in front of Amy Hall."

I nearly inhale my hot chocolate.

"Amy Hall?" I laugh some more. "Is that who everyone used to fancy?"

"Yup." Sam sounds sheepish.

"She's apparently addicted to crack now and has only half a head of hair," I say, remembering a past conversation I'd had with Mum.

"Oh, how the mighty have fallen." Sam laughs.

We fall silent and finish our drinks. The stars starting

to twinkle now the sun has fully fallen. It feels like it's already way past my bedtime as I yawn and sneak a look at my watch without exposing my wrist too much. I'm surprised to see it's only half nine.

"Time feels different out here." Sam says, hearing my surprise. "We wake with the sun and sleep with the sun. There's no rush to be doing things because we're not accessible twenty-four seven. This whole lifestyle that people have adopted, it's not healthy. Imagine being at the beck and call of your workplace every minute of every hour because they know you're checking your emails, or they can see read receipts. Imagine not having to reply to texts from friends within seconds because you're worried they'll think you're ignoring them. That is *not* something I miss."

"You're at work now and it's practically the middle of the night," I say, prickly, because he has just described me to a tee, except the friends part, I don't have enough of those to be texting me all the time.

He's right though. But I don't want to admit it. I live for my work. My job is fast-paced and exciting. I can't stand not being in contact with my emails to check rates and sales and this is the longest I've ever gone without it since I started working in finance. Yet the longer I'm away from it, the less I miss it.

"Touché," he says, and I can hear the disappointment in his voice.

The silence this time feels like it has a pulse. I want to tell Sam that I can see why he's at work now, that he's in a job where he can lie on the top of the world and stare at the vast expanse of starry sky, and why would anyone not want to do that. But the longer the silence goes on, the harder it is to fill.

"You know Frank fancied Amy Hall more than I did," Sam says eventually, and I wish the silence to come back again.

"Right guys," James shouts, startling me and saving me from the conversation. "Are we all finished with our drinks and ready to settle down for a night of stargazing?"

"Are we not going to brush our teeth?" Maya cries and I can hear someone muttering *oh my god* under their breath.

"Did you bring your toothbrush up with you, Maya?" James asks and Sam laughs. "One night won't make your teeth fall out."

"My dentist wouldn't agree with that sentiment," she says, but I don't think she's saying it unkindly, it's hard to tell when you can't see people's faces. "Though I have been known to chew on a liquorice root before, when a toothbrush was not close at hand."

A different kind of darkness descends as James covers over the fire. It's like a blanket. All consuming. Suffocating even, if I let my mind focus on it too much. A gentle hush falls over the group as one by one we lie back down and follow James' relaxing voice as he talks us through what we're about to witness.

As my eyes become accustomed to the darkness, the sky starts to pop and come alive. What had been a blanket of darkness is now alight with millions and trillions of stars. They're all different sizes and shapes and brightness. A wash of colours that are also somehow all white.

Everywhere I look there are layers upon layers of star, as far as my eyes can see. The vastness of it all, the depth and the stretch of the sky is making me feel dizzy. I lean up a little on my elbows as my head begins to spin, and they're the same beyond the stretch I could see when I was lying down. It's beautiful. It's magical. Without the light pollution of the cities and the cars, the stars come into their own. I have never seen anything like it.

"You know," Oliver's soft voice slices through the night. "I always find it fascinating that I can be looking up at the night sky and someone a thousand miles away can see the same stars as me. It's like, oh hey, there's the big dipper up here in Scotland but if I messaged my Grandma, say, back home in Cambridge, she could see it too. If I had my phone maybe I would, I miss her."

A crushing feeling of inadequacy presses hard on my chest. I lie back down and squeeze my eyes tightly shut. I wonder if Frank can see the same stars as me right now. The world descends into darkness as James starts to tell us all about Ursa Major and Ursa Minor and a constellation called Draco who—up until now—I thought was just a character in Harry Potter.

# Chapter Twenty-One
## Day Six

It's all going too fast. I feel like the time is slipping away from me and I'm not experiencing this trek in the same way as everyone else. The excited energy around me is almost palpable, the camp site is buzzing with voices that belie the fact there's only six of us here and one of us isn't making any noise at all.

I fold my clothes into my backpack and throw it out of my tent so I can roll the sleeping bag and squash it into its tiny sheath. After my second attempt to puff the air out, I manage to squeeze it away and my tent is barren once more. Ready for Sam to collapse and pack into the minibus to take to our next destination.

I know this is a trek and we're camping in lots of different places, but it seems like only a few hours ago we arrived at the river and I had grand plans to actually swim here and try my hardest to forge new friendships. But, yet again, I've spent most of the last two days tucked away on my own and haven't been anywhere near the river except to fall in it.

My bones feel achy and cold from sleeping out last night, despite the warmth my sleeping bag gave me. I think I nodded off before James had even finished talking us through the different constellations, his voice is calming, maybe I'll ask him to record it for me and I can play it back on those nights I can't use a glass of red to help instead.

"Right gang," James shouts from the now defunct fire as I wriggle out of my tent, sleeping bag in hand. "It's time to get going again. This trek will take us back towards the coastline. I'm so excited about our next destination. I think you're going to love it."

Maya flicks her hair over her shoulders and flutters her huge eyes at Oliver as she requests his help with her rucksack. Begrudgingly he hoiks it off the floor, glancing briefly in my direction, and holds it as she slips her arms through the straps. She looks different this morning, not quite as luminous. Though god knows what I look like these days, with no access to a mirror I've thrown off the usual cares about how large my hair is or how pale my skin. I strap my own sleeping bag to the bottom of my rucksack and throw it over my shoulders. Used to the feel and weight of it now, my centre of balance can cope with the change. We set off. James at the front as usual.

We've been walking for a while over the moors when I realise that I have no idea what the time is, but better than that, I don't care. My stomach is guiding me on when to eat the snacks in my bag and sip at my water, and so far this trip I've woken when I've had enough sleep, not because I'm being screamed at by an alarm clock designed to give even the deepest sleeper a heart attack. I'm no longer reaching for my absent phone to sneak a look at my emails or Twitter. And I think I may have managed to not think about work now for a solid few hours at a time. In fact, if I start to think about it now, in this vast landscape of mostly wilderness, I wonder why on earth anyone is bothering to sell stocks and shares that they can't even physically hold or see or touch or smell. What is it I'm really doing?

*Is this the existential crisis I was promised?*

If it is, then I'd like it to stop before I do anything stupid like quit my job, though that would be hard from the middle of nowhere. I can't very well carrier pigeon my resignation all the way to London. I need my job. It's who I am right now, it gives me purpose. And my lovely house can't pay for itself.

Luckily the terrain we're travelling over today is gentler than our previous trek. The moors feel soft and squidgy underfoot and the sun is shining on us again. I feel a sense of lightness, that I can carry the weight of my rucksack now without a strain on my shoulders. Bri trudges past me, her own feet like lead. She's lost a little of the spring in her step and can't bounce quick enough to catch up with James anymore. Her activewear has been swapped for a tracksuit that drowns her tiny frame like a sack, her hair lacklustre and falling around her face. I hold my hand out to tap her shoulder as she passes me, but it brushes gently without her noticing and she trudges onwards alone. On the other side of me Oliver is practically hanging off the path to walk as far away as possible from Maya as she tries to talk to him. He really doesn't like joining in with the whole team thing. He catches my eye and gives me a little side smile which makes my stomach tumble like a washing machine. I can't help but fancy him a little bit more as he huffs at something Maya is saying and I wonder if she's coming on to him.

I make a split-second decision to put him out of his misery. Bold as anything I walk up to him and start to chat, ignoring the death stare I get from Maya.

"Hey you," Oliver says, his face lighting up as he sees me approach. "This is pretty easy going isn't it?"

He nods, indicating the spongy moss underfoot, and I nod back.

"And the sun is shining," I say, smiling.

Maya scoffs and jogs up the path a little to join Bri. And somehow now, the talk about the weather and the soft ground doesn't seem quite enough.

"Will you help me?" I blurt out before I can stop myself.

"Sure," Oliver says, eager to agree without even knowing what I'm about to ask.

"Can you push me in the water at the next location so I can at least join in with the swimming?"

Oliver laughs and stops walking. I stop with him. Out of the corner of my eye I see Maya's own step falter, but she carries on with Bri.

"Of course I can," he says, looking down at me as he

runs his hands through his overgrown mop of hair. My stomach tightens.

His facial hair has also been growing like he's been feeding it with the fresh Scottish air. The stubble is now almost thick enough to run a comb through. I'm not normally a fan of beards, since my parents read me The Twits when I was younger and always imagined them to be full of food saved for later. But Oliver's jaw can definitely cope with it.

I start walking again, not wanting Oliver's gaze to be directed at me, scrutinising me, seeing right through me.

"I'm finding this harder than I thought I would," I say, as we trundle on, our arms brushing against each other, magnetised.

"Yeah, it's been a bit obvious that you're not all that comfortable with people." He gives me a look; side-eyed and small smiled.

"Says he!" I raise an eyebrow at him. "I'm just not used to it, that's all."

"Single child?" he asks, talking again so I don't have to answer. "I'm one of five boys, I'm used to there being a lot of people and not a lot of privacy. Plus, I was living with an ex-girlfriend up until about two months ago, and she was pretty full on, even after we split."

"Oh no, sorry to hear that," I say, keeping the conversation about him.

"No, it was for the best. And I thought this would be the perfect trip for me to clear my head."

"Yeah," I say, as the sea comes into view over the hill we've just mounted.

"Wow." We say in unison, both stopping again and looking at the ocean as it sparkles a bright turquoise blue. Our hands almost touching, I can feel the heat from his skin, and my heart flutters.

We're high up, a soft-edged cliff between us and the water, but it looks so clear I feel like I can see the bottom of it from where I'm standing.

"It certainly makes you feel a small and an insignificant part of the world, doesn't it?" I say, pointing at the water.

Oliver turns to me, his eyebrows crinkled.

"Insignificant?" he asks. "*That* makes you feel insignificant?"

I nod, feeling a bit silly now I've opened up to him in such a vulnerable way.

"It's just so huge, and I'm just so small," I say, quietly, my heart now hammering.

He takes a moment, looking like he's rolling my words around in his head.

"But what about if you think of it differently?" he asks, his eyes darken as they look into mine.

"What do you mean?" I almost whisper.

"What about if you're *not* the one who is insignificant," he says throatily. He looks away from me and I catch my breath. "You're a part of this amazing world, and what is *actually* insignificant is the part you give yourself. Be it your job, your relationships."

I snort but Oliver carries on talking.

"What if you're exactly who and what you're meant to be, but you're not giving yourself the chance to be significant? Take this ocean, or the stars last night. Looking at them, lying beneath them, we're shown a world that is totally different to what we're used to. And, yes, size wise we're tiny. But our actions have implications that could change the ocean or the stars. Like the butterfly flapping its wings that causes a hurricane, though I don't want to start spouting chaos theory at you because that's not what I'm trying to get at here. I can't quite find the words to say what I mean."

He moves closer to me, taking my hands in his, and I think all of those chaos theory butterflies have found themselves in my stomach.

"Instead of feeling like this vast world makes you insignificant, can you see it as a way to feel *free*? That the hugeness of it gives you the ability to *do* anything you want to do, *be* anyone you want to be, that there are endless opportunities because the world is so vast?"

I can feel the tears pricking my eyes as I shake my head. I want to tell Oliver why I can't feel free, and why I can't do anything or be anyone, but I can't because if I tell him he'll look at me differently and I've come to like the way he looks at me.

## Chapter Twenty-Two

The rest of the group have marched on ahead of us. I can see Maya's bright red coat flashing in the distance as they navigate the undulating mossy hills, walking far too close to the cliff top.

"We'd better catch up," I say, not wanting to get lost but not really wanting Oliver to let go of my hands either.

"Yes. Yes!" He looks over at the others and drops my hands as if coming to his senses, turning on his heels and pacing away.

I skip a little to catch up with him as we power towards the rest of the trek. Rounding the top of the next hillock I see the familiar sight of the tops of our tents. Set out circularly this time, around the roaring fire in the centre. We're situated in the dip where four peaks meet at the bottom. Over the peak to the left of us I can hear the sea roaring louder than I would have expected from way up here. The sounds send prickles all the way up my neck and makes my scalp tickle.

"Here we are," James calls out to all of us, as Oliver and I finally catch up with them. "Campsite number three, and if I'm honest, it's my favourite out of the lot of them."

Sam is waving from down at the campsite, his ponytail now secured into a man bun right on the top of his head. He looks tanned and happy as the sun's rays shine directly on him through gaps in the misty, blue sky. A cormorant swoops down near him like a feathered pterodactyl before soaring so high it's nothing but a black dot against the sky. Bri waves back and starts to run down the side of the hill, shaking out her shoulders and squealing excitedly in the way she does that I have learnt to love. The laugh she gives halfway down the hill is music to my ears, her renewed happiness an anecdote in itself.

"Looks like fun," James chuckles, he gives a shrug, then starts his own fast descent down after her.

I half expect Maya to ridicule them, but she doesn't, she hoiks her own backpack firmly on her back, holding the straps by her shoulders, and sets off down the moss herself.

"I know how to have fun too," she shouts back, screaming with laughter.

I can't imagine joining them, I'd feel like an idiot running down the hill like a child, or I'd topple over and break an arm. But it's only Oliver and me left up here now, and I can see from the eager look in his eyes he wants to join them.

"Come on," he says, reaching out a hand to me that I don't take. "What have you got to lose?"

I really don't want to do this, no matter how fun it looks, and no matter the great big wave that Sam is giving me from the bottom.

"My dignity?" I say, biting my lip.

"*Fliss*," Oliver says, shaking his hand hard to make me notice it and take hold. "You left your dignity on the tarmac at Heathrow with the rest of us. Run with me."

I can't decide if running down the hill with Oliver is worse than being left alone and trudging down to join the rest of them half an hour late for the party but with all my limbs intact. Before I can make the decision myself, Oliver is gripping my hand tightly in his and starting to walk briskly towards where the hill begins its slow decline. I shift the weight of my rucksack and hold onto it as best I can as our pace increases with the descent. Soon we're running. My hair flowing out behind me, the wind in my face. The ground under my feet is spongy and light and my legs don't feel like jelly anymore. They're powering over the floor of the hill as fast as they will carry me, my hands my own as Oliver lets go. He's right. This *is* fun. I feel like I can carry on running forever. I feel like I did as a child when I used to chase Frank down the road out the back of our house. Free.

Oliver whoops beside me and I join him, whooping though my lungs are burning with the exertion. I whoop and I whoop and with each whoop I feel a great weight being expelled from my body. I bounce down the hill with no grace or decorum whatsoever and my body is thanking me for it. The stiffness in my neck through years of hunching over my insecurities is unknotting itself with each step. The close, controlled, clipped movements of my limbs is long forgotten as my arms swing wildly, mirroring what my legs are doing. It feels amazing.

As we reach the bottom of the hill, the campsite in clear focus now, Oliver slightly ahead of me with his long legs, I start to slow down. My face is a huge smile, I can feel muscles in my cheeks that haven't worked this hard since I got a Tiny Tears doll for my seventh birthday. We come to a standstill by the back of the circle of tents, my chest rising and falling with the exertion, my heart pounding so hard I'm surprised it didn't reach the destination before me. Oliver grabs me up in a big hug and lifts me off my feet. Everyone around us cheers and I feel all at once a part of their group. I wrap my own arms around Oliver as he puts me back gently on the floor.

"Well done, Fliss," he whispers in my ear. "You did it."

"I did it," I whisper back, my skin tingling with the feel of his breath in my ear.

We release each other and I can feel droplets of sweat pooling at the bottom of my back. Stripping my backpack off and throwing it to the floor, I lift my jumper over my head. I know that my face must be the colour of pickled beetroot right now but I'm not worried. Which is a first for me.

"Where's the swimming at this camp?" I ask James who is smiling at me through the gap in the tents as he sits with Sam by the fire. "I'm roasting."

"That, my loves," James replies, getting up and holding out his arms like the king of the world. "Is why this campsite is so special. Grab your swimmers and follow me."

We all dart to our tents, knowing without having to read which one is ours now. I throw my suit on, determined to at least get my whole body wet this time, and not just my feet or my backside. I grab my neoprene gloves and boots as, no matter how warm I am now, the water will still be bloody freezing. Throwing my dry robe around me, I'm the first one back out.

"Nice to see you so keen, Fliss," James says, coming to stand beside me as we wait for the others. "You're going to love this."

I can feel the heat radiating from my body and I hope I don't smell too much. I keep my arms down by my sides, just in case. James still smells like Gaultier, and he's even managed a recent sneaky shave by the looks of it. His boyish grin isn't hidden away behind a mass of hair anymore. He smiles at me and I grin back, endorphins still rushing around my body.

With the rest of the group eager and ready, James starts the trek back up the hill in the opposite direction we have just run from. We follow, silently but buzzing with energy.

"Just over here," he says, pointing to the peak.

And as we all reach the top of the hill the sea comes into full view. It's turquoise, as though we've walked over the hill onto a Greek island. Golden sand stretches for as far as I can see. Little inlets gather the tropical looking water as it splashes gently down onto the beach. As we stop, almost directly underneath us the waves seem to disappear into the hill. The echoing of the waves that I'd heard earlier are much louder now, much closer. James walks us to a dip in the floor and peers into it.

"This, my friends," he says, turning back to us and beaming with pleasure. "Is Malfar Caves."

I edge a bit closer, my heart back in my mouth but for different reasons now. There's a gap in the cliff, as though a meteor has bashed through the rock into the sea below. It's probably only a couple of meters in diameter. The edges of the gap in the hill cascade gently from mossy grass into grey granite, softened over the years by rainwater that has moulded it into a benign curve. But it opens out after a drop of a few feet into a voluminous cave. Even from where I stand, as far back as possible, I can see the sea below, undulating and dark. The sun must be shining in from the cave opening at the bottom though, reflecting off not only the water but the stone walls, giving the cave an eerie blue glow.

"This is bloody insane," Bri cries, her brow crumpled, her feet so close to the edge I want to grab her and pull her back. "How far down is it?"

"Just over six metres, or twenty feet in old money" James says.

"And how do we get down there?" Maya asks, her eyebrow raised as if sensing my wildest fears. "I can't see a pathway."

James makes a noise like an excited penguin.

"We jump," he laughs.

I laugh too, there's no way he is being serious.

"There's only a few months in the year when it's not safe to jump in," he adds, and I'm getting the sinking feeling he's not joking. "When it's frozen at the edges, or when the waves are taller than me. August tends to be an okay month and Sam checked it out when he arrived at the site earlier, so we are good to go!"

My tongue feels thick.

"Oh my god," Bri grabs James' arm as he gets closer to her and pretends to push her over. "What? I can't do that."

She looks even smaller than normal as she clings on to James like a life preserver. Through all of her cheerfulness and enthusiasm, I can see how the world around her - the camping, the foraging, the lack of creature comforts - has ground her down to a shell. I want to hug her and tell her it'll be okay. But the words pot and kettle spring to mind. Oliver is looking at me and I feel like I want to ground to swallow me whole. Not here though. Somewhere where there isn't the threat of the sea to engulf me when I'm falling.

"Okay," James says, extracting his arm from Bri and moving us all away from the edge. "A few ground rules. Make sure you land feet first, no fancy dives or mid-fall loops unless you want a broken neck. Keep your arms tucked into your chest like this when you jump."

James demonstrates a look that could be an indication of what Dracula looks like when he's tucked up asleep in his coffin. It's not helping my nerves.

"Make sure there is no one underneath you when you

jump. And move out the way as quickly as possible when you surface below."

It's like one of those rides at theme parks I was never allowed to go to when I was younger. But then snuck to Alton Towers on a school trip and spent the entire day holding everyone's bags as they risked their lives on the aptly named Oblivion or Nemesis. All the signs dotted around the park telling the teenagers that they're basically doomed to a life-changing accident if they so much as looked at the rides. Why would I risk it? Life is risky enough without placing myself directly in the path of danger.

"Lastly," James adds, addressing both Bri and my petrified face. "Only jump if you want to. There's a path down to the beach just over this hill and a ledge to walk on that takes you right into the cave. This isn't for everyone, I get that."

I smile as best I can. I'll let them all jump first then hot foot it down the path to the cave from the beach. I can avoid the death jump into the sea if I do that.

"Okay," James says. "I'll go first so I can be there for you all when you jump, and Sam will bring up the rear. See you on the other side."

He walks up to the edge of the hole, drops his dry robe, and leaps as though he has absolutely no fears. There's a whoop of joy and—what seems like a very long time later—a loud splash. Silence envelopes us as we all look at each other, wondering who's going to be brave enough to go next, when James' voice shouts through the void.

"It's amazing," he yells. "Come on down."

Bri looks like she's about to wet herself and I start towards her to offer her company on the walk down to the beach. But before I can take another step, she's stripping off her robe.

"This girl can," she says, her voice wavering but there's a real strength to her conviction under the fear.

Then she leaps, screaming in hysterical laughter as she falls. I want to get closer to the edge to watch her landing, to try and grab some of the courage Bri must be exuding as she drops to the water, but I'm scared I'll slip and fall.

"Are you going to jump?" Oliver asks me.

I shake my head and get closer to him.

"Not a chance in hell," I whisper so Maya and Sam don't hear me.

I expect him to laugh at me or call me out for being a coward, but he doesn't, he just looks at me, heavy lidded, lopsided smile.

"I'll see you down there in a bit then," he whispers back, before stripping out of his robe, taking a huge deep breath, and jumping into the chasm.

This time I do edge closer to the hole. I watch as Oliver's head sinks towards the water like a lead balloon, my skin prickling with fear for him. Then he lands, sending waves up and over the others who are treading water by the ledge that James spoke of. I hold my breath, waiting for Oliver to surface. Hoping he's okay because I'd like to spend more time with him.

As his head bobs to the top he looks up at me and waves, then starts swimming towards the ledge.

"I'll walk with you, Felicity," Sam says from across the gap where he can see my petrified face. "Let me just make sure Maya is safe and we'll go together."

I fill my lungs, grateful to my childhood friend and start to lean back up so I can move out of the way of Maya. My foot catches on something solid. It knocks me off balance and I'm tumbling forwards. My arms flail out but there's nothing to grab hold of, nothing to get a purchase of to stop me toppling further towards the hole. Then I'm falling into the gap, chest first, arms still outstretched, the sea rushing towards me like a dark concrete floor. And I close my eyes and hope for the best.

## Chapter Twenty-Three

I hit the water with a thump that knocks the air clean out of my lungs. That was definitely not feet first. But luckily my arms are still outstretched, trying to find something to stop me falling even as I land, so they reduce my velocity with a crack. The pain is outweighed by the realisation that I am sinking faster than I should be. My dry robe is soaking up half of the sea and dragging me down as it gathers momentum. A kind of calm descends over me, the echoing of my heartbeat in my ears the only sounds I can hear as the water deepens.

I know there are two outcomes to this. I strip out of my robe now and surface, or I keep sinking. I think how easy it would be to keep sinking. The cave is deep, and no matter how quick a diver James is, he's not catching me now. He might not even realise I didn't mean to jump. It might take a moment before the rest of the gang realise too, including Oliver who *knew* I wasn't going to. Things would be easier if I kept sinking. I think of my stressful job, my expensive house with nothing in it except me, Frank, especially Frank. As the water darkens around me I see him, a vision of flashes and fear, his arms outstretched towards me like claws, his face twisted. I screw my eyes closed and my parents' faces pop into my head instead, making my decision for me.

    I struggle against my robe as it clings with the annoyance of a wet swimming costume when I'm desperate for a wee. My legs start to kick, slowing my descent a little. I pull one arm free, then throw as much weight as I can behind the other. My lungs are burning, and for the first time in my life I am not just glad but indebted to the early morning swims, the training I did when I was younger that is probably keeping me going right now. Muscles have memory, and right now my lungs are remembering those times I pushed myself underwater, from one end of the pool to the other. As my robe falls quickly away from me, I kick with all my might to the surface. Bursting through the waves and gulping down air as quickly as I can. I can't tell if my face is wet from sea water or tears, but I have no energy left to swim to the edge.

    I feel a strong pair of arms around me, tilting me backwards, floating me to safety and I close my eyes and lean into whoever it is rescuing me.

    "Fliss, what happened? You're okay now."

    I can hear voices around me, feel the heat of bodies near me and someone must have leant me their robe as it's laying over my body as I'm spread out on the cold, stone ledge. The sea splashes against the edge, spraying my face with the occasional lick, as if asking me if I'm alright.

"Fliss." James is by my side, holding my hand as best he can on the small ledge. "Thank god. How are you feeling? Any double vision or red-hot feeling in your body anywhere?"

I have no idea of the answer to his question. I daren't move again because my arm hurts too much and I'm worried that other parts of me will scream out in pain too.

"She tripped over her feet and fell right in. I recognise the voice as Maya without looking.

"Was there nothing you could have done?" James asks. "She could have drowned."

"Don't be ridiculous, I've seen her swimming, back at the hotel, and she knows what she's doing," Maya says, scoffing.

"But she wasn't ready to jump." That one must be Bri.

"She wasn't *going* to jump." And that one Oliver.

"Let me near her, I'm first aid trained." That's Bri again, though I can only tell because of her Welsh accent.

"You're an influencer, did someone give you a St Johns Ambulance badge for free too?" Maya says.

"I've also just qualified as a bloody dentist," Bri says, and I can hear the water splashing near me. "I was only on the 'Gram to pay for my training."

I turn my head and open my eyes. She's there bobbing in the water beside me, her eyes looking me up and down. As she places her palms on the rock ledge to haul herself up out of the water, Oliver's hand touches her bare shoulder.

"I'm a surgeon," he says, pushing himself up to the ledge. "If it's okay, I'd like to check her over."

Bri nods and squeezes my hand before she swims away.

James, who had been sitting on the ledge beside me, slides off into the water and I watch him swim away too.

"Have you got any pain or pins and needles in your back?" Oliver asks, his face paled and drawn.

I shake my head, I can feel the cold stone through my swimsuit absolutely fine, that's a good sign, right?

"Can you try and wriggle your toes for me?"

I tentatively move my toes and am relieved to feel them wriggle in my neoprene boots. I nod.

"Good," Oliver says, his eyes washing over my body. "And can you squeeze my fingers?"

I lift my left hand over and grab his fingers. My grip must still be pretty good as Oliver winces when I squeeze.

"My other arm is a bit sore," I say.

As I lift my right arm a sharp pain radiates all the way from my elbow to my fingers. I cry out and grab my elbow with my good arm.

"You hit the water with that elbow," Oliver says by way of explanation. "Well, your elbow and your chest. Do you mind if I have a feel?"

"Of my chest?"

Oliver nods sheepishly. "I am obviously first aid trained; I don't just want to cop a feel. I want to make sure you've got no pain in your ribs. A broken arm I can deal with, ribs are a bit riskier. They could slip and puncture a lung."

"Oh jeez," I say, trying not to breath as heavily, or at all. "Yes, please check them."

He moves his fingers deftly over my collar bone. In other circumstances I'd be quite enjoying this. Luckily there's no pain as he moves his fingers along each rib bone, feeling gently and carefully for anything that shouldn't be there. My skin ripples through my swimsuit as his fingers venture down past the neckline and carefully avoids my actual breasts which are poking up towards him with the cold and the sensation.

"Any pain?" he asks as he reaches the last of my ribs and places his hands on my stomach.

I shake my head, not able to speak in anything but tongues. I remind myself that, as a surgeon, it's his sworn Hippocratic oath to make sure I'm okay.

"Okay," he says, running his hands down my legs and puffing out a breath. "I think you're okay. Let's get you sitting up so you don't catch a chill."

He holds out an arm for me to lean against. Tentatively I use my good arm to push up from the stone ledge, holding Oliver with my sore arm. I await my head to start throbbing again as I sit up, but it doesn't come, it just feels a bit dizzy. I stretch my sore arm out, seeing how far I can push it without the pain sending vomit inducing stabs. But this time it seems okay, it's hurting, but not debilitating pain. All at once I feel a bit daft for the panic on Oliver's face.

*Maybe I should pretend it hurts more, so I don't look like an attention seeking loser.*

But watching Oliver watch me, I can't do that to him. The cold has been seeping into my skin for however long I was lying on the ledge, I can feel my teeth chattering. Oliver leans over and wraps his arms around me, it's an awkward angle for him but I appreciate his body warmth. As he rubs his hands gently up and down my back I can feel the heat almost immediately. Over his shoulder I see James and Maya talking animatedly, half submerged in the water.

"Maybe we can look at it positively," Maya says.

"What's that supposed to mean?" James asks, and he sounds a bit short with her.

"She did it, she got in the water," Maya replies. "It's what she asked *Oliver* to help her with back at the top of the hill. She said to him, and I quote, 'can you push me in the water at the next location so I can at least join in with the swimming'"

"What?" James says. "I don't think she would have meant it literally, Maya. She's probably just feeling like it's harder for her to join in with us all and was asking for some assistance to do that. Not an actual push."

Maya huffs. "Well, it wasn't a push, was it? Like I said, she tripped over. I was just trying to think positively, that's all. Isn't that what we're supposed to do on this trip?"

James shakes his head and swims away.

"Come on guys, what happened to togetherness and

looking out for each other?" Sam asks, getting in between his colleague and Maya.

"Well, *she* never looks out for any of us," Maya says, quietly now as she bobs up and down in the water.

I want to get in the water now too. Maybe Maya is right. Maybe my fall *was* a good thing. I've landed in the sea and I made it out. I wasn't carried off to the Outer Hebrides by a tide I couldn't swim against or dragged under by a wave. I tripped and fell and then was dragged down by a human-made robe, but I still made it out. I made it. And I want to take from that all the courage I can while I still have it.

I wriggle free of Oliver's warm embrace just as James swims back towards me.

"Thank you for saving me," I say to James, remembering the feel of his strong arms around my neck as he pulled me to safety.

He looks sheepish, and glances at Oliver.

"It's my job," he shrugs, though I know it's more than his job to throw himself in after a drowning woman.

"I think I'm going to swim off the aches and pains."

"Are you sure that's a good idea?" James' eyebrows knit together. "You're cold and we still don't know what damage your arm has taken."

The paler James gets, the younger he looks. He turns to Oliver as if he needs permission for me to get back in the water.

"I'll take it easy," I say, wanting to get in before he changes my mind. "And I'll swim straight out the cave and onto the sunny beach to warm up, promise."

He nods and swims aside to let me slide into the water. I ignoring the stabbing feeling in my elbow until I'm all the way in. It's no colder being in the water than out of it. In fact, being submerged feels really good right now. I roll over onto my back and kick with my legs, letting myself float on the gentle bob of the waves.

## Chapter Twenty-Four

We traipse back to the camp site as a disjointed group. The soaring feeling I had for overcoming my fears of the sea were soon squashed when I realised I no longer have a dry robe to my name. Oliver had wrapped his robe around my shivering shoulders and had jogged back from the top of the hill in just his swimwear, Sam close behind him.

I slip into my tent and throw on an all-in-one thermal suit, two jumpers, two pairs of socks, and some waterproof trousers. As a last-minute thought, I grab my cashmere bobble hat and head back out to the fire. I'm feeling the chill now. Though I was only in the water for a few minutes, the time we were down in the cave has worked its way right into my bone marrow and settled there like an unwelcome visitor.

Peeking from my tent flaps I can see Sam is around, so I go and sit with him by the fire. Huddling around myself to try to warm up a bit.

"That was some entrance," Sam says, stoking the fire and balancing the kettle on the wood.

"You know me." I say, trying to make light of it, then immediately regret it.

"Like I said at the last campsite," he says. "I knew the old you."

"The hay bale climber?"

He stops poking at the fire for a moment, the flames flickering on his face in the dusky light.

"Not just that. I knew the fun, carefree, crazy girl. The girl who would race me down the road on her bike. The girl who used to beat me at wheelies," he says, and I laugh because I'd forgotten about that bit.

"My bike was a lot lighter than yours."

The road I grew up on was a dead end, though it wasn't supposed to be. The parents had decided to put large planters across the tarmac to stop the boy racers who would use our small road as a cut through to their joy rides. It was only a side road really, it didn't lead anywhere because there were streets and avenues either side that lead to wherever they needed to go. The boy racers stopped screeching their tyres past our houses and the children who lived there started playing instead. Soon the planters were so heavy with the trees and bushes our parents had filled them with, that we couldn't move them out the way even if highway maintenance forced us to.

Sam and Frank and I used to race each other on our BMXs. But when they grew too old and strong to race against, I'd challenge them to who could stay up the longest on one wheel. I always won. And I'd forgotten all about that, until right now.

"Your bike was a BMX!" Sam laughs. "I had my Dad's old street bike. Do you remember? The wheels were so rusted that I practically had to run along holding it off the floor with my knees."

We both laugh now, at the thought of Sam knock-kneed with a bike between his legs.

"What happened to that Felicity? The Felicity with no fears?"

I'm not laughing anymore.

"She's long gone," I say, sadly. "Just boring old *Fliss* now, who worries about stocks and shares and falling to death on a holiday I thought was going to be relaxing and good for my wellbeing."

"An adrenaline pumped holiday," Sam says as though that's what I'd signed up for.

"Nope," I say, shaking my head. The kettle is starting to rattle now, and I'd kill for a cuppa. "Okay, maybe it did advertise itself as not for the faint-hearted, but it also said a relaxing, wellbeing, secret destination holiday. To be honest with you Sam, I thought I'd be heading to the Maldives on an all-inclusive two-week scuba-diving trip."

Sam gets off the seat and grabs his stick. Levering it under the kettle handle he lifts it to safety.

"Tea or coffee?"

"Coffee, please."

As he pours the water over the freeze-dried granules, he looks at me with one eyebrow raised.

"You did read the small print of the holiday you were booking, didn't you?"

My scrunched up face tells him everything he needs to know.

"*Hidden Holidays* offer two types of secret destination holidays. Both of them for the brave souls, yes. But with marked differences between them. One: a wellbeing break designed for those who like to relax and unwind. Two: an adventure packed adrenaline-filled trek where anything goes."

*Oh my god!* "What?"

Sam's face looks fit to burst. "Did you not wonder why your welcome email told you to pack thick socks and thermal undies?" he splutters.

"Well, yes," I say. "I did think that was a bit strange. But then I just thought that maybe we would be going to the Andes or something."

"Oh, Felicity."

"Oh my god, what an idiot. I booked it in a hurry because my parents wanted to do something for my birthday and the thought filled me with horror. I must have pressed on the wrong booking button."

I see Sam's face fall, he always got on really well with my parents, but I don't want to get into all that now.

"Where would I be if I'd clicked the right button?" My face is in my hands now, my eyes peeking out through my fingers. "Or do I not want to know."

"I hate to be the one to break this to you, Felicity. But you'd be in a villa for ten on Ibiza. A yoga retreat I think this one was. Full of Sangria and olives, with your own en-suite room and a heated pool."

"You have to be fucking kidding me?" I scream through my hands.

"You'd have to bear your deepest darkest secrets on that one, though," he adds, spluttering trying not to laugh. "But it would be in the luxury of a teepee in the grounds replete with blankets and cushions and your very own therapist."

Sam is bent double now, his head shaking with fits of laughter. I don't know whether to join him or go and throw myself down the hole again. I feel my lips creeping up, my cheeks stretching.

"Oh my god," I say again, this time with a big smile on my face. "Please, *please* don't tell anyone. I'll never live it down."

"Tell anyone what?" It's James, he's freshly washed by the looks of it and dressed in a comfortable looking track suit and beanie hat.

"Sam," I say, sternly.

He holds his hands up in surrender.

"Okay, okay. Nothing, James. Nothing at all."

James looks bewildered then catches sight of my coffee.

"Pour me a cup would you, mate?"

Sam gets up to get James a drink and James sits in his place, wrapping an arm around my shoulder.

"How're you feeling, Fliss?"

*Like an idiot.*

"Yeah, okay thanks. I'm a bit warmer now, and my

arm isn't aching as much. Thanks again, James. For pulling me out of the water."

"Couldn't let you sink now, could we?"

A lull falls over the three of us as we sip our hot drinks. No one else has come out to join us and I hope that I've not caused a rift between the members of the group.

"Maybe I did myself a favour by tripping over my feet, though I'm not sure it was my feet to be honest."

Sam snorts into his coffee. "You *did* do yourself a favour?" he cries. "Though I would recommend holding off on any further attempts at reacquainting yourself with the old Felicity I used to know. The one who would have jumped feet first right into that hole and looked for the dangers later."

"So, tell me," James says, holding his hands out, his own drink sloshing over the side of the tin mug. "How do you two know each other?"

"Used to," I say quickly. "A very long time ago."

I want to steamroller any possibility of a conversation about my past, so I keep talking.

"I wanted to swim this time, then when I realised it would be in the sea, I kind of chickened out. I'm not a big fan of the sea since… well, anyway. So without my giant leap for mankind with assistance from my size sixes, I wouldn't have swum. And I'm glad I did. Got me over my teenage phobia."

I shrug again and sip my coffee.

"Oh god," James says, his head in his free hand. "So

you not only risked your life, you gave yourself a quick dose of aversion therapy to go with it."

"Well, I didn't mean to," I say, surprised James doesn't just want to let this go. It's his business at stake. If it got out that guests were putting themselves in peril, shares may drop quicker than I did down the hole in the cliff top.

"Wouldn't be having this argument in Ibiza," Sam says wryly.

"Shut up," I laugh.

James gives us the side eye and goes off with his cuppa, I assume in search of the others.

"I'm going to do more," I say to Sam now we're alone. "Make my tent tidier, make tea, forage for more food, that kind of thing. Maya said I hadn't been looking out for anyone and she's right."

"Maya's not exactly been Mrs Hinch while she's been here, either," he adds. "Her tent is always littered with crap when I pack them away."

He leans into me conspiratorially and lowers his voice to a whisper.

"For someone so *at one* with nature, she's got a hell of a lot of luxury toiletries." He winks as he moves back.

## Chapter Twenty-Five
### Day Seven

"Fliss." The voice jolts me from a dream about tidal waves and sinking ships with cats at the helm.

"Fliss, are you awake?"

I groan and roll over onto my back, my sore arm protesting in pain.

"I am now," I hiss back.

The zipper on my tent starts to move up and a blast of fresh air hits me right in the face. It's not icy cold, thankfully, but it reminds me to pull my sleeping bag up around my neck as I'm not wearing a top. I'd woken in the night, sweating like I'd been doing two hours of Bikram so I'd peeled my thermals off and slept in just my sleeping bag. I feel a bit exposed now.

Bri's head pokes in through the gap in my tent flap. Her usual tightly braided hair is falling in soft waves around her face, making her eyes look bluer and her new freckles pop over her nose.

"God, you're tidy," she says, creeping in and sitting down by my feet.

"Morning Bri," I say, bemused.

"I wondered if you'd be up for an early morning swim with me?" she asks, looking down at her fingers. "I feel bad about what happened to you yesterday and I wanted to make sure you're okay."

There's joie de vivre about Bri again, but it feels different. As though her discomfort with the situation has been set free along with her hair.

"There's nothing to feel bad about, Bri, but thank you." I shuffle up a bit and try to sit up without flashing my boobs. "Like Maya said, she saw me swimming back at the hotel. I knew I wasn't going to drown."

*I didn't know that until I was shirking off my dry robe and gulping air as I surfaced.*

"You're so brave, Fliss!" she says, grabbing me in a hug.

"I'm really not," I say, laughing as she lets go. "But I'd rather people think I'm brave, than a clumsy idiot who plunged though a gaping hole to the dark, depths of the ocean. Though…"

I don't want to mention to Bri how the more I think about it, the less I think it was my own feet I tripped over. I'm not clumsy by nature.

"Swim then? From the beach?" She leans over and hugs my shoulders.

"Okay," I nod. "But you'll need to give me a chance to get dressed first."

"Sure," Bri says, crossing her legs. "No hurry. It's still mega early anyway."

I watch her for a moment, waiting for her to leave me to slip into my swimsuit.

"Bri?"

Her face drops.

"Oh, sorry," she splutters. "You want me to actually get out."

She scrambles to the flap and steps out into the sunshine.

"All yours," she sings through the door.

I throw on my swimsuit, hiding my scarred torso.

"Right," I say, climbing out my tent in my swimmers with Oliver's dry robe wrapped around me; I'll give it back to him next time I see him. "Let's head to the sea. Though I'll need to detour for a wee on the way there!"

The sun reflecting off the water hits us both in the eyes as we mount the top of the hill. Its beauty takes my breath away. I hadn't fully appreciated the beach yesterday, as we'd walked back from the cave. I'd been too cold. Too aware that I'd had to force myself not to sink into the sea, and at one point, wasn't sure which way to go. But this morning, it's as though we're in Ibiza after all. The sand is as white as can be. The water turquoise and dapple green. Transparent all the way down to the busy seabed.

"I can't believe you're a dentist and you didn't tell us," I say, remembering her coming to my aid yesterday, as we head down to the cove where the waves aren't even tickling the shoreline it's so calm.

A few gulls fly overhead, squawking loudly at each other as they duck and dive together. They're huge. I wouldn't fancy my chances if I had a bag of chips. The sun's rays are warm, and I feel a tug in my chest as we get closer to the sea, a jolt of happiness that I take a little while to process because it's been so long.

"I thought influencer seemed more glamorous, more me, you know?" she replies, the bounce back in her step. "But the longer I am here without my bloody phone, the more I'm enjoying it."

I look over at her.

"I can tell," I say, and I really can tell, she's glowing.

"Thank you," she smiles. "I thought I was going to fail at the first hurdle when I realised what was in store. As we were collecting cockles that first day, I wanted to jack it all in and run off to the Bahamas, you know?"

I nod. "I'm glad you didn't."

"Me too." She looks wistfully at the deep turquoise waters. "Though we could be in the Bahamas now for all I know. Look at it."

We throw off our dry robes and fold them neatly on the sand. Bri is already waiting for me by the water's edge by the time I've worked out how to fold it so the arms aren't hanging out. As I go and join her, I'm struck by the total opposite of how I'd normally be feeling right now, with the sea ahead of me looming in its vastness. There's no sense of sickness or dread, just a buoyancy running through the middle of me that will probably come in quite handy with my sore arm.

"Well, it may look like the Bahamas," Bri says, her toes in the water. "But it's still bloody freezing."

I dip a toe in and wince at the feeling shooting up my feet into my leg.

"I say five minutes max," Bri continues. "Right now you don't want to add chilblains to your list of ailments!"

The sound of splashing draws our attention to the far end of the cove. Whoever it is swimming, is coming from the direction of the cave entrance. We stand and watch as they get nearer, then he spots us, and stops to tread water and wave.

"It's Oliver," Bri squeals, waving back. "Hiya. God he must have been up and out early."

I sigh at the sight of his strong arms powering through the water again before I can stop myself. "Yep, yep, he must have been," I say, loudly and quickly to hide the sigh.

"What?" Bri turns to me as the splashing from Oliver's strokes gets louder.

"I was agreeing with you," I say, keen to stop this conversation before my face self-combusts.

"What?!" Bri says again in a staccato voice that may attract the wild dolphins over to join in our conversations. "Oh em gee, Fliss. You and Oliver?"

"Shush," I hiss, flapping my arms at her as she grins towards Oliver with a knowing look on her face. "Me and Oliver nothing. Like, literally nothing."

I think of the walk to this campsite. How he held me and promised to look out for me. The looks we have shared. The night in his tent. The way my pulse flaps about whenever he's near me.

"Nope," I add. "Nothing at all."

"Whatever, Fliss," Bri says, a wry smile on her face now. "Your luminous cheeks are giving you away. He's a surgeon, and he's hot, for an older guy I guess."

"He's probably my age," I yell. "Stop with the old!!"

"What're you girls talking about?" Oliver asks as he walks out of the sea like Daniel Craig's James Bond, only more brunette and less clean cut.

"You're out early," I blurt, not wanting Bri to even contemplate telling him what we were talking about.

"Yes," he says, his eyes twinkling as he steps closer to me. "Someone once told me I need to be up and out *at* the crack of dawn if I want to see the real swimmers. I guess they were right."

I smile, feeling my face heat so much I no longer need a dry robe. Oliver, on the other hand, is turning blue as we stand here speaking. I run back and pick up his robe, handing it to him as he follows me up the beach.

"This is yours," I say. "Thanks for the loan."

As he reaches out for it our fingers brush, the energy could have sent me flying all the way back to the campsite. Neither of us move our hands away. His eyes meet mine and against all my better judgement I don't look away.

"Right," Bri says from somewhere nearby. "I can see you guys have a lot to talk about. I'll be getting in the sea then."

Oliver wraps his robe around his shoulders, and I feel a bit naked standing here in just my costume.

"Will you walk with me?" he asks.

It's a split-second decision to make. I barely have time to think about it and normally big decisions like this take me ages to make. I pity my poor mum when she was rushing to get me out the house in time for school and I'd still be trying to decide if I wanted knickers with hearts or flowers that morning.

"I think I'm going to swim with Bri," I say, surprising even myself.

Oliver runs a hand through his hair, water drips down through the gap in his robe and onto his chest. It's all I can do to stop myself from diving in there too,

"Okay," he says, looking down at me through wet lashes with a tug of mischievousness. "Enjoy the water, it's clear and cold and wonderful."

"Thanks."

I'm doing the right thing. Bri asked me to swim with her and that's what I'm going to do. My priorities cannot change at the temptation of a man, despite the fact he takes my breath away. He'll still be there when we get back to the campsite and maybe we can walk and talk then. Bri is already powering through the water now, and I don't want to miss our five minutes swim together, so I head towards the sea myself.

"Oh, Fliss," Oliver shouts as I'm tiptoeing carefully into the icy cold water. "I'll leave this here for you. Don't want you catching a chill."

He strips out of his dry robe and throws it next to

Bri's. I smile a thanks. I'd answer properly, but I'm too busy watching him jog away in his neoprene boots and swimming trunks. The muscles in his back ripple with each step.

*Jeez, Felicity. Get a grip.*

I dunk myself down into the water to cool off. Forgetting for a second that it's not only icy enough to shake me from the revere of Oliver's muscles, but also cold enough to ice over my eyeballs.

## Chapter Twenty-Six

"Surprised to see you in here," Bri says to me as I swim up and tread water next to her.

The water is so translucent I can see just how red my legs have turned already. James' words of advice circle in my head and I'm wary to not get too cold.

"Not as surprised as I am, trust me," I say, my teeth already chattering together. "I'm doing quite well for someone who is sea-phobic. Is there a word for that? Being afraid of the sea? Because up until I fell in yesterday, I hadn't really set foot in the ocean since I was a teen."

I'm doing that thing where my teeth are chattering so much that words are pouring out of my mouth like a neurotic exerciser strapped to one of those gyrating band machines.

"Yes," Bri says, her own lips tinted blue. "Thalassophobia. Though it's normally caused by a traumatic event. What did the sea ever do to you?"

"Nothing," I say quickly, it pains me to remember so I rarely do, but the memories that surfaced during yesterday's dunk in the water have fought their way back.

We swim around a bit more. I'm trying my hardest to warm up so I can feel my extremities.

"But I wasn't talking about your conquered phobias," she says, catching up to me. "Though well done. I was talking about Mr Muscles."

She nods her head in the direction of where Oliver has just jogged off up the beach, but she needn't have. I knew what she was talking about as soon as she said it.

"Yeah," I chatter. "I don't want to cause a rift in the gang by being caught walking with Oliver. Besides, you asked me first."

"What?"

I swim away a bit, not wanting to admit that I think Maya has feelings for Oliver, like a love triangle that harks back to school days. And no matter what Bri said to me this morning, I know that her and Maya have formed a close bond.

"I think we should get out now," Bri says, waving me towards the shore. "I can't feel the end of my nose!"

My arms power through the water, still so clear I can see all the way down to the sand and the seabed. It's not too deep here, and the colours are beautiful. Like precious jewels out in their natural habitat instead of chipped away at and stuck into fastenings so we can wear them on our bodies to make us look pretty and desirable to others.

## Wild Swimming

I think of the four of us trekkers. Stuck out in the wild, not our natural habitat, but quickly becoming accustomed to it. Do we shape ourselves like these quartz and agates into a mould we think is desirable? And only out here, without the constraints of the world and our own histories, can we be ourselves. We've all changed, in the short space of time we've been on holiday. We've all merged back into our old natural shapes. Except I can feel myself not willing to let go, not willing to go back to the shape that I was born as, and I'm not willing to accept the reasons why. Maybe we reshape to protect ourselves too.

I reach the shore before Bri, my swimmer's instinct like a muscle memory, never too far out of reach. I emerge from the water into the heat of the sun, which isn't really that warm but compared with the water it feels like a steam room. I pull Oliver's robe around my body, stamping my feet and clapping my hands to get the blood circulating, just as James had shown us on that first evening back in Loch Rosingar. As the feeling of pins and needles flood my toes, I draw myself into the robe and bury my face in the hood. Even though he only had it on for a minute or so, the robe still carries a hint of Oliver. His smell igniting in me what I've been trying to dampen down.

"That was invigorating," Bri says, rubbing her arms and covering herself in her robe.

"Yes," I reply. "Thanks for the invite. Shall we walk back?"

We head on up the beach and back onto the mossy

hill, walking slowly back to camp around the peninsula of the furthest peak.

"What did you mean about not wanting to cause a rift by going for a walk with Oliver?" Bri asks, taking her hair out of its band and retying it in a high bun.

I'm probably never going to see Bri again after we fly back to London. Now's a good a time as any to talk, I suppose. We step single file over a rocky bit of terrain, my neoprene booties not quite as supportive as my walking boots. But I like the feel of the ground under my feet. I've always gone barefoot when I can and it's nice to have the sensation of it for a moment.

"I'm not great with forming friendships or relationships. The last relationship I had ended five years ago. It was with a guy I thought I was in love with," I start to talk as Bri is ahead of me. It's easier, somehow, that she's not looking at me. "We went to uni together. I thought we'd get married and have kids. Grow old together. But he had other ideas. He told me after six years that he never really knew me, and he needed to get away to clear his head and have some space. The next day he left for Australia and I haven't heard from him since."

"God," Bri says, stopping at the top of the hill and looking down at me. "What a dick."

"Yup," I say. "But I can't help but wonder if he was right. I wasn't all that fussed by the end of our relationship, so maybe I never did let him in. I've been on dates since, on and off dating sites, but I just can't seem to do it. Am I really that hard to get to know?"

Bri chews on the inside of her cheek and doesn't

answer immediately, giving me more of an answer than any words would do.

"I've known you just over a week." She says eventually, starting to walk again. I follow. "So, I'm probably not the best person to ask. But you've been quite a closed book. Let's just say that."

We walk on in silence for a moment.

"Do I seem like I'm not trying?" I don't really want to know the answer to that but after Maya shouted it for all and sundry to hear while I was lying in the cave wondering why my life hadn't flashed before my eyes, I need to know.

"Look Fliss," Bri says, stopping again and turning to me. Taking my hands in hers. "Not everyone wants to share their life story with a bunch of strangers and that's okay, especially here where we've been told not to really. But there's a fine line between being an introvert and being standoffish."

She doesn't say which side of the line I stand on. She doesn't need to. But she hugs me anyway. A deep, friendly hug that makes my eyes fill with tears for all the hugs I've missed out on so far. For the fun I've missed out on.

"And," she continues, her arms still wrapped around me. "Your story is sad, but it doesn't explain why you didn't go with Oliver and why you don't want to get in a muddle with the gang."

"Oh yeah," I laugh as she lets me go. "I got a bit sidetracked with my inability to forge friendships. So, after Mark—the ex—fled to the other side of the world to get some space from me, and I have failed again and again at online dating, I figured maybe it wasn't for me. And that's okay, you know. I'm happy not sharing my life with anyone. At least, I thought I was. These feelings for Oliver have thrown me for six. But two weeks in a confined space with someone isn't the best place to work out my fears of getting close to someone again, is it? Especially when I have no idea how he feels, and I *think* Maya might quite fancy him too. I definitely don't want to annoy her, especially when… well, I just don't want to annoy her."

Bri nods. The campsite is in view now. The rest of the gang are sitting around the fire, their hands cupped around hot drinks.

"What were you going to say?" she asks. "About Maya. Especially what?"

I look at Bri again, wondering if I can trust her with this.

"I don't know if I should be saying this to you," I say, eventually. "But I'm not certain that it was my own feet I tripped over yesterday. I think maybe I was tripped deliberately."

"What?" Bri looks incensed and I'm wondering maybe I should have kept my fears to myself. "If it's true, that's terrible. Jeez."

"I'm probably just being over dramatic, forget I said anything. Just be thankful she hasn't got her eye on James, hey?" I say, trying to make a joke of it.

"I don't know what you mean?" she says, with a side

smile and a quick glance down the hill to where James is busy prepping breakfast.

"Has anything happened between you two?" I ask, trying to change the subject, but I'm also interested.

"Nope," she says. "And that's not for a want of trying. I think he's too professional to get it on with a client. But maybe when we're back in the real world I can sneak him my number. I'd just like to have a go on that gorgeous six-pack, you know?"

A laugh bubbles up my throat and I can see James' six-pack quite clearly in my memories.

"Yep," I sigh. "I know exactly what you mean."

The look she gives me is playful.

"Careful," she says, stepping closer to me. "One wrong step here and you could roll all the way down this hill into that campfire."

I smile and throw my arm through hers.

We head off down the hill towards camp and the delicious smells of breakfast have me walking a bit quicker than I would normally. Bri squeezes my arm as we near the others.

"Don't worry," she whispers. "I'll look out for you."

And I feel an affinity towards the young woman who has just offered me more friendship than I've known for a long time.

# Chapter Twenty-Seven

Oliver catches up with me later that morning as we all disperse after a lunch of freshly caught seaweed soup. I'm walking towards the idea of my sleeping bag and forty winks when I hear his feet jogging up to me.

"Fancy that walk, now?" he asks, coming to a halt beside my tent.

Maya peeks out from her doorway at us before zipping it closed with such force that I think she's going to trap her head.

"I'd love to," I say, quietly, not wanting to upset her.

I grab my hoody out of my tent and pull it over my head, relishing the warmth of the extra layer now I've left the heat of the fire. The coldness from the sea still sitting in my bones. Oliver offers me his arm, and we head out the circle of tents and up the valley, retracing the steps of yesterday's run.

"Thanks again, for checking me over," I say, matching Oliver's strides on the soft grass as we head up the hill.

"It's quite reassuring to know we've got a medically trained professional on the trip."

"Not that you're planning on doing anything else quite so dangerous, though, right Fliss?" Oliver asks, a smile in his words.

"Of course," I reply, throatily, remembering the way his hands had gently worked their way across my whole body, checking for injury and breaks.

"And I'm sure Sam and James have a fair degree of training too," he adds as we round the top of the hill and watch the skyline soar away in front of us.

"A week of first aid training is *not* the same as ten years of medical school and practise," I say, sliding my arms out of Oliver's and walking to the edge of the cliff.

"And neither would be enough to help you if you were to slip and fall off *that* cliff," he says, still smiling, but I can hear the inflection in his words that tells me to stop before I get any closer to the sheer drop.

"Don't worry," I reply, looking back at Oliver over my shoulder where he is standing a safe distance from certain death. "I just wanted to look at the view."

And it has stopped me in my tracks. The ocean below — as blue as the sky — is licking gently at the sand, salted and cool I can almost feel it on my skin with the memory of yesterday's accidental dip and the memories of a childhood untarred by later events.

I shake the feel of Frank's hand painfully gripping my arm and try to concentrate on the much nicer way the hairs on the back of my neck are tingling as Oliver gets closer. I can't hear him, neither of us are speaking now, and I can't be the only one holding my breath, but I can feel his presence in the air as my whole body prickles with energy.

"The view is better from where I am standing," he whispers right behind me, his words tickling my ear.

I drop my head, exposing the nape of my neck to his breath and feel like I am about to self-combust with the need for him to touch my bare skin.

"Oh, Fliss, look." Oliver's voice is loud, startling me. "Out there, look."

He is beside me now, an arm outstretched, finger pointing out to sea. I follow his gaze to a pod of dolphins frolicking on the waves. They skim the water, darting between each other, flying up into the sky as they play. It's incredible, there must be twenty of them, flitting in and out of the sea. Almost as incredible as the idea of Oliver stroking my neck. I take a sideways glance at him, relishing the happiness on his face at the sight of the dolphins and the pinkness in his cheeks.

---

"It was a dark and stormy night."

"Wait, that's cheating," Sam cries, slapping his thighs, and tucking his hair behind his ear as it falls over his eyes. "You can't tell a Paul Clifford and pass it off as your own scary story."

"No, you can't!" James adds. "Besides, that's a melodramatic, purple prose opener. Go with your heart.

Surely you've got a lot of horror stories about being a dentist!"

The fire burns brightly in the middle of the group, providing warmth and light now the sun has disappeared. Bri holds a lit stick under her chin and illuminates her face, the shadows of her contours flickering eerily in the wrong direction. She drops her arm by her side and illuminates her Lululemon instead.

"That was burning my chin hair right off!" she says, throwing the stick onto the fire. "Okay, from the heart."

We all lean forwards ready to hear what Bri has to offer to our evening repertoire of ghostly stories. James has already given us a cackling episode of an Eastenders-esque Slender Man replete with a slanging match and tawdry shenanigans that I didn't think Slender Man would be physically capable of. Sam, on the other hand, told a story that made my neck creep with the feeling that someone was up on the mossy hill, watching us. When he stopped talking the silence was so thick he had to bash through it to explain it was a story he'd read on CreepyPasta and he was sure it wasn't real. I think Bri had been trying to lighten the mood with her *dark and stormy night*; and thank goodness it is working.

"There were four campers and two tour guides, sitting around a campfire and telling ghost stories."

"At least we know it can't be us," Oliver pipes up, rubbing his hands in front of the flames, his sleeves rolled up to just under his elbows showing off his tanned forearms. "There's only three of us and our tour guides tonight."

He is right. Maya hasn't joined us this evening. Something about a sore head and a chill from the length of time she had to spend in the water earlier, had her turning in after we'd finished our dinner of fresh seaweed we'd all collected from the beach and a massive trout that Sam had dragged back from the river late this afternoon. We haven't seen her since.

"Speaking of," James says. "I'd better go and check on our patient. Make sure she's okay."

He puts his cup on the floor and heads past me and Bri towards the tents.

"Thank god," Bri says, hiding her hands inside the sleeves of her huge sweatshirt. "I'm rubbish at ghost stories. Ask me for a juicy tale of gore and real-life crime stuff and I'm your girl. But my creative juices are as dry as a nun's gusset."

Sam chokes on his hot chocolate with Bri's words.

"Jeez," he says, once he's stopped coughing. "That's an image burned onto my retina that I never knew I needed."

"Sorry, love," Bri says, leaning over and patting his knee. "But better than picturing a wet one."

Sam screws up his face and shudders.

"On that note, Oliver?" He looks over the fire to where Oliver is sitting.

"Sorry, what?" Oliver says, looking up from his hot chocolate. "You want me to tell a story now?"

His face looks like his thoughts are miles away. Sam nods.

"Okay," he says, his face lighting up. "No problem at all, there's nothing dry about my creative juices."

He smirks and somehow makes something so innocuous sound vulgar.

"Oh my goodness, you guys," Sam cries, covering his ears with his hands.

We all fall about laughing. My sides ache with the feeling. It's a good ache to be having.

"Poor Sam," I splutter though tears of laughter. "He's an innocent. Look at this place, he was brought up in the middle of nowhere where females are scarcer than hens' teeth."

"Shut up, Felicity," he croaks. "As you well know, I was brought up down the street from you in a desirable road in Kent. Plenty of girls. I only moved here once my innocence was well and truly squashed by Anthony's older sister."

"Smelly Susan?" I blurt, without even questioning the hideously cruel nickname the girls had given poor Susan who was hitting the primes of puberty when she started the secondary school and was stuck with it throughout her time there. "No way."

Sam nods. "She had her claws in me after I befriended Anthony because he had a new Sega Megadrive and the latest edition of Fifa. I didn't stand a chance."

I squeal with laughter now, tears running down my cheeks as I picture a late to develop Sam cowering under the gaze of an older girl.

"That's every boy's dream, isn't it?" Oliver asks. "To be taken under the wing of a more experienced woman and shown the ropes."

"You never met Susan." Sam's face is puce even beyond the flames of the fire reflecting on his cheeks.

We all break down in fits of giggles again. Even Oliver, who all afternoon had been stony faced and monosyllabic, is now holding his ribs together, his eyes wrinkled and his face bright.

"What's got you all high as kites?" James is wandering back to the campfire, his hands in his pockets as his hips sway.

"Alright, Mary Nightingale," Bri says, patting the space next to her as she scoots over. "How's the patient?"

"Yeah," Sam asks, his lips curving. "Took your time. Did she need some extra TLC?"

A flash of something flickers over Bri's face but is gone before it's really there.

"As always," he says pointedly at Sam. "I was ever the professional. She'll be fine. Some sleep will help. So, tell me, why are you all laughing like hyenas?"

I can't help but notice the flush creep up James' neck, but he's just sat right next to the fire, perhaps it's the heat and the reflection.

"Just comparing creative juices," Oliver says, stifling a laugh now. "You know?"

That's too much for us all to take, as we break down into giggles again. It wasn't even that funny. I think it's a mixture of the situation and the tension that had been gathering between us all. Thrown in together as total strangers who now know each other's toileting habits and strange odours. There's a collective strength in us now. The way an express friendship with no place to hide will do that to people. We need an outlet and tonight is providing a perfect one. It's helping me that Maya isn't here stalking my every glance at Oliver. I can't help it. He's just so magnetic, my eyes are drawn to him. I can't help it that both Maya and I may have fallen a little for this handsome stranger. A holiday this intense, I suppose it was bound to happen.

"Right." James looks a bit put out that he's not in on our joke and I watch him flounder for a bit. For once I'm in the inner circle and it feels good. But, being a natural leader and entertainer, James isn't on the wrong foot for long. "So, who wants to help me get my creative juices flowing, then?"

He looks at Bri. The look he knows will gather him back up into the folds of the circle and back to the centre where he belongs. It's a tried and trusted look, and something tugs at my insides for Bri. I watch, enthralled, at the game they're playing between them. Vicariously living through their flirting. She's playing it cool though, her eyebrows raised, a small shrug of one of her shoulders. I can feel the tension pulsing between them from across the fire. Then my eyes flicker like the flames, over to Oliver. His face hidden behind the burning embers, occasionally coming into view between golden, red peaks of crackling fire.

"Oliver," James says, interrupting the moment. "Tell us a little about your work as a surgeon."

Oliver's languidness clears as he shakes out his arms and I feel the breath fall from my body.

"I work at Addenbrooks," he says, picking up a stick and poking the bottom of the fire. Small dashes of charcoal float up into the sky. "In paediatric oncology. It's tough, you know, seeing babies and children with cancer. But I love it, and I wouldn't do anything else."

He stares into the fire, caught somewhere between work and the trek.

"I chose my job because I'm good with numbers," I say quietly across the fire. "I love being in control and numbers help me do that well. What made you choose to help children?"

Oliver's face pinches almost imperceptibly, his eyes still fixed on the flames.

"I am one of five boys," he continues. "When I was a teen, my youngest brother was diagnosed with Acute Lymphoblastic Leukaemia, cancer of the blood, basically. He was in and out of hospital so I'd stay with my grandma to get away from the stress of home. My parents weren't the nicest to each other at that time, there was a lot of shouting. I guess they were stressed and tired and I can't even imagine how awful it was for them.

My brother healed, thankfully. The hospital and doctors and nurses were all amazing. He's living in America now, herding cattle on a ranch. I guess he was the reason I chose to help kids."

"I'm so sorry you went through that," Sam says, nodding at Oliver. "It's admirable taking on a career that could potentially be quite traumatic given your history."

Oliver smiles sadly.

"I was so young that I think I took it in my stride, the way kids tend to do if they're protected from the worst of what could happen. Sadly, my parents couldn't seem to get over the stress, they split up not long after my brother was given the all clear. I stayed with my grandma a lot more after that happened. She is my rock. Once, she told me that to live is not necessarily to enjoy every single moment, but to know there is enjoyment happening for others. She's so right. What day is it?"

His question throws me as I realise I also have no idea what day it is.

"Friday," James replies.

"Friday." Oliver stops poking the fire and picks up his drink to raise in a cheer. "Ever since I broke up with my ex, Grandma has been keeping me company a couple nights a week. Happy takeaway and movie night, Grandma. Hope you're watching Crazy, Stupid, Love this week so I don't have to again when I get home."

He raises his cup to his lips and takes a sip. Bri, James, and Sam raise their own hot chocolate and say a salute to Oliver's Grandma, but I'm paralysed, drawn to the eyes of the man sitting opposite me, the way he took the trauma of his childhood and turned it into good, the way he helps people, the way he talks about his family and his grandma, and it's too much for my poor heart. The itch of desire I'm feeling for him deepens as Oliver catches me looking, his eyelids look heavy, his mouth parting slightly.

I clear my throat and stand abruptly.

"I'm just going for a wee," I say, blind to the fact that only a matter of days ago I'd be mortified if people knew I was about to empty my bladder.

"I'll come with you," Oliver says, upright before I can say anything. "It's dark, and there're great big holes in the ground around here. Can't be too careful."

I nod, not trusting myself to speak coherent words. Bri is so focused on James that she barely notices I'm leaving, but as we're heading off into the darkness, she shouts over to me.

"Don't do anything I wouldn't do" Which makes my heart rush up into my throat.

Oliver stops at his tent, unzipping the flap and heading in. "How desperate are you?"

I want to shout it's been so long that I've gone past the point of desperate. My hymen has grown back. I'm a quaking mess of excitement and angst. I inflate my chest with a good dose of bravery and go to follow Oliver deep into the unknown. Almost unknown; I do remember the night we drank ourselves silly inside his tent. The chemistry even then had been undeniable, despite my spiky exterior. As I get closer to the zipped opening his head pops back out and I jump back.

"I have this cool head torch that will stop us falling foul to any more hidden caves," he says, his head bobbing up and down out with a light attached to the top of it that burns my retinas clean off. "I just wanted to make sure I had time to pick it up before you wet yourself."

"Desperate for a wee?" *I'm such an idiot.* "Oh, yeah, not that desperate. Not at all. Really don't think I need."

"Well, we're out now," he says, the light illuminating the moors. "Let's go, shall we?"

Thank god I didn't follow him inside and start ripping off my clothes. Or his. He links his arm through mine and we walk away from the camp. The light firing its way out of Oliver's forehead like an angler fish makes the moor look eerier that it did in the dark. Now I can see a large round patch like it's daytime, yet the edges are muffled, wrought with only the concepts of what might be there. With every step I get the feeling that something is going to appear in the circle of light and make my heart stop its infernal pounding in my chest.

"There's a good hill just up here," Oliver says turning and blinding me. "Oh crap, sorry."

He turns his head back and I blink a few times to rid my eyeballs of the two glaring spots.

"Is this your first holiday with a head torch?" I ask.

"How can you tell?" he says, his voice dripping with irony. "You know, I thought I'd be good at this wilderness shit. But all it's really showing me is how much I need my home essentials."

"You seem so at home, though."

"Do I? I feel like one of Sam's poor trout. I'm a walker. I run. I'm healthy and fit and youngish. I thought this would be easier than it is. But I miss proper coffee so much. And my bed. Oh god, I miss my bed."

"Urgh, me too."

"Didn't know you'd ever been in my bed. I'm pretty sure I'd remember that."

I wallop his arm.

*I wish.*

He stops walking, the light wobbling as he tries to fiddle with the switch. Then the night envelops us in a darkness so complete it takes my breath clean out of my body.

"Fliss," Oliver says, his face must be close to mine, I can feel his breath on my mouth.

I don't move. Oliver reaches out and finds my arms, clasping my shoulders then drawing his fingers up towards my neck. My whole body feels alive. My skin tingles, my lips part. There is no one here to see us. Even if Maya was standing right next to us, she wouldn't be able to see through the darkness to Oliver's fingers as they find my lips. I let out a moan and Oliver mirrors me. I can sense his body moving closer before I feel it up against me. A hand reaches the back of my head, pulling me in, fingers running through my hair. Oliver's body is solid against my own.

"Can I kiss you?" he whispers into my hair, sending electric currents down my spine.

I don't wait to answer him, my lips reach up towards where I think his face is. I kiss him hard. On the stubble that has grown all over his chin.

"Ow, shit, sorry," I giggle.

"Fliss?" It's Sam's voice. "Oliver?"

Oliver mutters under his breath, his hands leaving my hair and my face. I take a step back from him.

"Yes Sam, we're here."

"Oh, thank goodness," Sam says as Oliver flicks his light back on. "You vanished. Your light went out. I thought I'd better check nothing had happened."

"Nope," I say, feeling alive and deflated in one fowl sweep. "Nothing happened. Nothing at all."

# Chapter Twenty-Eight
## Day Eight

I went to bed last night feeling frustrated and fizzing and in desperate need of a wee. And woke feeling cold and grubby and in desperate need of a hot shower and some Egyptian cotton, and still desperate for a wee. We're two thirds of the way through our trek. One more location left to go and then I get to go home and start up my old life again. As I'm pulling on yesterday's thermals, their armpits being the least offensive, I feel a pull in my stomach at the thought of travelling back to my stressful job and my empty house. I'm starting to enjoy it here.

It's three days until my birthday. The penultimate day of our trek. I haven't mentioned it since we were in the minibus, so I hope everyone has forgotten about it by now. I don't want a fuss. That was the whole reason for running away on a holiday for one, even if I should have been in Ibiza. I'm laughing to myself as Bri pokes her head in my tent with a smile and a welcome mug of something steaming in her hand.

"Morning, rise and shine," she says. "Coffee?"

"Ahhh, Bri," I say, taking the cup and moving over so she can squeeze in with me. "You're a lifesaver."

"Not me, technically. I didn't drag you from the depths of the sea or run my hands over your body to make sure there were no broken bones."

"Coffee trumps both of those, to be honest," I say, though the memory of Oliver's hands running along my collar bone is a pretty close second.

We laugh and we sip, savouring the drink even though it's pretty vile. I'm kind of used to the three-in-one sachets topped with camping kettle boiling water now. Sweet and pretend milky and nothing like the ones I make at home. But at least this one was made with love.

"So?" Bri asks, sipping her coffee and elongating the vowel sound.

"So? What?"

"You and Oliver?"

"What?" I cover my burning face with my mug.

"What happened to you last night? After Sam went to find you, James told me to go to bed! I was gutted to be honest; it was really romantic just the two of us by the fire."

"Sorry." I think back to standing on the hill with Oliver. The way his hands and his words had made me feel and I can't help my lips as they curl into a smile.

"I knew it," Bri says, shaking her head in excitement.

"Shhh," I say, whispering now. "We're in a tent and I don't want the whole of the Scottish Highlands to know."

"Especially not." She nods towards Maya's tent then zips her mouth closed.

"Preferably not. Though, I mean, nothing actually happened between us. But I just get this feeling, you know?"

"Oh yes. I know exactly what you mean," she sighs, tilting her head back and shutting her eyes

I know she does. I've seen the way she looks at James.

"I want to have sex with him in the sea," Bri says, hopefully about James. "Or on the ledge of the cave. Uhhh."

"You'd catch hypothermia, and I'm not sure any man would be able to, er, perform in such cold conditions." I waggle my little finger around to highlight my point, Bri peeks one eye open and snorts.

"Okay," she says, curling her free hand into a ball of frustration. "His tent then. Anywhere. I just want to jump him."

I laugh. I've never had this kind of conversation before. My girlfriends and I don't talk about who we'd like to sleep with in the ocean. We don't even really talk about men all that much. We talk about work, because that's how I know them. It's fun, having this kind of connection with someone. As though the quick, intenseness of our relationship means it's open all access because of the newfound safe space we have formed.

"Though," I say, with a new-found permission to be cheeky. "From the feel of it, Oliver wasn't that cold last night."

Bri squeals and hits her knee with her hand.

"Fliss," she says, incredulous. "I knew you were in there somewhere."

Her words hit me right in the solar plexus. She's right. I am in here somewhere. And this trek has me fighting to get out.

"So," she continues. "You can't say that then not tell me more."

"Literally nothing happened. Sam interrupted us. But I think I might have snogged Oliver's beard."

We roll over in fits of giggles.

"It's a gorgeous beard, I'll give you that. But his lips look less chafing."

"They're pretty gorgeous lips, aren't they?"

"He's hot, Fliss. Not as hot as James mind."

"They're both hot. And they're both really decent human beings. What's going on?"

Bri shrugs her shoulders right up to her chin. "I know, right? Anyway, I'd best be off. We're having one last trip over to the cave today. Then packing to leave for our last camping spot. Wonder what it'll be like. I hope I can manage the last trek okay, I'm pretty exhausted."

She chews her lips as she manoeuvres herself out of my tent.

"See you in a bit, Bri," I shout after her. "And thanks."

She pokes her head back in through the flap.

"You're welcome, Fliss. It's nice to finally meet you."

. . .

## Wild Swimming

Oliver and I are doing that thing where we both look sheepish and coy whenever the other is in sight. It's building; the tension between us. We're at that delicious stage where I know something is going to happen and the anticipation is fizzing around me like Mentos in Coke.

The whole gang is marching up the hill towards the cave entrance. Sam's by my side, he's already said he'll walk around to the beach with me once everyone has jumped in. Grateful though I am for Sam's company, I can't help but sneak a look at Oliver. I want to catch up with him, to talk to him about what almost happened between us last night, but James holds his attention with a conversation that sounds suspiciously like a football chat. It's weird to listen to. As though I'd forgotten that the real world is still out there, going on without us. Football matches are being won and lost while we're all up here finding ourselves. My work is still buzzing from eight til eight. My parents are still going to be celebrating the birth of their babies. I push that last thought out of my head as Maya treks up behind us, her arm looped into Bri's.

"Glad you're feeling better, Maya," I say, trying to sound upbeat.

I've decided I like this new part of me. The sociable part who chats to other girls and talks about cold willies.

"Yes," she says talking rather loudly, her usual smile not so easy to come by today. "It was just a headache. Not sure why everyone was so concerned. James certainly didn't need to check in on me last night. I'm very glad he did though."

And only a few seconds into being sociable, I'm reminded of why I find friendships so hard. I see Bri's forehead crinkle and want to gather her up and tell her that this is what girls do. We taunt. We push buttons. We pit ourselves against each other for men we don't even want. Just to come out on top and be the victor. The heady need to be desired providing enough impetus to tread on each other as we do so. We can't help it, it's how society has taught us to behave through cleverly masked subterfuge of women in television, press, and magazines.

"He's just doing his job as a trek leader," Bri says, prickly, trying to remove her arm from Maya's with varying degrees of success. "He needs to make sure we're okay. He did the same for Fliss when she wasn't well, didn't he? And Sam went to look for Fliss and Oliver last night when their light went out."

She knows as soon as she's said it that she shouldn't have. Maya's body almost imperceptibly stops and jolts in my direction. But she rights herself quickly. As we keep walking towards the fateful drop, I feel dread sitting heavily in my stomach. Like I want to explain Bri's words to Maya, to placate her. I know I've done nothing wrong and I don't need to tell Maya what we were doing. But she gives me a look and I can't help myself.

"Oliver was just shining the light so I could go for a wee," I blurt. "The light went out so I could have some privacy."

Maya raises her eyebrow at me, it's lighter now it's not pencilled in, but still just as scathing. I figuratively kick myself, my feet feeling heavy.

## Wild Swimming

We reach the cliff top, the cave entrance hidden well behind the moss and growth of the wild grass. We've been really lucky with the weather the last couple of days. It's warm and sunny again today. Almost hot. Over the hill the sea looks inviting. Which is something I never thought I'd hear myself saying. It twinkles at me, welcoming and encouraging. I'm still wearing Oliver's robe, and I sneak a sniff at the collar which I think now smells less like him and more like me. Unfortunately.

"As per," James says as we gather around him. "I'll go first, and Sam will bring up the rear. Anyone not wanting to jump can walk around with Sam to the beach entrance."

We all strip down to our swimmers. Everyone's feet and hands are covered by black neoprene this time. I think we're all starting to feel the coldness, unable to shake it from our bodies after so long in the elements. Oliver walks over to me and puts a warm hand on my shoulder.

"I'll walk down with you if you'd like me to?" he says, a curl falling over his eye.

"Thanks, but you jump. It's the last chance we'll have to do it and I'd hate to take that away from you."

"I want to be with you," he says, leaning in and whispering in my ear.

I look up at him. His dark eyes trained on me, getting darker by the second. There's a raw feeling building up in me. And I want nothing more than to be alone with Oliver now too. But I also know that I can't let lust get in the way of an opportunity like this.

"I can't," I whisper back, my heart hammering in my chest. "You need to jump."

We both step back from each other, breathing heavily, a pulse of energy between us.

"I'll go first," Maya says, once James has taken the leap. "I'm not afraid."

And she looks directly at me as she says those words. As though they will hurt more than falling in did. And I think they do.

Bri rubs my arm.

"Why did you do that earlier? she asks, once Maya has jumped. "Placate Maya about Oliver? It's not your place to make excuses for yourself and a man who you'd like to snog."

She's talking quietly, but I still feel like the whole of the northern territory can hear her.

"I don't know," I shrug. "I feel bad that we both like him, maybe?"

"Right, well," she says. "Don't bloody do it again!"

"Yes mum," I laugh, then feel a stab of guilt because I would never have conceded so easily to my actual mum.

"I'll go next," Bri says. "Otherwise I'll chicken out."

And she peers over to check it's all clear then jumps in. I can feel my resolve growing. With Oliver's words of kindness, Sam's reminder of what I used to be like, and Bri's friendship I feel like I can do anything. I fell in the cave and was fine. Maybe I should just jump.

"Do it," Sam says, looking at me intently.

"What?"

"I can see the hunger in your eyes," he says, nodding towards the cave entrance.

Oliver looks at me and the hunger is now probably ravenous.

"I can't," I say.

"Why? You've done it once," Sam asks.

"What if I hurt myself?" My eyes are still glued to Oliver as Sam replies.

"You can't miss out on adventure because you're too worried you'll hurt yourself. Think of everything out there that is riddled with risk that you'll miss out on." I tear my eyes away to look at Sam now.

"Like breaking my neck?" But Sam is right. I have spent my life worried about hurting myself. About dying. "You don't understand."

I'm talking to Sam, but it's directed at both of them.

"Stop being afraid." Oliver says, his voice husky. "Take a chance."

So I do. I walk towards the edge. The water below is crystal clear and the others are out of my way. And I jump.

# Chapter Twenty-Nine

It's so different to the last time. I feel a sense of relief quickly followed by a rising of emotion in my chest. Though that could be my breakfast coming back to greet me.

I hit the water with my neoprene boots and glide gracefully under. The darkness doesn't fill me with dread this time. There are no unwanted memories. There are no images of Frank reaching out to me, his eyes as black as tar, his hands wretched in their shape. Instead, I feel calmness descend as the world is blocked out by the water. I flipper my feet to the surface, breaking out into the cave I take a deep breath and choke back a sob. I haven't hurt myself. I'm fine. More than fine. Luckily my tears blend in with the salty water and I swim towards the cave entrance rather than the ledge where the others are waiting. I power through the calm sea, swimming as though I'm back in a pool practising for a competition. I'm back in my teens. There have been no failed relationships reminding me I'm useless with people. There's no stressful job that I do to block out the memories and the world. There's no executive house empty of everything important and filled with expensive goods. And, most importantly, my family all still love me.

I swim out of the cave and into the open water. The feeling of the sun on the back of my head is wonderful, taking away the cold, damp feeling that had permeated my skull and sat heavily on my neck. My shoulders feel smooth, my stroke as good as it always had been back when I was younger; like riding a bike.

The rocks from the cove jut out so I swim past them and round into the cove where the sea is turquoise and the gulls swoop with ease to catch their own breakfast. It's beautiful. The way the purple moss twinkles with dew. The sand a perfect white, stretching across the cove and to the edge of the peninsula like a crescent moon. I stop swimming and flip over onto my back. Watching the gulls, listening to their cries. The water rocks me and I shut my eyes, feeling the warm sun on my face. As I'm drifting, I feel the water undulate beneath my back, the waves getting faster. I can hear the splashing of someone swimming towards me. I turn my head and peel open an eye. It's Oliver, and he's swimming fast.

He's beside me and treading water, his breathing heavy. There's no one else around in the cove. They must all still be in the confines of the cave. I push my legs down so I'm treading water beside him. The waves push us closer together. I could push myself away with my feet, swim towards the shore, but I don't. I let myself be carried by the sea, crashing against his chest. He reaches out to me with one hand, the other sliding back and forth through the water to help keep him afloat. As his fingers cup my cheek a large wave pushes me right up to his chest and all the air escapes my lungs.

I tilt my head towards his and he kisses me. The urgency with which his lips find mine is exhilarating. I push back, needing to taste him, to kiss him. I grab his face in my hands, my legs paddling heavily under water, so I don't drag us both underneath. We're lost in each other for a moment. Our lips crashing together, our tongues fighting to touch. And when we finally draw apart my eyes feel as heavy as Oliver's look. I want to keep kissing him. I want to feel his hands over my body, to touch his naked chest and to trail my fingers down to his shorts. But it's cold. And I can hear the voices of the others getting louder as they make their way towards the cove. So I flip over onto my front and power to the shore. Unable to keep the smile from my face.

"Well, I have to say," James says later as we're all warming up by the fire, wrapped in layers of clothes with our lunch on our knees and the sun beating on our heads. "I am so proud of how far you've all come."

We smile at each other. And I'm glad of a reason to smile that everyone is privy to, because my cheeks are sore with the effort to keep my face neutral.

"Think back to Loch Rosingar. The dark water and

the striking backdrop. Did any one of you think then that you'd be jumping off a cliff into the sea?"

"Not me, that's for sure," I say, grinning. "Even setting foot in the sea was pretty much a no-go for me before I arrived here."

"You're certainly looking different after that swim, Fliss," Bri says, rubbing my knee.

"I feel it." My eye catches Oliver's and I bite my lip to stop myself looking like a Cheshire cat.

"It's *okay* to grin like a loon, Felicity," Sam says, his own grin quite curious. "That's the grin I remember and it's amazing to see it back on your face."

So I let myself smile widely and fully for the first time in years.

"I feel like a million dollars, myself," Bri says, her hand cupping her cheeks and I notice her nails are now bare and short. And it's true, she now looks a million dollars sitting there in her old jogging bottoms and a rain coat. We all do. Despite the lack of good coffee, the permanent cold, and the lack of sleep. And I feel great. I know my fitness levels have increased ten-fold with the hiking and the swimming. And the fact I'm not stressing about what I look like because of the lack of mirrors has helped my confidence in ways I would not have imagined it to.

We have been eating well, there's hardly any sugar and our meals have all been freshly foraged and caught. Though I'm not ruling sugar out when I get home, it's practically one of my main food groups, maybe I'll just cut it down a little.

"I feel amazing too," Maya says, though she seems to have lost her perma-tan while we've been away. "My skin is glowing, and I normally get eczema on my breasts and that's all but cleared up, look."

Before any of us can avert our eyes Maya has whipped up her hoody and thermal vest and whatever other layers she has on which definitely don't contain a bra and flashes the most perfect pair of breasts I think I've seen. Not that I've seen a lot, if I don't count my own then it's just ones on television. But Maya's are pert but large and not ravaged by gravity. It's like a car crash that I can't not look at.

Sam clears his throat. "Glad to hear it, Maya."

Over the flicker of flames, I can see Oliver shake his head, though a stab of jealously hits me when I realise he can't draw his eyes away from them either. A real stab of pain in my ribs has me looking away from the perfect mammaries and to Bri who's jabbing me in the side with her pointy elbow.

"Stop giving her what she wants," she says under her breath.

"But I think I want her boobs," I whisper back, and we giggle in stilted gasps looking around guiltily when all eyes fall on us.

"Right," James says. "Well that's certainly sent me right off track. But thanks Maya for your honest review of the Scottish fresh air."

He clears his own throat a few times too.

"And giving us the evidence to back it up," Bri says. "Always one for a bit of clinical reasoning."

Everyone laughs this time.

"And it's not like we haven't seen each other naked anyway," Oliver pipes up, his face more a grimace than a smile.

A rush of heat floods my cheeks as I picture him and Maya naked together. Has something happened between them already? Why is he admitting to this in front of everyone now, after we kissed this morning? Couldn't he have just kept his mouth shut? Both times?

"Ah yes," James says, oblivious to my embarrassment. "Talking of skinny dipping." *Oh, yes, thank God, not a sexual encounter after all.* "We will be trekking to our final location tomorrow, very early doors. And hopefully we'll all feel free enough to get our clothes off as a final thank you to our bodies for the work they've done this fortnight. We've all done ourselves proud and I think our skin deserves a chance to really connect with the nature around us. I'm so excited to show you the final destination."

"I hope it's not like the film," Maya says, sort of under her breath but loud enough so we can all hear.

"Nope," James says. "Not unless we all escaped sudden death on the flight over here. Though now I think of it, I'm pretty sure we did. I've never been thrown around in my tiny airplane seat so much as I was on that flight."

"I think death has skipped Fliss again already then, seeing as she didn't get hurt when she *tripped* into the cave," Bri says, as brazen as anything.

"Ah yes," James says, ignoring the connotations of

how Bri has just said what she said. "Fliss. Our holiday birthday girl. Remind me when the big day is again?"

All eyes drop on me again. So much for keeping it a secret.

"The penultimate day," I say. "But I really don't want to do anything. I don't want a fuss. That's why I came away. To avoid a fuss."

"No fuss, necessary. I just wanted to make sure we didn't miss it, that's all."

"Oh come on," Maya pipes up, smiling sweetly at me. "Of course you want a fuss. It's not like you haven't already caused a great deal of fuss, is it? What's one more day?"

"Me? Fuss?" I say, my face heating as I think back to the times when James and Sam have singled me out to help me. "Sorry, look, I really don't want to celebrate it. A swim or a walk will do me fine."

"It's okay Fliss," James says. "The next location will provide both of those in abundance, as you can imagine now we've been in the Scottish Highlands for so long. But there is something extra special that we will hopefully get to witness there too. Not saying it's there for your birthday in particular, but when you see it, you'll be hard pushed not to feel celebratory."

"See," says Maya, her lips curling into a smile. "You can't get away with not celebrating it now, can you?"

"I guess not," I say quietly, my stomach clenched. "I guess not."

But I don't want to celebrate, and I have very good reason not to.

# Chapter Thirty
## Day Nine

"Good morning, good mo-or-orning," James is singing what sounds like right in my ear but is probably just outside the tents. "We've talked the whole night through. Good morning. Good morning, to you."

He sounds happier than I think he has all trek, which is no mean feat seeing as he's one of the most upbeat and positive people I've ever met. Nothing like a bit of Gene Kelly to remind me of what a miserable old sod I am. I check my watch and groan into the pillow of my sleeping bag.

"It's four thirty. It's not morning yet," I yell back.

"Oh but it is, dear Fliss," he says, unzipping my tent and poking his smiling face inside. "Oh but it is."

He had told us last night to pack up our stuff and be ready for an early call. But I thought he meant seven am, not the middle of the night when some people are still dragging their bodies to bed after a wild night on the town. Not me, of course. But that fact that someone somewhere is, is enough for me.

"It's not," I hear someone else shout from their own tent.

"Time to rise and shine we have a boat to catch."

That got everyone's attention.

And James wasn't kidding. By half five, all six of us are clinging on to the sides of a rickety old motorboat, bouncing over the white tops of the sounds between mainland Scotland and the upper tip of the Isle of Skye. The tents and bags are roped together, held down by fisherman's knots and an old bench I'm not sure will withstand the weight of all our worldly goods if the sea gets any choppier. Poor Bri is looking a bit green around the gills, and her head is wobbling like an already sprung jack-in-the-box as Maya rubs her back.

When James had mentioned a boat, I had been picturing a ferry, or at least something with a roof. As it is, we're all soaked to the skin with the spray battering us from the bow. It's like a slower version of a water ride at a theme park, only not quite as safe. Though as I'm cowering behind Oliver's broad shoulders to try and protect myself a little from the elements, I can't help thinking it's more than a little exhilarating. Oliver is behind James who is sitting at the peak of the bow, if that's even what it's called. The pointy bit at the front where the two seating benches come together. He occasionally puts his arms out by his sides and whoops about being the king of the world, but we're all too busy holding on for dear life to pay him much attention. Even Bri is momentarily distracted by her misplaced sea legs. Sam has his eyes fixed on the tents which is thankful. I don't want to be sleeping under the elements after being pummelled by them across the sounds.

"Nearly there, aye," says the old, bearded man wearing galoshes and faded yellow waterproof bib and braces that I swear James must have made him wear to look authentic. "Lovely smooth trip."

Bri looks like she disagrees, a trickle of vomit dribbling from the corner of her mouth into the choppy waters.

It's weird how bumpy the journey has been given how smooth the water looked at the cove where we set off from. But apparently because the channels between the mainland and all the islands are relatively small, the water can bash against both and cause larger waves in between. I, for one, will never moan about having to go in a rowing boat on the Thames ever again. Not that I would have any reason to go for a row on the river, but if someone was to ask me, I'd not have an issue with it.

We're dropped off on a desolate looking beach surrounded by even more desolate looking moorland. Some sea foam and a few bits of driftwood are our welcome party. I'm not getting the sense of excitement that James promised about our final location. Not yet anyway. My legs feel like they're still on the boat as I go to pick up my rucksack from where the surprisingly strong boat driver has thrown it. I've got that weird sensation I sometimes get if I've stayed on the treadmill too long, only the world isn't going too fast, it's moving from side to side.

"Land sickness," James says, seeing me swaying. "It'll pass."

"And the sea sickness?" Bri asks him, wiping her green sweaty face with the back of her hand.

"Should be gone in a few hours." He throws his bag over his shoulders as Bri groans into her zipped up coat. "Follow me, everyone."

A light drizzle doesn't make any difference to how wet I already am, but this trek will be harder given that we're having to carry our tents as well as our bags because the minibus wouldn't fit on the fishing boat. I trudge behind Bri and Maya as one consoles the other, until Oliver comes up behind me and places a hand on my back.

"Do you want me to take that for you?" he asks, gesturing to the tent that I can't work out how to hold without it bashing against my shins.

"No thanks," I say, hoiking it up so it can bash against my hip for a bit instead.

I'm not being deliberately obtuse; I'm genuinely enjoying carrying my worldly goods across a flat open expanse. My walking boots squelch in the mud as we traverse the moorlands. I'm a bit shivery with the wet from the boat, and I can't wait to get changed and warmed up by the fire. It's the first time I've looked forward to the fire, rather than craved my hot water bottle, my slanket, and my central heating.

## Wild Swimming

"Can we go for a walk later?" Oliver asks me, his eyebrow raised as my tent clashed with my rucksack and ends up wrapped around my knees.

"Yes," I say, trying to untangle myself and keep up with the group who are now jumping over a small running burn. "That'd be lovely. If I've still got all my limbs when we arrive at the campsite!"

"Ha," Oliver barks. "Yes, might be helpful on the moors."

"Maybe after we're dry and warmed up a bit?"

Oliver nods at me and we walk in silence for a few steps. I hop over the burn myself, enjoying the feel of the squelchy mud at the other side as my foot slips a little. Oliver's there by my elbow before my backside hits the floor. As I right myself, he slips his hand around my back and pulls me in for a hug. He smells comforting now, like a favourite jumper that sits on the edge of the bed waiting to be pulled on after a hard day at work. In a quick flash he lets go and we carry on walking as though it hasn't happened. But my grin gives me away.

We must have been walking for over an hour, the landscape now forming undulating hills, when we reach what looks like a craggy mini mountain. Oliver and I catch up with the rest of the group who all look at us as we do. James clears his throat.

"So, gang," he says. "Here we are. Our final camping spot is just up this hill."

I raise an eyebrow and James spots it, coming over to me so he's standing at the back of the crowd now and looking up at a particularly grey-looking rock face.

"I know exactly what you're thinking," he winks at me.

"No," I reply. "I'm pretty sure you don't."

Because what I'm actually thinking is how long it'll take us to scale this dreary looking wall and put up our tents because now I just want to strip Oliver down and warm up the fun way. And if James can read my mind when I'm thinking that, then what I actually want is the wall to topple and crush me.

"Well, I can guess it's on the lines of *but you said it was so special, James?* Or *that's not a hill that's a rock face!*"

*Nope.*

"Maybe a little bit," I say, not wanting to hurt his feelings, and he is a little bit right. This craggy hill is more foreboding than the first location.

"Just wait until we're over the top, then come to me with your complaints."

I want to tell him that I wasn't complaining at all, and in fact, he put those words in my mouth. But looking at his demeanour and the way he's skipping about on the balls of his feet I think he wanted to tell us all and just needed an excuse to do it. I can tell he's thriving on the expectation and possibility of what's over the ridge, even though he knows. And I love him a little for caring enough about us as a group to hold so much stead over the reality awaiting us.

"Right, gang," he says, clapping his hands and reminding me of the first time we all met him. "There is a knack to getting up and over this overhang, and it takes teamwork and a little balance. First thing's first, you need to all throw your tents as high as you can up and over."

"Up and over?" Maya says, looking at the height of the target. It's the first time I've seen her looking defeated.

"Your tents are lightweight, I'm pretty sure you don't need to be a famous Highland Log Flinger for it to work."

"Caber toss," Sam corrects, his hand on James' shoulder.

"Not in company, Sam," James laughs, and Sam rolls his eyes in jest. "Here, seeing as you know the correct terminology and are pretty much a native of this fine country now, why don't you show us how it's done?"

Sam throws his rucksack from his back and gets his tent. Knotting his fingers together underneath the end, Sam flings his tent as high and far as it will go and it flies out of sight on to the top of the craggy rock face.

"Good job I know what's up there," he says, standing back and admiring his handiwork. "Otherwise I may have thrown it right into a peat bog."

"I bloody hope there's no peat bogs where we're going," pipes up Bri as she takes her place by the rock face.

James and Sam share a look that doesn't help put her mind at rest. Bri's eyes widen in faux horror. I'm pretty sure her newfound love of adventure will be able to deal with it if we're about to go and give ourselves a mud treatment with the old non-decomposed plant life festering away up there. Even if that does sound painful.

She drops her own bag and demonstrates the perfect tent toss of someone who must have enjoyed athletics at high school. A well-deserved round of applause follows.

I step up to the mark, feeling like I used to during high school athletics, and just hope my tent doesn't land back on my face. I can't imagine there are any plastic surgeons nearby who could reset a squashed nose. I need not worry though, it's surprisingly easy, and when my own rapturous applause follows, I feel a warm glow of achievement. Dampened only slightly by Maya asking Oliver to throw hers because he's seen her throwing and her tent is liable to end up back on the mainland. Then James asks us all to pick a partner.

"Bagsies Fliss?" Oliver says, indifferent to whatever it was Maya just whispered in his ear.

"Okay," I smile.

"Right," James continues. "The lightest of the pair goes first. I want you to get a leg up to the top and haul yourself up from there."

I raise an eyebrow but hoik my bag back over my shoulders and take Oliver's proffered linked hands with my left foot.

"Three, two, one."

I place my hands on the surprisingly smooth rock and on the count of *one* feel Oliver's strong arms literally toss me upwards like the proverbial log. I grapple, not expecting to go so quickly because I'm a sucker for a good pastry when I'm at home, and my hands find purchase on some soggy moss. Hauling myself and my rucksack upwards, Oliver's hands still pushing at both feet now, I bounce up to the top of the ridge, my heart bouncing there a few seconds before me I'm so exhilarated. I did it. I got a leg up. Something I've always declined whenever the chance has arisen—though admittedly not a lot since I left school—because I always felt too ashamed of my weight or my feet or just my general body to let anyone have that much responsibility over my wellbeing.

I look around and see that James and Bri are up here with me.

"Shall we run off and leave them?" James asks, conspiratorially. "Run off to Acapulco and a beach bar with all-you-can-consume rum from coconut shells?"

"No!" I say without thinking, and for the first time since we came away, I actually want to stay here. I'm no longer hankering after an all-inclusive with loungers by a pool and waiters bringing me a Sex on the Beach every five minutes. The wilderness has won me over.

"Well then, get on your knees and give the man a hand up," James says, his smile as wide as my own.

## Chapter Thirty-One

It's magical. Actually magical, not just magical because this is the first time I've ever been north of the Midlands and the scenery all looks like it's from a picture book.

The ridge we all climbed up, some easier than others, has led us to a large open semi-circle of tall hills surrounding a flat wide expanse of land with a crater smack bang in the middle. It is such a huge gap that I have visions of alien crafts lying prone at the bottom, or a giant imprint of a dinosaur foot. What I actually see when we troop over the springy soft ground, fragrant with lavender and bell heather, is the gentle gushing of a waterfall springing from a hidden river. As the water cascades over a gentle slope in the rock, the vision of where it lands is as though there's a photoshopped version in front of my eyes. It's a giant pool of water so aqua-green it's like it's soaked up the ink from a Bic colouring pen. Yet I can still see all the way down through the deep, deep water to where the rock bed forms the base of the pool.

There are four of them. Four brightly coloured pools of blue and green water, swirling together like there's a sheen of petrol on the surface. All open to the elements but sheltered from the rest of the world by this crater that we're all standing wide-eyed and gawping at the edge of. The waterfall could be a mirage, it's so quiet. I've been to Niagara Falls and I had to shout to be heard over the roar of the water. Not here. This water is a gentle as the rest of the surroundings.

"There is a famous group of pools just like this one," James says. "They're called the Fairy Pools and tourists come from miles around to see them and swim in them. They're south of the island and easier to get to. These, on the other hand, are far away from the beaten path. Our boat trip and our trek here—wall climbing inclusive—is what sets these pools apart from the rest. And what means we have them all to ourselves."

Oliver picks up a large stone and throws it into the nearest pool. It sinks and we all watch it through the crystal-clear water until it hits the bottom.

"By the waterfall, the water is deep enough to jump from this height," James continues. "But don't try it anywhere else or you'll come a cropper. And further down the way, the hill and the pools meet, so you can walk down and enter the water there."

"How is the water so clean and clear when it looks like there's no outlet and the only inlet is that waterfall?" Bri asks, stunned as I am.

"Good question, Bri," James says, a twinkle in his eye. A creep of a blush rises on her cheeks. "This water is said to have healing properties because of the cleansing plants growing here. The heather in abundance, bog myrtle, tormentil. There are so many plants that are rich in minerals and salts and other medicinal properties. I mean, don't drink the stuff, but after a few swims you'll notice your skin as soft as anything, and your joints supple and as bendy as a child's."

"And they cleanse the water too, do they?" Maya asks, her own soft skin looking slightly patchy in places, a tell-tale sign of a botched fake tan attempt.

"Well, I'll let you in on a secret because *health and safety*, you know? There are underground rivers that mean the water is always flowing. You'll feel the pull of the water when you're down there so try to keep away from the outlets. But the fact that the water mostly flows underground means that the temperature is a few degrees warmer than it has been in the previous sites. You should still look out for the signs of cold-water stress and after-drop but you are free to swim for more than a few minutes here."

He motions to a flat patch of land just past the drop to the pools.

"This, gang, is our last camping spot," he says. "Now you can either attempt to erect your tent with a little help from Sam and myself. Or you can head off for a little walkabout and we'll do it for you."

Maya drops her tent at Sam's feet and grabs Bri's hand.

"I'm going swimming," she says, grinning towards the pools. "You love the water and a bit of adventure, don't you, Bri? You can come with me."

Maya doesn't ask the rest of us, yet she's looking directly at me. Bri looks between James and Maya, her face wrinkled in decision.

"It's fine to go off," James says to her. "There's no brownie points for staying and putting up your own bed for the night. I just know that by this point in the trek there are some people that like to be more hands on with this side of things."

Bri drops her tent on top of Maya's and shouts thanks as the two girls run off down the hill to where the pools are easy to access.

"See you in a bit," Bri shouts over her shoulder to me as she's dragged away by the hand.

I wave then look at Oliver. His eyes have darkened, and his cheeks look flushed.

"Shall we walk?"

I nod, not really wanting to wait for a warm fire and a change of clothes now we're up here.

"Is that okay?" I ask James and Sam and they grab the two extra tents.

"Of course, it is," Sam says, winking at me.

I smile and shake my head at him, just a tiny movement to let him know I don't want any gossip, and hand over my tent and sleeping bag.

"We're doing locally caught venison for supper tonight, I snagged a few steaks from the captain of the boat, but come back for some lunch of noodles when you get hungry!" James says, already making his way around to where the tents will be.

"I thought we'd be eating a lot more noodles than we have done, this trip," Oliver says as we walk slowly, following the path that the girls ran down moments earlier. "But the food has been surprisingly tasty and nutritious. I didn't realise how much could be foraged from the wilds."

"It's a good job, wouldn't want bits of you turning into a noodle," I say, thinking about his fingers going all long and floppy, then I realise what that could have been interpreted as and feel my tongue swell in my mouth as I try to make amends. "Though I'm sure it won't. Not that noodle shapes are bad. You know. It's not the size of the boat, it's the motion of the… It was quite a trip today wasn't it?"

My face feels as though it's on fire, and I can feel Oliver's eyes on me, but I can't face to look at him.

"God, you're cute," he says, grabbing for my hand.

No one has ever called me cute before. Normally I'm spiky, or prickly, or like a headteacher with an attitude. Cute? That's not me, but I'm not protesting, because I quite like it.

"I had actually been thinking of long noodle fingers," I say, quietly, wiggling my own hands out in front of me, my fingers like juicy worms.

Oliver laughs a loud bark of a laugh. As he stops walking, he grabs my shoulders and pulls me into him, his lips finding mine with urgency. I'm momentarily stunned, but it doesn't take me long to find myself kissing him back. I can feel his, distinctly un-noodle-like arousal as he holds me close to his body and feel a laugh bubble up through my own lips.

"Let's get out of the public eye, shall we?" I say, and grab Oliver's hand and start quick-marching down the hill towards the lower entrance to the magical pools.

I can feel little rivulets of sweat starting to form at my lower back, my shoulder-blades prickle with heat. It's remarkable really; just under two weeks ago I was shivering with cold and wrapped up in more layers than my mum when she's trying to save money by not putting the heating on until the windows crack with ice. Now, when we're walking, I feel the burn of my own energy through just two simple layers. There's a good chance the heat is radiating from much lower than my shoulder-blades right now, though. But it's fine as long as I'm not shivering cold with a runny nose. Not a good look.

There's no sign of Maya and Bri as we turn the corner into the hidden pools. From this angle, the waterfall looks even more magical. The water of the pools glistens from the very bottom. Almost enough to take my mind off what I might be about to do. Almost.

I relinquish Oliver's hand only for long enough for us to walk single file down between the pools to the back of the crater. The waterfall's rushing sounds louder down here, the noise must be syphoning out through the front, through the gap in the hills that we've just walked through. The noise of the water crashing against the pool echoes around my ears and blocks out anything else. Even Oliver's loud sighs as he pushes me against the wall, the waterfall so close the spray is battering me from the side, gratefully cooling my cheeks. We grab at each other; the ferocity of the water matches our hands; fumbling with buttons and zips and finally feeling the warmth of skin and hair.

We slide down into the water, occasionally pushed under by the falls. Oliver pushes me through the pool so my back is against the wall, right under and behind the waterfall as it covers our lust like a curtain. And as he kisses my neck and my collar bone, his hands guide him cleverly and we rock together with the movement of the waves.

## Chapter Thirty-Two

It's the calm after the storm. The moment I normally dread in case I did something stupid or moaned too loudly. But sitting here, out of the water and back on the mossy grass, wrapped in my clothes and Oliver's arms I feel a certain kind of peace. The sun beats down on my face as I turn it to the sky. This moment, this picture, could quite possibly be perfect.

He reaches down and kisses the top of my wet hair. I close my eyes and let myself just be. Trying not to think about what this means. I came away to escape. I wasn't expecting to end up somewhere where I had no chance to hide away from others. Where I had no capacity to remove my real self and project who I wanted people to see. The tiredness and the realness of everything around me has made it difficult to pretend any longer. So escaping from myself, the one person I've always kept at arms' length, has been impossible.

Keeping my biggest secret is taking all of my left-over

stores of energy. Sam isn't helping, I'm expecting him to ask me about my home life, my parents and Frank any second, and I'm holding on to the fact he left Kent before anything happened.

This trek, the camping and the swimming, the nature in its finest state, it's all amazing. But it's all so intense. I've known these people for less than two weeks, yet in some ways I've been more honest with them than I have with my so-called real friends at home.

I feel like we've all been thrown into battle and the battlefield has stripped us of our armour. We've talked about life, death, and bowel movements. We've laughed and cried together. Yet I have no idea where some of them come from, or what they do in their spare time, I still have no idea what Maya even does for a living. There's no getting away from the reality of people when you're sleeping less than a meter apart.

Oliver moves an arm and reminds me where I am. I sigh and he holds me tighter. I was never meant to fall for someone here. But without my defences, I have actually found it quite easy. I kiss the bare bit of skin between his jumper sleeve and his hand, the fine hairs tickling my lips. I could stay here all day, but the distant giggles of the girls has my body tensing and pulling away from Oliver, as though he's made of ice. His strong arms keep me by his side.

"I can hear the others, don't you want to keep *us* a secret?" I ask, my eyes roaming for signs of them. They can't have been in the pools or else we would have seen them, wouldn't we? So I scan in the opposite direction.

"I don't think I have the energy to," Oliver says, kissing the top of my head. "Why? Do you? We can if you need to?"

*Maybe! I don't know. It's a holiday fling, isn't it? Something to fill the time and pass the days.*

But as I'm thinking it, I know I don't feel like that. And maybe that's what scares me more than people here finding out about us. I wriggle myself out of his grip and shake out my wet hair, noticing the dark mark it has made on Oliver's jumper as I have been laid against his chest. There's no sign of the girls, though their voices are getting louder, Maya's jabbing tones overshadowing Bri's laughter.

"Oh God, look who it is," Maya says, and I jerk my head around and see them emerge from the grass beside the pools.

Bri waves at me and I feel a hot pool of shame gurgle in the pit of my stomach.

*They were in there. They must have heard us.*

"Shit," I whisper to Oliver. "Do you think they saw us?"

He shrugs, nonplussed. I think back over the weirdness between Oliver and Maya and the possibility that something has already happened between them too. Maybe Oliver wanted them to hear us. Maybe that's why he dragged me down to the pools in the first place, because he saw them heading this way. Maybe he's on a mission to sleep with as many of us as possible to chase away the demons of his ex. That's why he's here, after all, to get over her.

"Hi guys," Maya waves coquettishly, fluttering her eyelashes.

Bri looks at me and winks. I close my eyes and hope everyone will disappear. Like an ostrich, I don't want to surface until the danger is over.

They come over, and Maya sits right next to Oliver, her hands on his knee.

"Oh Ollie," she says, way too cosily for my liking. "Doesn't this bring back memories of our first holiday together in Santorini? The lush looking water. The hot pools, the hot sex under that waterfall in our suite. Though it was a private suite and a private waterfall, no onlookers. Respectable, you know."

She directs the last line at me. I can feel the residual warmth from Oliver's body sapping from my own, my face sags with understanding. Bri lets out an exclamation of shock but I can't look at her. I can't look at any of them

*He's not trying to bed us all. Just whoever he can to make his ex jealous. His ex who he's brought with him on this stupid trek.*

I scramble to my feet, uncaring that my shoes are still where I left them and run back into where the pools and waterfall are casting judgmental shades over me. I don't hear the details of the shouts from either Oliver or Bri as I run. They're drowned out by the rushing water as I near the falls. I can't believe I was so stupid to fall for his kindness and my lust. After so long keeping people at arm's length, this is what I get for finally letting someone in. Maybe it's a testament to my own cowardice that the person who chipped away at my exterior was only doing it for his own agenda.

I can see Oliver running towards me. I don't want to talk to him. I don't want to have to listen to his excuses of how he only did it because he felt awful at being dumped. I'm better than that.

Still in my clothes I slide quietly into the water and glide over to the far wall of the waterfall where I can't be seen from the banks of the pools. It's hard to tread water here, with my woollen jumper soaking up the crystal water and my trousers trying to fill with air because they're waterproof and they're not designed for swimming in with absolutely no sponge-like qualities at all. I can feel my bottom half trying to float, my top half being dragged under. It's ridiculous. I must look completely stupid. But I'm not going to surface now, I'm not giving Oliver the satisfaction.

From through the water that not so long ago we were both encased in, I can see Oliver scan around. Looking for me. It doesn't take him too long to give up and walk away. I watch as his sloped shoulders leave and push myself off the wall to warm up a bit. I swim through the clear water of the biggest pool. It's safe, everyone has left me. Bri surprises me though. I thought she had been on my side. That one hurts perhaps even more so than what Oliver has done.

I can't feel the cold from the water anymore, my feet and hands are moving and I'm still propelling myself forwards, but I'm not sure if they're just too cold to feel. My heart is hammering but I think it's probably my anger. I won't stop. Not yet. Just a few more laps to work out the anxiety in my head. It's what I used to do in the mornings. I'd swim to take my mind off how awful everything was. It's sort of working now. My brain can't focus on a lot at all.

It's only when my teeth start clattering together so loudly I think there must be a mutant rook nearby that I realise maybe all of my symptoms aren't anger and anxiousness after all, but the beginnings of hypothermia. I paddle to the edge, realising the water now feels as thick as treacle, and drag myself out. Rubbing my arms with my numb fingers, I place one foot in front of the other and try to navigate the small walkways between the pools without falling in and giving myself even more hypothermia, if that's at all possible. As I round the edge of the hill, the sun dips behind a cloud and my teeth feel as though they're going to shatter if I keep shivering at such a rate.

*It's good though, to be shivering. Keep shivering. That means you're still alive, Fliss.*

I stagger up the hill towards the top of the waterfall where we all stood looking down what seems like an eternity ago. I can picture the way Oliver looked at me, as he grabbed my hand and dragged me down towards where he knew Maya would be watching. This had better not be my life flashing before my eyes, the moment before death. I want to be picturing fun things like my first cat, and the times Frank and I would race down the street on our bikes, not fuck-boys playing with me like a toy. But the images are gone and replaced with a calming kind of fog, descending over my thoughts like a warm blanket. *At least my brain is warm*, I think, as my feet shuffle forwards, my clothes dripping onto my toes that look a bit purple and mottled.

"Fliss?" A voice shouts over the fog and I hold up my hand as if to say *I'm fine, just a bit damp that's all.* "Fliss, shit, what happened to you?"

It's James, he's looking me up and down. Assessing me for damage I imagine. Though he'd better not look too closely or he'll see that I'm completely beyond repair. And that's without the impending hypothermia. The look on his face tells me he's not liking what he's seeing. And I can't say I blame him.

## Chapter Thirty-Three

"Come with me," he says, taking my elbow and leading me, not without some force towards the tents and Sam who's stoking a fledgling fire.

There's no one else here yet. They're all still off somewhere laughing about me.

"Felicity?" Sam says, getting up to his feet.

"No, don't," James cries. "Get that fire roaring, we're going to need it."

Sam flings himself back down to the kindling, blowing frantically at the base of the fire. I'm quite enjoying the drama. It's taking my mind of the aches in my jaw, and the stinging sensation of my hands and feet.

James drags me to his tent, hauling me inside and double zipping the door up behind us.

"This is going to seem a bit forward," he says, as he starts to peel off my wet coat. "But I'm doing this to save your life. If you feel at any point like you want me to stop, please tell me. But speed is of the essence and I want to get you warm before you become hypothermic."

He's helping me unzip my thermals, his own hands stingingly hot on my cold skin. But my fingers are so fat and numb now I don't think I could manage them myself. All the while he's talking to me about what he's doing.

"You're experiencing what we call afterdrop," he says, gently peeling my trousers from my soaking wet legs. They're matching my feet in purpleness, spreading quicker than proverbial wildfire. "Where your body carries on cooling down once it's out of the water. If it continues cooling down, we'll need to get on the radio for backup, but there's a few things we can do first. And the most important thing is to get you completely dry."

I feel a blush creep up my neck, but it can't get any further because my face is too cold and my blood vessels too constricted. James is pulling down my large cotton knickers, they're sticking to my damp, cold thighs that don't have enough gap in them to help any.

"Right," he says, carefully averting his eyes away from my naked body whilst also laying me down and wrapping me up in his soft downy sleeping-bag. "Time to get friendly."

*Get friendly? Is stripping me naked and getting me in your sleeping bag not friendly enough?* I giggle at the thought.

I can feel my scar tighten across my chest as my skin starts to slowly defrost, throwing thoughts of Frank at me, which is actually quite distracting. It's itching like crazy, but I don't want to draw attention to it. Though if James had managed to get me naked without seeing it, he's less *should have gone to Specsavers* more *Mr Magoo*. The coldness has drawn out the whiteness of the thick tissue and it is glaring out from under my breasts like a lighthouse warning sailors to mind the hills.

A Mars Bar is thrust in my face, and with my hands still tucked inside the sleeping bag, I tentatively take a bite, chewing as quickly as my numb face will allow.

*Feeding; this I can deal with.*

James throws my wet clothes out of the tent, and zips it back up before any of the damp, cooling air weaves its way in. Then he starts to pull off his own top.

*Where's he going with this?*

Naked from the waist up, James brings me another bite of Mars Bar. Then he starts undoing his boots. I watch, not quite as bashful as maybe I should be, as James' tight stomach muscles contract as he bends over to pull off his socks. The trickle of blonde hair from his chest to the waist band of his trousers looks so soft from where I'm lying. Nothing like the thick, dark hair I had been running my hands through earlier. Who would have thought I would be seeing two men naked in the space of only a few hours? Certainly not me!

James is down to his boxers now and as his hands grab the elastic he falters.

"Is this okay?" he asks. "The more body heat the better, and most of my body heat comes from my balls."

I'm so taken aback that I burst out laughing, the action taking my lungs by surprise and I descend into a fit of coughing. I try to nod in agreement at the same time and he must understand my weird body language because he whips off his Calvins and climbs in the sleeping bag with me. It's the most ungraceful angle I think I've ever witnesses a man from, and I try to avoid grimacing as his heat source swings near my face.

The feeling of James' skin against my own brings a sweet sort of relief. The warmth is almost instant, even his feet, but I think that might just be because mine are the temperature of the arctic. He pulls a hat down over my head and snuggles in next to me so we are lying face to face. It's perhaps the most awkward and the most grateful I have been all at once.

After a few minutes and another few bites of sugary malt chocolate, I can feel my extremities again. I wiggle my fingers, then immediately stop as they are at an unfortunate height and I think I may be waking up parts of James that don't need any encouragement. I stick with moving my toes and enjoying the pins and needles that flood my arms and legs.

"Do you want to tell me what happened?" James asks, his breath sweet with mint. "Did you fall in? I should have warned you about the slippery moss between the pools, I'm sorry."

I could go with that. Pretend that I fell in the pools. But I don't want to pretend anymore. I'm sick of it. I've had a lifetime of pretending.

"No," I say quietly, happy that my teeth are no longer trying to break each other. "I… Oliver and I… well we got into the water together. You know. And we didn't have our swimmers on or keep a good track of the time."

"Oh, riiight," James says, just as I think this couldn't get any more awkward.

"And after we got out and got, um, dressed, I found out rather unceremoniously that Maya and he used to be in a relationship."

"What?" James' whole body jerks with the news.

"Yep." I shuffle my elbow down a bit so I can get my arm out from under my side where it's going a bit tingly. "In fact, I think she's the girl who he came on the trek to get away from. Ironically enough."

"Sheesh," James says, sucking his teeth. "Well I like to think I'm a good reader of people, but I didn't see that one coming. What a low blow."

"Yeah," I say. "So I ran off."

"Oh yeah, you guys had just," he starts but I cut him off before he puts it into words.

"And when Oliver came looking for me, I hid in the only place I could find at quick notice."

"The water?"

"The water." I nod. "And it was so lovely I thought I'd have an actual swim. It's what I used to do to clear my head, before…"

I stop, there's only so much unpretending I can do. James shuffles over a bit, rustling the sleeping bag between us. The arm around my shoulder is starting to cool a bit. I think I must be sapping his heat quicker than I'm regaining mine.

"Are you okay?" I ask him.

"Yeah," he says, though his eyebrows are knotted together. He shakes his head, noticing my worry, his face smiling again. "Yeah. I'm fine. Just worried about you, that's all."

"I meant, temperature wise," I say, wriggling my toes against his. "You're starting to soak up my hypothermia?"

He laughs, not unkindly.

"No," he says, wriggling his own toes back. "It's just our bodies becoming the same temperature, that's all. It probably feels cold to you because I felt so hot to start with."

"Are you calling yourself *hot?*" I giggle.

"Of course," he says, smiling. "My hotness saved your life. I can't help being so hot. What can I do?"

He half shrugs, as well as he can do wrapped in my body and a duck down cocoon.

"I think this is the first time I've ever taken my clothes off for a guy *before* a first date!"

"I should come with a warning."

I don't fancy James one bit, but the banter is making me feel less aware of my nakedness. More at ease with the situation. And my brain is finally starting to defrost from the fog that had descended.

"How long do we have to stay like this before I'm out of the woods?"

"I'd say until your lips turn back to a normal colour."

I chew my bottom lip, wondering what colour it is now that means James is still sharing my space.

"Maybe just another few minutes," he says, smiling, reading my mind. "How're *you* feeling?"

"Like I'm regaining feeling in my extremities again," I say.

"Good. And how're you *feeling?*"

I raise an eyebrow, which is hard to do in a woolly hat.

"What?" James asks. "Think of me as your camp counsellor. I don't want you to have a bad trip just because of one bad experience. Did Oliver say anything about why he might have put both you and Maya in the situation he has?"

"I'm fine," I say, thinking I probably will be if I never have to see Maya or Oliver ever again in my whole entire life. "Honestly."

"Hmm," James says, his eye going a bit crossed as he tries to focus on me in such close proximity. "So Oliver didn't say anything at all to you about Maya?"

"No," I say. "Why would he do that when it would have probably meant less excitement for him? I think they're probably here to play games with other peoples' hearts to be honest. And, now I have had time to think about it, I don't think my trip into the cave was as accidental as maybe it seemed."

I huff and James looks shocked. I think I would be too, in his position. So much for a luxury retreat. Still, the blame can't be laid at James' feet. It's all my own doing.

"At least it got my adrenaline racing. As advertised," I say, trying to lighten the mood that had dropped a few notches.

"I heard you didn't want your adrenaline racing?" James grins.

"Sam told you I didn't read the small print?"

James nods, and I make a mental note to go and

throttle Sam when my hands are working properly. I wriggle my fingers again, to see if they're defrosting as quickly as my face, forgetting their proximity to James' groin.

"Oh, jeez," he says, his face ruby red. "Can you not do that, please."

"Eeek," I cry, trying and failing to pull my hands up out of the sleeping bag. "Sorry."

"You're still moving your hands a bit close to me," he says, trying to reposition himself. "I can't be held responsible for what my body does!"

I'm trying so hard to remain straight faced, but I can't. Something about this whole situation is making my cheeks rise up into a grin. Which turns to a laugh. It's the kind of laugh that used to get Frank and me in trouble at school. Once it takes hold I just can't stop. It's bellying out of me now and must be contagious as James' own face is screwed up in a smile too.

We're laughing so loud that we obviously don't hear the zipper on the tent slide up until it's too late.

"Sam told me to bring you this, James," Maya says, holding out a steaming cup. "Oh, I see you have company. Sorry."

I immediately pull back as far as I can from James, which ends up being only about a foot because we're still entwined in the sleeping bag.

"Maya!" James cries. "Thanks. Just leave it there."

She places the cup on the floor at the entrance to the tent then stands back, holding the tent flap wide open.

### Wild Swimming

Outside I can see Oliver staring, but, even worse, I can see Bri as her eyes widen and her face turns to thunder.

## Chapter Thirty-Four
### Day Ten

"Happy birthday, dear Fliss. Happy birthday, to you."

The cheer couldn't be less celebratory if we were all at a distant relatives' funeral. As everyone takes a turn to hug me, I can't help but think this isn't quite how I planned to spend my birthday, no matter how alone I was hoping to be.

At least the fire is giving off warmth, which is more than can be said for pretty much everyone gathered around it for my birthday breakfast. Bri won't come near me and hasn't done since yesterday when she eyeballed my nakedness wrapped around James' nakedness. I've tried to explain to her what happened, but she keeps fleeing like an Olympic speed walker whenever I get nearby.

Oliver, who has no right whatsoever to be annoyed with me, is giving me a shoulder cold enough to reignite my almost-hypothermia. But that's fine with me, I don't want anything to do with him. His recently acquired sad-looking puppy dog eyes do make me want to go and hug him, but he can get any solace he needs from Maya, who weirdly is the only one giving me the time of day with her snarky smiles every time she sees me. I should have stayed at home. Even a party organised by my parents couldn't be as awkward as this.

Could it?

"Can you pass around the birthday sausages, please Bri?" James asks, holding out a tray of browned chipolatas that he must have been keeping cool somewhere to whip out and have as a treat. Bri takes the tray and passes it on like a mutant hot potato. Maya takes a couple and passes the tray to Oliver, flashing her pearly whites as she does. No matter how annoyed with me Oliver is, sausages are too good to pass up when his main source of protein recently has been a locally picked or caught produce with not a hint of added extra MSG.

The smell of them has my mouth watering and I take the tray gratefully when he offers it; his eyes not quite meeting mine, his smile forced.

"Thanks for this, guys," I say, directing my thanks to James and Sam only. "I'd almost forgotten how good food is when it's filled with additives."

It sounds snidey, and I don't mean it to. I'm genuinely grateful for the thought they put in to finding and bringing celebratory food along for my birthday. But as I take a bite, the salt makes my throat constrict and I choke out a cough.

Now they're all looking at me as though they wish I'd succumbed to the cold and been whisked away by air ambulance to the safety of whichever hospital is the nearest.

"Just a bit hot," I say, fanning my closed mouth as I try to make noises that give the impression that I'm enjoying my breakfast.

We eat in a silence that grows more awkward by the second.

*Maybe I should just come out with it and say what happened right now?* I think, shovelling my sausages in so I can escape as quickly as possible. Then at least everyone will know.

But if I come clean and tell everyone that James and I were only naked in his tent as he was saving me from losing my fingers and toes then I have to come out and tell them why. And the more I think about it, the less I want to. What if Maya and Bri didn't see Oliver and me at it under the waterfall? What if Sam starts talking about the Felicity who he knows who would *never* let a guy treat her so badly? What if Oliver doesn't believe me anyway? And what if Maya pipes up and tells me all about her and Oliver? I don't want any of that to happen. And while I'm keeping quiet about it, James and Sam have to as well.

Clearing my plate, I get up off the mossy floor where I've been sitting and brush my hands down my waterproofs; my fingers leaving greasy stains down my legs like slug trails.

"I think I'm going to head out for a birthday walk," I say.

Noone replies. Not that I want them to, the last thing I want is an offer of companionship.

"Have fun," James says as I walk away to my tent to lace up my boots and grab my coat.

I try not to let the sounds of laughter and talking hurt me as I make my way down the hillside towards the entrance to the pools. The tight band of tension that has wound its way around our group, so stifling at breakfast it's given me indigestion, sounds like it's been cut now I've left the campfire. Tears prick my eyes and roll down my cheeks freely. I decide against walking through the pools. Instead, I think I'll follow the path as it leads further down the hillside. The water of the pools twinkles enticingly at me as I pass, singing as though a siren lives in its midst. It takes all my willpower to ignore it, though my whole being is screaming at me to swim. Despite what happened yesterday, I do want to swim.

There's only one day left of our trek. Tomorrow we walk back to the edges of the island to be picked up by a large boat who will be taking us to the mainland and to our minibus, our hotel, and our plane home. The harsh reality is that I may never get a chance to swim again in these healing pools or walk again on these hills. This was my chance to get away. Despite it being a comedy of errors from start to finish, I had actually begun to enjoy myself, to let myself relax a bit.

I dip a booted toe in the nearest pool and watch as the ripples of water spool out away from me. Repelled by my own fair hand—or foot in this case—like everything else in my life. Pulling my foot out I carry on the route down the hill. The slope starts meandering down gently, but soon takes a sharp turn. I don't remember walking so much uphill to get to the campsite, but that was from the other direction. Perhaps this way leads to the south of Skye in more ways than one. It's beautiful. When the hill falls away in front of me, I'm left standing overlooking a valley full of the colours of a Scottish summer. Purples and greens and vibrant blues. Large cormorants, who must have flown in from the coast are magnificent in their flight.

The path narrows, cut deep through granite and flint. I keep following it, downwards, towards the valley but still not quite getting there. It looks miles away as I watch it while I walk. Wondering what it would be like to live here, in the middle of nowhere with no-one around to judge or to hide from.

"Happy birthday, me," I say, licking salty tears from my mouth. "Happy birthday, Frank."

I round a corner and come to an abrupt halt. In front of me is a small, round pool. No bigger than my back garden at home. But it's deep. I can tell by the way the light green quickly turns to inky blue. I pick up a stone and toss it into the pool. Watching as it descends into the darkness.

Without thinking too hard about it. I strip down to my bare skin, neatly folding my clothes by the edge, and slip slowly into the freezing water. Its icy fingers close themselves around me, gripping at my chest and constricting my breathing for a sweet second before I remember how to breathe through it. It feels painfully cleansing. Much better than drinking myself into a coma which is normally what occurs on my birthday. I take a few strokes out to the middle of the water, wondering how deep it goes and what's underneath me. But the more I swim, the greater my mind fills with positives. How free I feel right now, how amazing this trip has actually been for me. How I feel not scared for the first time in almost nineteen years.

*That's not right*

I swim harder, dunking my head under the water, feeling its pin pricks of cold through my scalp.

*I shouldn't be feeling positive. I'm not allowed to feel positive. What about what happened with Frank?*

I can feel the hands of the sirens stroking my toes and my fingers and know it's time to get out. Swimming back to the edge of the water, my tears mixing with the cool fresh-water on my face and making it taste like the ocean, I feel a smile pulling itself onto my face and try to bat it away by biting on my cheeks until I taste something tangy.

I pull myself up onto the side of the pool, wrapping Oliver's dry robe around me, dragging my hat down over my wet hair. And I sit for just long enough to dry off my feet and pull on my boots. I gather up the rest of my clothes in my arms and start to walk quickly back up the hill. My body temperature warming with each step. I have learnt what my limits are and I am sticking to them. If there's anything that was worth learning while I'm here, then that may well be the most important.

When I reach the edge of the path overlooking the

valley again, I stop for a moment and take in the silence, my heart pounding in my ears. I'm dry now, the robe soaked away all of the pool water just like the pool water soaked away all of my fears. Now it's damp and heavy with the weight I have been carrying around with me for too long. I strip it off, feeling the warmth of the day on all of my body. My scar glistens like the sun itself. I throw out my hands, my arms reaching out as far as they can and I tip my head back. Then, from a primal place that I haven't reached into since I was a child, and my self-consciousness wasn't yet covering me like a shroud, I let out a mighty cry into the depths of the valley.

## Chapter Thirty-Five

"Well guys," James says, as we all sit under the stars, our faces flickering in the light of the fire. "It's our last night."

We all make noises as though we're sad to be leaving, and I wonder if it's just me who is trying too hard. Bri and Maya hug each other. I glance quickly at Oliver who must have already been looking my way, as his eyes dart towards the fire.

"It's been one heck of a crazy trek, this one," James continues as all eyes turn to him. "We've had some great times. You've all come out of your shells. You seem to all have embraced the outdoors, the nature, the way it can heal and protect, whilst at the same time stripping you completely bare and open up some visceral wounds."

I laugh ironically then bite my lips close. No need to let go now, not when I'm so close to the finish line. Just shut up, pass go, and collect my £200.

"There's one last fun thing we have planned for you before we head off tomorrow, though of course we have a last swim tomorrow morning for those who want to," James says, looking directly at me. I didn't tell him about the pool I found. I want to keep something for myself. "But tonight, we will once again be sleeping out under the stars. It's our last chance to really connect with nature. To ask her for forgiveness and favours for the future. I want you all to go home feeling like you're renewed, and the sense of vastness under the sky this far North will certainly make you question a lot of things about your life."

Maya sniggers.

"I know I have," she says bitingly. "I'm much freer than when I arrived."

I shuffle down a bit in my seat, my face heating. I don't want anyone to mention Maya and Oliver or Oliver and me. The damage is done, it's not like I can do a lot about it now but move on.

"Me too," Oliver pipes up in a stubborn and not so subtle reply to Maya.

It's like a slanging match with no shouting or swearing. Just two possible exes getting one over on each other at the expense of whoever gets in their way.

"I've got so much out of this trip," Bri says, sadly. "A newfound love of adventure and being outdoors, new courage to do things I never would have back home, new friends. And it's been heaven not having my phone as an extra appendage. I'm going to cut back on my usage when I get home. Maybe kill the influencer career. I mean, I've graduated now, about to be let loose on people's teeth, maybe I don't need that part of me any more."

"Extra appendages always just get in the way," Maya says, gripping Bri's hand. "Cut them loose as soon as you can, I say. Appendages think for you, in ways you'd probably not, if the appendage wasn't there."

For literally everyone sitting around the campfire, it's fairly obvious that Maya is not, in fact, talking about a phone. Oliver shifts uncomfortably around in his seat while the two tour guides look at the floor and probably wish that our trek was over already. I wonder if they've ever had this much drama before. Or this much secrecy.

"Well," Sam says, clapping his hands together loudly enough for the sound to echo around the hills. "Gather up your sleeping bags and some extra layers and we'll head off."

Under his breath I can hear him mutter *before anyone loses their appendage* and laugh to myself at the thought of Maya going after Oliver's penis with a pocketknife. Like a Grizzly Adams John Bobbett.

With my hat, gloves, two pairs of extra thick socks under my boots, and Oliver's dry robe that I had dried by the fire when I'd gotten back from my swim earlier, I am ready to go. I tuck my sleeping bag under a free arm and grab my stash of birthday chocolate that I had been carrying with me for my birthday night treat, and head out into the night.

Sam comes over, his sleeping bag wrapped around his shoulders. He gathers me in for a hug and squeezes me hard.

"I'm glad you're okay, Felicity," he says. "Imagine having to tell your parents you'd frozen to death because you were having cold water sex."

He laughs into my hat and my whole body freezes.

"Yeah," I say, thinking that would be the end of my parents. No doubt about it. Not the sex bit, they're not prudes. Just if anything happened to me. I'm their anchor, I keep them tied together in a world that has already been upended. Without me, they'd float apart and quite happily sink.

A familiar heavy feeling settles in my chest.

*Welcome back, old friend.* I think. It's probably about time, seeing as I'll be returning to normality tomorrow.

Sam's arms release me, the rest of the group as ready as I am. Maya lifts an eyebrow and less than subtly whispers to Bri that I'm working my way around the whole group and she should be glad I'm not starting on the girls next. I roll my own eyes and shake my head. I can deal with this for less than twenty-four hours now. Bri catches my eye and her face drops with sadness.

Our campsite for the night isn't too far away. The fire is still visible down the valley by the top of the pools. The moon is a sliver of nail, making the sky brighter with stars than I've seen it all trip. We all lay our bags out, I stay on the periphery of the group again, where I belong, and flap my sleeping bag out of its roll. Sam comes and lays next to me, his own bag fitting in the space I'd left once again. He has a canny habit of making us feel inclusive even if we don't want to be.

We all take our places, snuggling down into our

warm cocoons. I hope that James' has dried off properly after my soaking wet body dripped all over it. He had said he slept without it last night and I'd felt terrible because the nights drop to a temperature fit for a penguin. I prop myself up on my elbows and look over the hillocks of downy bags to the far end where James is nestled down next to Bri. He looks cosy enough. My worries put to the side, I sink back down onto my back. Remembering at the last minute about my chocolates.

I rummage around in my coat pockets, and pull out the bag of M&Ms. Not the most refined chocolate in the world, but they've always been my favourite. And it is my birthday, after all.

"What's that?" Sam says, the rustling of the bag giving my game away.

I don't much feel like sharing, not with everyone anyway. But I don't want to cause a scene.

"Birthday treat," I say, holding the packet up so he can see what I'm stashing. "Want some?"

"Oh my god, do I ever!"

We are at risk of flying right up to the stars above us if we eat too much, given our limited sugar intake this trip. But I'm throwing caution to the wind as I rip open the packet and grab a handful.

Sam takes the bag from my hands; I can see him pull back a little so not to snatch even though his instincts are to act like a child in a sweet shop. He takes a few and pops one into his mouth, groaning like he's having sex. Maya snorts from where she's lying next to James. But before she can open her mouth and diss me any more than she already has done, Bri gasps in joy.

"Oh," Bri cries. "Look."

I think she's talking about my birthday chocolate for a split second before something in the sky catches my eye and sweeps the breath right out of my body.

It's alight with swirls of green and yellow, flashes of purple split in and out as the waves of colour move through the sky. I fall back down prone and watch the sky with a heavy weight on my chest. Aurora Borealis. The sights Frank and I promised we would watch together. It's the most beautiful thing I have ever seen. Heavenly. And filled with sadness.

"Isn't this a wonderful birthday gift?" James shouts across the bodies.

But it's not. It's a reminder of all I have lost.

"Hey," Sam says, sitting up on his elbows and looking over to me. "Do you remember when you and Frank and I used to sit out on a summer's evening and eat M&Ms and stare at the sky waiting for something exciting to happen? Frank always used to wish for an electrical storm, thunder or lightning, do you remember? I think he even said he wanted to see this, even at a young age, if my memory serves me?"

*Do I remember?*

"You used to get annoyed with us for stealing all the chocolate." Sam is still talking, unseeing my distress because his eyes are fixed upwards. "You should tell him about this, maybe he could come on a trek, if he's up to the walking? Or he could just fly up to Scotland and watch it from there. No need to do the trek."

I can't speak, my throat is so thick I can barely breathe. Tears are flowing down the side of my face and onto my pillow and there's nothing I can do to stop them. I don't want to stop them. I *should* be feeling bad. I deserve the pain that's stabbing me in the chest right now. I can't hold the sobs in any longer. With the sky on fire above me I try to muffle a keen that still perforates the air with such clarity my skin prickles with goosebumps.

"What the fuck?" Maya cries.

"Felicity?" Sam is holding my arm now, leaning over me, blocking my view of the sky. "What's the matter? What's happened?"

But I can't talk. My throat is clogged with over a decade's worth of secrets and lies that are trying to force their way out all at once. I pull at my sleeping bag, ripping my arms out and loosening my zip from around my throat, rolling over on to my side away from Sam so I can push up to sitting. Tears are cascading down my face as though they're the waterfall, but I'm silent, struggling to draw breath.

"It's okay, Felicity." Sam draws me into his arms, but I push him away, underserving of the friendship, of the comfort he is trying to provide.

"It's not okay," I choke out through sobs. "It's not…"

"Fliss?" I can hear Oliver over the sounds of my cries and know that I got what I deserved when he used me the way he did.

I take a breath, finally able to drag some air in

through my tight throat and fill my lungs. Resigned to the fact that everyone here hates me anyway, I start to speak.

"It's Frank, Sam." My words are stuttered, rasping their way out. "He's... he's dead."

Sam's eyes fill with shock and tears, then he gathers me up in a hug, and this time I let him, all the energy has been sapped from me and I no longer have fight left.

"It's okay, Felicity," he whispers into my ear. "It's okay."

"It's not okay," I say back, too tired to pretend. "It's not okay because it's my fault he's dead."

And my words cause a vacuum of sound that shuts up even the cutting voice of Maya.

## Chapter Thirty-Six

The stars twinkle on as if nothing is happening a million light years below them. The Aurora Borealis weaves its way in and out of the sky. The air is thick, at least it feels it as I try to fill my lungs with great gasps. Sam's arms are wrapped around me and for a moment I let myself feel quiet, knowing that I will have to emerge from their comfort and explain why I have just admitted to something that I've never spoken out loud before. I can hear Maya muttering about how I should have never been allowed on the trip and I agree with her. I should have taken more time to plan my birthday holiday, and actually gone somewhere I could hide away like normal. And if my parents hadn't decided to land me with a great big party, I would have done that very thing.

Sam rubs my back, he whispers something to James over my shoulder, and the next thing I know he's handing me a small silver hip flask. I peel myself away from Sam and unscrew the lid. The smell hits me right at the back of my throat and the taste isn't much better. The single malt warms as it drops down my throat and into my stomach. The sharpness of the hit is like a slap around the face. I take another sip and hand the flask back to James.

"Thanks," I say to James for the whisky before I look at Sam. "And thanks to you too. Sorry."

I look down at my fingers, turning red with the cold without my gloves to warm them. I know inspecting my nails won't distract from the fact I just opened my heart up, but it's giving me a little breathing space. My tears have dried up at least. James drags his sleeping bag over to the other side of me, so I'm now flanked by him and Sam.

"The last night is often when people fall apart," James says, snuggling back down into his sleeping bag and pulling his hat back down over his ears. "It's the emotions of the last two weeks all coming to a head, topped with the realisation that it's all ending tomorrow."

*So maybe it's not just me, then?*

"Yeah," Sam says, tucking himself in too. "There are always a lot of tears and outbursts. It's just your body's way of letting go of all the stress and tension it has been bottling up for the last thirty years. Let it out, Felicity. And anyone else who feels like they have come far enough to be able to. It's not a bad thing."

He pauses for a moment and looks over at me. I'm the only one of the group still sitting upright. Everyone else is back looking at the sky. I slide myself down into the warmth, tucking my hands under my bum to warm them up again. With the sleeping bag right up to my chin, I feel less exposed, not just to the elements but to the judgement that I feel from those around me for being honest for once.

"I have to say though," James says, crunching on an M&M. "We've never had anyone admit that before."

"Nope," Sam agrees. "That's definitely a new one on me too. I knew Frank when we were growing up, what happened, Felicity? Do you want to talk about it?"

"Probably," Maya mutters under her breath.

"Oh, shut up, Maya," Oliver barks, making me jump with the volume and tone of his words. "For once in your life can you please just shut up? You don't have to moan about literally everything, you know? We can hear you, we're not deaf. Let Fliss talk if it will help her. It's not like you've gone out of your way to make things easy for her now, is it?"

Maya huffs and her own sleeping bag rustles in the dark. My chest fills with something that I can't think about yet. I wasn't going to talk about Frank. I don't know if I *can* talk about what happened. But Oliver and James and Sam have all given me permission to, and it's dark and no-one can see my face, and I can't see the judgement on theirs. And I feel ready to talk about it. For the first time in fourteen years.

"Okay," I say, my voice small and projected into my sleeping bag. "Maybe I will."

I find the packet of chocolates and throw a few in my mouth to give me some strength. I picture Frank and me throwing them at each other, trying to get them in our mouths but deliberately aiming just too wide. I got Frank in the eyeball once, but he never shouted at me or got angry, despite being blind for a couple of days afterwards. The memory helps.

"Frank is my brother, *was* my brother," I start. "My twin brother. He was older than me by one hundred and seventy-five seconds and he used to tell me that at least once a week. Usually when we were fighting over who got to sit in the front seat with Dad, or who got to pick whether they washed or dried the dishes. We were premature, but not by a lot by twin standards. But when we had our new-born screenings, Frank was diagnosed with cystic fibrosis and somehow, I wasn't. It didn't seem fair. Why did I get away without having to do chest physio every morning, or take a handful of drugs just to get through the day? Frank never moaned about it, never felt it was unfair. And he *never* once used it against me. Never. Even those times when he couldn't come out and play in the street, he'd tell me to go and enjoy myself because it was no use both of us sitting around moping. I tried everything I could to make him feel better. I'd do his homework when he was too tired, our writing was so similar the teachers had no idea. I'd bring him sweets from the corner shop when he was too weak to get up there himself. Though Mum used to go mental at me because lots of sugar wasn't great, apparently. But who listens to their parents when they're thirteen?"

I take a deep breath. Knowing that the next bit isn't going to be quite so happy.

"It's okay, Fliss," Bri says from the other side of the row of sleeping bags. "Keep going when you're ready."

At that moment I know I'm forgiven and her compassion is just what I need.

"When we got a little older, Frank became less able to do the ordinary things. He didn't attend school every day anymore, he had his physio, these exercises he had to do every morning and they completely took it out of him. I used to cover my ears with headphones so I could block out his coughing because it sounded so painful and I couldn't help take away the pain. I started to hide away too, scared that people would look badly on me being out playing when my twin was at home barely able to draw breath.

"I wanted to do something more than just solve his algebra and rot his teeth. So, when I hit sixteen, the legal age to be able to, I offered myself as a living lung donor. As a twin, there couldn't have been a better match. Frank didn't want me to, and my parents said that I shouldn't, but I could tell deep down that they really did want me to at least try.

We had the tests, and I was compatible, so we went ahead and booked in the surgery. I think at sixteen I wasn't quite mature enough to understand what a huge surgery giving part of my lung would turn out to be. And it went well, but we were both out of action during the start of our A Level journey. I did a lot of my work at home, recovering. And Frank's school work, well, he just couldn't really do it anymore. He was so frustrated and bored."

My breath becomes lodged in my throat as I garner the courage to finish the story.

"So one morning, at the beginning of summer, I skipped school and we snuck out of the house and got the bus to the beach. It was stupid, crazy really, Frank was still recovering and I wasn't completely healed from the surgery. We were only supposed to paddle, but we started splashing each other and getting deeper and deeper. Before we knew what was happening, a rip current caught us."

I squeeze my eyes tighter as Frank's face appears behind my eyelids, the way he had reached out to me and tried to grab my arm, the fear on his face.

"Eventually, we got out by swimming parallel to the beach and away from the current, but we were cold and exhausted and we had to get the bus home. Frank pretended he was okay but just a few days later, the morning we were due to collect our AS results from the school, Frank developed pneumonia. I went to pick them both up. I was only out of the house for an hour, tops."

I can feel the tears starting again as I remember walking alone to the school gates. My friends had deserted me because I'd been off for so long and teenagers are fickle.

"I was holding my results envelope, not wanting to unstick it and look at what was inside and I felt something in my body just give-way. As though a piece of it just disappeared and I felt hollow, as though I'd never be whole again. And I knew at that moment Frank had passed away."

## Chapter Thirty-Seven

"What had happened?" Sam asks. The air around us so still it feels like the eye of the storm is passing. "To Frank, I mean."

Everyone is focused on me.

"Salt water from the sea had triggered the pneumonia and it tore through his body like a fire. Soon after I left for school that morning, Mum took him down to A&E, but they couldn't save him. His body was in shutdown, sepsis, infections, you name it. My donor lung had been rejected, my parents told me once that it was the lung that caused all the problems," I say, looking up at the swirling sky. "I couldn't even do that for him. Instead of making him better, I killed him."

The silence is palpable.

But instead of feeling like the world is crashing around my shoulders and pulling me down, I feel like I could reach up to Aurora Borealis and fly amongst her colours. The band that has been squeezing my head since I left home as soon as I could get away, has pinged off somewhere into the ether. I feel a whole stone lighter. As though Frank was still there with me, weighing me down. Though that's unfair, because if there was one thing he never did, that was make me feel like he was a burden.

"God!" James says, eventually, breaking my concentration. "Fliss, that's awful."

"Poor Frank," Sam says, making my head feel slightly squished again. "But Felicity, you did more than a lot of people would have done in your situation."

"Yeah," Bri pipes up. "I'd never give my sister a part of my body, no matter how much I love her. I'm loathe to even share my cinema pic-n-mix with her, let alone part of my lungs."

A light-hearted laugh ripples across our line of sleeping bags like a jolly Mexican wave.

"Has it left you with less lung power?" Oliver asks.

"Errr," James says, sitting up a bit and leaning on his elbows. I can barely make him out in the dark, but I think his eyebrows are a tad creased. "I hope not, seeing as you never mentioned it on your waiver form, and this would definitely class as something we'd need to know about."

I can't help a burst of laughter escape.

"No sir!" I say, as though he's my head teacher and I've just been caught smoking in the girl's toilets. "No, my lungs have healed themselves. It's why I was allowed to donate part of them as a living donor so young. Our bodies are pretty amazing. Even though I inhaled a lot of salt water that day too, my lungs were healthy enough to heal themselves within a year of the donation. They work just as well as any other healthy adult lungs would, better perhaps, because of all the swimming I did as a child."

"That's a good job, I'm not sure what would have happened to you when you… fell in the cave at the last camping spot had you not had good lung function," James says.

Maya huffs again, it seems to be her go-to when she's got no comeback. I don't retaliate. I don't feel the need to bring that back up again. She's won, hasn't she?

"I *used* to swim," I say instead. "As a child. Then I took it up again when I was fit enough, to build up my lung strength. Never in the sea though, never again. I swam in pools where I could control how deep I was going. It was my saviour, I think. Not just physically either. It got me out of the house from very early in the morning. Away from my parents who were a weird kind of stand-offish controlling when Frank died. Like they couldn't stand the sight of me, but still wanted to wrap me in bubble wrap. It was stifling.

"Then, as I got older and started uni and work and living a life away from my family and the constant weight of grief, I gave it up. So, ridiculous now I think of it, because it gave me a lot more than a chance to escape. Swimming in the different waters in the Highlands over the last two weeks has made me fall in love with it again. It's also made me realise just how scared I am to *live*."

"Your poor parents," Sam says. "How did they cope?"

I sit up a bit more.

"With the death of their son? I'm not sure they did."

"Not just the death of Frank," he says. "The death of a child is something that parents can never get over, I imagine."

He rolls over onto his side so he's facing me, I can make out the contours of his face, highlighted by the swirling lights from the sky. He's questioning me, his eyebrows kinked.

"What do you mean, then?" I ask, my arms getting cold out of my sleeping bag so I shuffle myself back down and wriggle onto my side to I'm facing Sam. I see the cheeky boy who used to chase me down the road on his rickety old bike and think how hard this must be for him to just be finding out about a childhood friend like this. "Are you okay?"

He nods as he lies sideways, wiping away a tear.

"Your parents not only had to deal with the death of a child, but they had to carry on living for you. They had to pull themselves together in a time when they naturally would probably fall apart."

My stomach contracts. He's right. Maybe the distance I felt was not caused by me. Maybe they just didn't feel able to express themselves how they wanted to, because they had to stay strong for me. What if all this time I've been thinking the total opposite of how they felt? Ignoring them because I thought that made it easier for them. Finding excuses not to see them because I thought my presence was too difficult for them, that they only did it out of a sense of duty, when maybe it was never that way to start with.

"I'm surprised they didn't want to spend your birthday with you," James says, and shame floods my body, heating my neck. "I'm surprised they're okay with you coming on a trek like this, to be honest. Seeing how dangerous it could be."

"Well I didn't know, did I?" I say, defensively. "I thought I was booking a relaxing spa trip, not a jaunt to the middle of bloody nowhere."

May as well be totally honest with everyone now.

"And my parents did want to spend my birthday with me. They always do, and I always decline. Only this year, they wanted to throw a big party, remember? They'd started planning it and everything. I think they'd even invited loads of friends and family there to celebrate with me."

"And?" Sam probes.

"And I haven't celebrated my birthday since Frank died. How could I?" I say, my lip wobbling with the selfishness of my actions. "I can barely even get through the day, but to have to celebrate it while I'm here and he's not, it seems… I don't know, evil."

"Evil?" Oliver asks from across the sea of bodies. "Fliss, I can't imagine you ever being evil."

A snort fills the space left by his words and I don't need the light of the quickly dimming Northern Lights to illuminate who it is.

"I ran away from my parents this year because I didn't want a big party. I didn't even want to spend it with them because all they talk about is Frank, as though they wish it was him still alive and not me."

"But what if they only talk about him to *keep* him alive," Oliver asks. "What if they feel okay talking about him to you because you're the only one who understands how painful it is? What if they're only doing what they think is best and you're shutting them out because *you* find it too hard to talk about Frank? It's not like you were open and honest with us about him until you were pushed."

Oliver's words sink in like lead. He's right. I hate talking about my dead brother.

"But…" I have no comeback to that. "What are you, a shrink as well as a surgeon?"

Oliver laughs gently. It's weird that I really have no idea what he does day to day, yet I know how his lips taste and how his hands feel as they run through my hair.

"Not quite," he says.

"Paediatrics make him easy to talk to." It's Maya again, marking her territory.

As the last of the light from the Aurora Borealis becomes still and the sky closes in on me, I wish I could call my parents and apologise. These four strangers, being reunited with Sam, this trek, they've all made me overcome my fear of being open to the extent that I don't know why I was lying in the first place.

"Is that why you're fawning over the men of the trek?" Maya asks sharply, and a deathly hush falls over the night. If I didn't know there were others here, there would be no way of telling I was surrounded by people. "Because you're looking for a replacement male figure in your life? You know, some people make partners with whoever it is they're missing. I learnt that on Oprah, or maybe it was Jeremy Kyle. I can't quite remember now."

"I'm not fawning over all the men on the trek!" I splutter.

"I don't know," Maya continues, perhaps the darkness is giving her more confidence to say what she really feels now. "You've been flirting with James since we got to the airport, Oliver here didn't stand a chance when you decided to get your claws into him. And Sam and you have been sharing insider jokes since we met up with him at the first location."

I actually laugh. It's amazing to me that people can see me so differently to how I see myself. Yes, I thought James was attractive when we laid eyes on him, I still do, but I don't fancy him in the slightest, there's only so much spouting about nature and healing that I can take in a day and he's also way too young. Oliver came on to me, I think, though the feeling was mutual. *Was*? And Sam and I are old friends. I could list all the ways Maya has me wrong, but I'm already drained of energy. But there is one thing I need to put right.

"Nothing has happened between James and me."

"Ha!" Maya shouts. "Didn't look like it to me."

"Maya!" Oliver says, his voice as cold as my nose. "Give it a rest."

"It's okay Oliver," I say, not wanting him to fight my battles. "Maya, as you well know, I was naked in James' sleeping bag because I did something stupid and I was at risk of hypothermia, not because I was trying to have my wicked way with him. He was *literally* just saving my life. Which is twice now on this trip because he dragged me from the water when I fell into the cave, which I'm sure *you* remember?"

I can hear Bri releasing a breath. It's pitch black now and must be getting towards midnight. Finally she says: "Hypothermia can be bloody awful, can't it? But it wasn't James who dived down to get you when you fell in the cave, Fliss. Oliver was already halfway towards you before James and I saw what was happening. It was Oliver who pulled you from the water, not James."

*What?*

"Yep," James says. "We'll have to share the cape; Oliver was your hero that day."

Oliver grunts.

"Oliver? Why though?" I ask before I realise that he probably doesn't want to talk about this in front of the whole group. "Why have you been so friendly with me? Why come after me when you and Maya are together?"

"Were together," Oliver shouts out, sounding at the end of a very frayed tether. "We *were* together."

I hear a crunching from somewhere beside me where James is tucking into my M&Ms.

"I may as well just tell them, Maya, while everyone is being so honest about themselves" Oliver says, exasperated.

"Whatever," Maya huffs.

"I booked this retreat as a getaway from my life because things weren't going too well at home. My work is stressful and I'm never really *at* home, and when I was there — at home, I mean — I wasn't there in mind and body. Something needed to change, I know that. So I get why Maya felt the need to find solace in my best friend, I suppose."

There's a sharp intake of breath from James before he goes back to his crunching.

"We broke up over two months ago. I haven't seen her since I asked her to leave and she swiped all the electricals from my apartment on her way out. Then when I turned up at the airport two weeks ago, she was standing there with her rucksack pleading forgiveness."

"I was already booked on to the trip, why should I miss out when we paid for it ages ago?" Maya says, sourly.

"Because we agreed that I would come," Oliver says. "You know, to get over the fact my girlfriend and best friend had been cheating on me. Plus, I was the one who paid for it."

"Well I thought I'd come on the trip too, to surprise you."

"You certainly did that," Oliver laughs ironically.

"I wanted to make amends," she says, her voice shaky.

The night falls silent again. The darkness and quiet a form of therapy.

"But our relationship was well and truly over, Maya, and I told you that time and time again," Oliver says eventually.

"I thought maybe with a neutral territory we could

start afresh," Maya says, quietly. "You need me, look at what you've done since you've been here, who you've gravitated towards. A complete nutcase if ever there was one. You don't need that, Oliver."

"Wait," Oliver says, and now I'm starting to feel a little uncomfortable in the midst of this argument, as it's looking like news of our tryst may well be fodder in the knives they are throwing at one another. "That's not fair. I wasn't expecting to fall for someone while I was away."

*Wait, what?*

My insides slip around each other. My mouth has shrivelled up and my throat feels like the M&Ms have stopped there to have a little party before they're digested. I swallow twice in quick succession but they're not moving. Oliver is still talking but his words echo around my head.

"Fliss is the most sane, honest person I've met, Maya," he says. "She's everything you're not. She's not pretending to be a wilderness expert who can't go anywhere without her fake tan and eyelash extensions. She's not the one harping on about travelling and using sticks as toothbrushes, when the most adventurous place she's been is luxury log cabin in British Columbia. You're so fake, Maya, but you don't fool me anymore."

Maya starts to retort but Sam intervenes.

"Maybe we need to bring it down a bit here, hey guys?" Sam says, and I can see a small movement in the corner of my eye as though he's waving his arms uselessly in the dark.

"Happily," Maya says, huffing.

"Right," Oliver adds. "Sorry guys."

And we're back to lying in the pitch black in total silence, the only sound I can hear is the rushing of blood in my ears.

## Chapter Thirty-Eight
### Day Eleven

A gentle nudge to my shoulder has me wide-eyed and surprised at how bright it is.

"Fliss," Oliver whispers as he pokes my shoulder again. "Are you awake?"

My whole body groans as I try to shift from the prone position I must have nodded off in.

"What time is it?"

"Just gone five."

"Well then I'm not awake."

I try to roll over onto my side, away from Oliver and everything I don't want to talk about right now.

"I need to talk to you," he says, his touch less poky now. "Please Fliss, just a few minutes of your time? Then you can go back to sleep if you want to."

In actual fact I'm wide awake and fizzing with a mixture of rage and excitement.

"Okay," I say, shuffling back and trying to sit up. "My body feels like it's done ten rounds with Fury."

"Tell me about it."

"You should see him though!" I add, flexing a frozen bicep.

Oliver laughs. I unzip my sleeping bag, glad of the five layers of clothing I put on to sleep out under the stars. Truth be told, I'm starting to feel tired now, my joints ache and my toes tingle every morning. Though that could be the two weeks wild camping in the coldest part of the United Kingdom, rather than my impending retirement age. He offers me his hand and I take it, glad of the help to get to standing.

"You're a doctor," I say, wrapping his dry robe around me which I have definitely claimed as my own now, and grabbing my hair up into a top knot. I dread to think what kind of state it's in after nearly two weeks with no conditioner. "Are we at risk of losing our fingers and toes after being out here for so long?"

We head down towards the camp, carefully stepping over the sleeping bodies. Our tents looking appealing after a night under the stars. The campfire is smouldering when we get there, so I throw some more wood on it and poke at it with the blackened stick thrown by the wayside. Soon the flames start slithering through the smoke.

"Here, you're quite good at that," Oliver nods at the fire as he warms his hands together. "You'll not be losing any fingers or toes anytime soon. You're quite the adventurer, aren't you?"

I shake my head and sit down next to him, feeling the heat from his body on my arm.

"To tell you the truth, I wasn't even supposed to be

on this trek," I say, swirling the kettle around, happy to feel the movement of water inside. I place it over the flames. "I booked this holiday thinking it was a wellbeing escape. Apparently if I'd booked the right one, I'd be sunning myself in Ibiza right about now. With a cocktail of healthy stuff in one hand and a tanned Spaniard on the other."

Oliver coughs.

"Well thank goodness you didn't book that one then," he says, looking up at me through his eyebrows.

I make a noncommittal grunt and poke the flames to stoke them. I need a cuppa if I'm up this early. The coffee granules and powdered milk are in a container beside the fire. Lifting the lid, I fill two of the spring-water rinsed metal cups and decant a sachet into each mug.

As a watched pot never boils, especially if it's below zero when the fire was lit, I nod towards the waterfall. Oliver throws me a small smile and drags himself up off the seat. We walk together in silence to start with. It's not a difficult silence, though I'm certain I don't know how to break it. As we reach the edge, where James had brought us only days ago, I sit down on a dry patch of grass and dangle my legs over the side.

I can feel the coldness seep through into my backside but it's okay for a minute. Oliver sits down beside me, dropping his own legs over to match mine. We sit for a moment. Watching and listening to the water as it falls over the rocks and disappears into the crystal pool below. The sun has risen almost up out of its bed now and is painting everything with a glow as though it's shining through pink Perspex. The mossy hills shine a vibrant purple and the water sparkles like jewels.

"Thank goodness I didn't," I say, picking a blade of long grass and popping the newly released end of it into my mouth. The dew is cool and refreshing.

Oliver cocks his head and raises an eyebrow.

"Thank goodness I didn't book the retreat," I add.

"Yes?" The lilt in his voice tells me he wants me to go on and explain why I'm glad.

I do, but it's probably not for the reasons he's hoping to hear.

"Yes," I say. "If I'd ended up in a villa in Ibiza I would never have experienced this."

I open my arms wide and take in the beauty of the nature around me.

"And I would never have opened myself up to all the experiences I have done over the last two weeks. God, I was worried about going to the loo behind a bush on the first day. To think how far I've come makes me so proud of myself."

Oliver takes my hand in his and squeezes it.

"You should feel proud, look at you!"

I turn to look at him as I can't see myself.

"What do you mean?"

"Your whole demeanour has changed. You're holding yourself upright. You're practically glowing. All signs of how far you've come. And that's just from my professional opinion."

I snort, but he's right. I do feel at least a foot taller

than when I stepped on to the tarmac at Inverness ten days ago.

"But you also would never have met a rude, arrogant, idiot like me," he continues quieter now. "And for that I am really sorry."

"Thank you," I reply, slipping my hand back out of his.

"I just wanted to apologise for the way I was to you at the beginning of the holiday. I never meant to be rude, I was just so angry with Maya that I couldn't think straight. I never thought I would meet someone who would make me question every single relationship I'd ever had. Someone who made me realise that friendship should be the foundation for love, not sex. Not that the sex wasn't amazing. It was under a real-life waterfall! Christ. Anyway. I just wanted to say I'm sorry."

I think he might want me to tell him it's okay. That I forgive him his unkind behaviour, that Maya's turning up unannounced is somehow penance for how he treated everyone else. For leading me on and having sex with me. But the words clog in my throat until Oliver breaks the silence again.

"Well, I'll leave you to it, then. Good luck, Fliss, with whatever comes your way."

I watch his back as he makes his way to his tent.

## Chapter Thirty-Nine

"Last one off the edge is a rotten egg," James roars as he strips out of his trousers and runs naked towards the top of the waterfall.

Bri squeals and hops on one leg, tearing at her long johns and trying not to unbalance. Maya trekked down from the hill and disappeared off into her tent just as Oliver left me, neither of them have made a peep since. Just as Sam comes hurtling from his own tent, as naked as the day he was born, a flash of bravery hits me like a fist to my chest and I jump up from the log and tear off my own clothes. I'm still in the million layers that I slept in and feeling the heat of the sun start to make my skin prickle with sweat makes me long for the cool of the water below.

We all run to the edge of the waterfall, listening to the birdsong until our screams send them all soaring up above us, circling the waterfall like something out of Lord of the Rings. The thought of the film conjures up memories of Frank as he'd wave a stick at Saruman on the precipice of the fiery pit that was actually our flower border. Instead of pushing it away, down to the tips of my toes so I don't feel broken in two with the pain of it all, I smile at the moment and try to picture what would happen next. Namely a squashed prize tulip of Mum's or a damaged leek of Dad's.

Bri grabs at my hand and we take a leap together. Barging past the boys so we're tumbling through the air first. I scream as loud as my lungs will let me, Bri screeching in my ear at the same time. It makes my skin feel alive and my eyes prick with tears. Though that could be the air as we fly towards the rushing of the water. Our hands part as we reach the pool below and I fill my lungs with air before I hit the water. It's cold. Refreshingly so. But it's so much more than that. My body has become accustomed to the biting pain of the freezing water. It no longer feels like a weight around my neck, dragging me under with its icy fingers. It feels like a life preserver. Someone breathing air into my lungs. The kiss of life.

As I kick towards the surface, I see two streaks of pinky blue rush downwards past me. My head bobs above the water and I breathe, kicking my legs to take me away from the pounding waterfall and towards Bri where she's leaning with her elbows on the edge of the pool, her legs kicking out in front of her.

"I wish I could bottle this feeling and take it home with me," she says as I push my hair back from my face and lean next to her. "I'm so in love with this place, it's unreal."

## Wild Swimming

Our legs float out in front of us, the water crystal enough to be able to see my huge mass of pubes and my wobbly stomach and my boobs. Next to the svelte and smooth body of Bri I look like I could be her hairy auntie. But I don't care. I feel free. I thought the cold and the lack of a decent bed or coffee would make me close in on myself and hide away, eager to get it over with and get back home to my luxuries. But after a while it's done the opposite. I feel freer than I have done in forever. And I know it isn't just the lack of luxuries that have done that, my mindset is now somewhat different. But I have this wild expanse of Scottish Highlands to thank for that, and this group of people who I would mostly call friends. *Real* friends.

My heart stretches as I think of Oliver. And what might have been if he had trusted me with the truth in the first place. But Bri starts to talk again before it hurts too much.

"Maybe I can bottle a bit of this pool? Sell it off a pipette drop at a time. It is healing, after all. I could have a little side hustle as a dentist."

I laugh, my body sinking as my lungs deflate. With my arms still leaning on the edge, I kick my legs and my toes surface again.

"I thought you were done with side hustles?" I say. "Getting rid of the influencer persona and concentrating on Bri, the nature loving dentist."

"Certainly some things about nature I love more than others," she says, as we eye up the two men bobbing about in the water.

We laugh, and my head dips below the water as my lungs empty of air. As I surface again, this time swimming around to face Bri, treading water to stay afloat, her face looks relaxed.

"I don't think I need to get rid of the influencer," she says, tilting her head back to look at the beautiful blue sky above. The birds are still circling and I think they may be looking for casualties of the drop. They'll be looking for a lot longer as Sam and James swim towards us. "I think I just need to be more honest about who I am. I don't need to pretend anymore because this has shown me I am more than enough."

"Me too, Bri," I say. "Me too."

"What's going on here?" James asks, wiping his hand down his face. "Can we join in?"

I feel momentarily self-conscious of my nakedness, but it flees as quickly as it surfaces. Bri pushes off from her elbows and sinks down to her chin in the water, causing small waves to rock us all gently.

"I'm not sure," she says, turning to me. "What do we feel about conversing with waterfall *losers*?"

With the last word she flicks water into James' face with her fingers and swims past his body, her legs powering her back to the middle of the pool. James looks momentarily shocked, blinking to free his eyes of the assault from water. It doesn't take him long to twist his own body around and power after Bri, shouting something about revenge. Sam shakes his head at me and we tread water together for a moment, watching James as he reaches Bri and dunks her under.

"They suit each other," Sam says wistfully. "He's never bonded so well with someone on these trips before. And he's certainly had them flinging themselves at him, that's for sure."

"She's lovely," I say. And I secretly hope that something will happen between them, they both deserve it.

"How're you feeling this morning?" Sam asks, as we swim together slowly around the edge of the pool. "I was worried when I saw your empty sleeping bag up on the hill."

"I'm good, thanks," I reply, for once actually feeling it too. "I feel like I can finally breathe, you know? I was remembering Frank and I wasn't trying to run away from my memory. Does that sound cheesy?"

"Not at all." Sam shakes his head. "I was really sad to hear about what happened to Frank. He was a good friend when we were younger, we all had a laugh together, didn't we? But, Fliss, I'm glad you opened up last night. Holding all that guilt inside you must have been eating you alive. You've never been to blame, Felicity, your parents know that."

I look at Sam and his floppy pony-tail and smile.

"A lot of people leave this trek feeling like they're littering these beautiful islands with their unwanted baggage." He smiles back at me.

"So much for *not leaving a trace*, hey?"

Sam laughs.

"I don't think emotional baggage leaves a trace. Though imagine if it did! These highlands would be rife with bad energy and in need of a good soul cleanse themselves."

I flip over onto my back and let the sun warm my skin.

"Here," I say, my hands like flippers keeping me afloat. "That would make a great horror film! The Scottish Highlands come alive with peoples' negative energy as it rampages through the hills sucking the goodness from hapless holiday makers."

"What is it you do for a living again, Felicity?" Sam asks, manoeuvring himself so his body is upright.

"Investment banking," I say, laughing.

"Well it's wasted on your quite obvious pitching skills,"

I thump him gently on the arm, the momentum of the water hindering my movements.

"I like my job!" I say, my teeth starting to chatter. "It's fast paced and fun. And actually, I think I'm looking forward to getting back, which surprises me."

"That's great," Sam replies. "But I think we'd better be getting out now, your lips have gone a little blue and my fingers are stinging."

I look around the edges of the pool and wince as I remember where I left my clothes.

# Chapter Forty

"So, gang," James shouts over the roaring of the water as the boat bounces back across the sound to the mainland. "I think we can safely say that was a success, can't we?"

His eyes avoid Maya's stony glare and land on me and my easy smile. Our bags have been chucked on the bed of the boat, and even the spray from the water and the soaking wet hair dripping down my face can't tear the smile away. My chest is swelling like the ocean. My head as clear as the pools we have just waved goodbye to.

"It's changed my life, James," I shout back.

"Mine too," Oliver shouts from the back of the boat, his own face beaming and glossy with spray.

He gives me a smile, the dimple in his right cheek collecting seawater as he lifts his lips.

"I am so glad I came here and not the luxury villa in Ibiza you offer too," I shout as the boat gives a violent lurch and I grab hold of the side with white knuckles trying not to lose my breakfast.

Maya's head jerks towards me with a raised eyebrow.
*Oh, she didn't know about the alternative holiday either!*

"We're glad too," James says, as he hangs on the prow of the boat for dear life. "Even if I may end up in the middle of the sea before the trip is out!"

Bri shifts on the bench next to James, they're sitting almost touching, and the gap between them speaks volumes. Much more so than if they had been squashed together with their thighs rubbing. Bri's hair is messy and her eyes are aflame. She wraps her green rain coat around her body and splashes her feet in the puddles at the bottom of the boat.

"You know," I add, as the shoreline comes welcomingly into view and the waves mute themselves to a gentle rocking motion. "As much as this wellbeing holiday has been the making of me, I wish I had given my parents the chance to celebrate my birthday with me too. I have avoided them every birthday since I left home. But what Sam said about the pain they must have suffered in staying alive for me, it made me feel awful about the way I have treated them. I think I'll make it up to them when I get home. Maybe even organise a belated do with them."

The idea doesn't send chills down my spine as once it may have done. I can picture a large gathering and I don't want to run and hide. The fresh air and cold water swimming have done me a world of good.

The captain of the boat steers us around the rocky shoreline and heads towards a small wooden jetty where our minibus stands waiting like an old friend. Sam shifts his weight in the boat, grabbing the long, thick rope that's tied to the metal cleat and unwinding it. As the boat comes alongside the jetty Sam jumps onto the wood, taking the rope with him and pulling us gently towards him. He deftly ties the rope to the mooring on the jetty and heads up to the front of the boat to grab the second rope thrown to him by our Captain. When we're safely attached to the jetty and the boat is bobbing gently beside the wooden structure, James starts lifting out our bags and tents. They drip on to our heads with the water collected at the bottom of the boat, but everyone's eyes are on the minibus and the bittersweet knowledge that there is heating and comfortable seats waiting for us.

Maya steps over my feet and shirks James' offer of a helping arm. She is shooting herself in the foot by shrugging off Sam's offer too as the boat wobbles too much for her to find her footing. With a slip slide, and a moment where my heart was in my mouth, because as unkind as she has been, I don't want to see Maya end up in the sea, she makes it to dry land and hot foots it to the bus.

James helps Bri out next, as she grabs his hand the looks they share could light up the sky just like the Aurora Borealis. She makes it out the boat and stands on the jetty, lifting her bag from the pile.

"Leave those, Bri," Sam calls over his shoulder. "We'll load up the van."

Bri walks over to the edge of the jetty, leaving room for me to clamber out of the boat.

"Fliss," James calls to me, his hand ready and waiting. "Your turn next."

"It's Felicity," I say, realising with a bolt that there is no longer any need to pretend anymore. Felicity is who I've always been and there's no need to hide her away or reboot myself in order to fit in or forget. "My name is Felicity."

"Well then Felicity," James says with a wry smile. "It's time for you to disembark."


The hotel is just as grand as I remember it. I picture my claw footed bath and the little bottle of bubbles included in the pot of goodies and sigh a breath of relief as I climb off the minibus. My top is still damp from the crossing and my feet ache, and the cool wind from the ocean is whipping around my ankles in the carpark.

A great sense of happy exhaustion washes over me. Tears spring into my eyes and I try to wipe them away before Sam wraps his arm around my shoulder and walks through the sliding doors of Glasmakirk Hotel and Spa.

"Well done, Felicity," he says, squeezing me hard. "Not everyone could have done what you've done and still come to the same conclusion about your parents and your party as you did."

"Thanks Sam," I say. "It's not every day you risk life and limb on a wilderness trek to find yourself."

Maya storms past us, dragging her bag behind her and harassing the hotel receptionist who is already typing as fast as she can. James intervenes and steps in front of Maya, using his ever present charm to win back the receptionist's smile. Maya sounds as though she's going to self-combust as a result.

I feel Oliver walk up behind me and Sam quickly slips his arm away from me and goes to placate Maya. From the groan he lets out, Oliver is as glad to be thawing out inside the hotel as I am. Either that, or he's had enough of the whole thing now and just wants to be back at home, wherever home may be.

"How did I ever put up with all that childish behaviour?" he asks me, nodding at Maya who is grabbing her key from James.

"A pretty face and amazing boobs?" I offer.

Oliver huffs out an ironic laugh. "I am more discerning than that, I'll have you know. Not that long ago I was falling for someone who hadn't washed in days simply because she made me laugh and I could talk to her for hours at a time."

"Touché," I concede, my heart hammering.

We move towards the reception desk as James ushers us forward. James passes me a large key fob that I take gratefully.

"The rooms are yours for the night," James says to us all. "Feel free to use the facilities again, and this time the spa is up for grabs too. Go and massage those tent aches and pains out of your necks and steam the mud out of your pores. You've got the rest of the day today, and all of tomorrow. Our flight isn't until the evening."

James divvies out the rest of the keys.

"Oh, and we have a dinner tonight," he adds as we're heading off to the large staircase that dominates the space. "Please be ready for eight, and try to look smartish, we have a few surprises left in store."

Oliver grabs his key, and we head up the stairs to our rooms. I can feel the heat of his arm through his shirt sleeves as we occasionally bump into each other following the long corridors to our wing.

I can sense that neither of us want to get there because we're both walking at the pace of as snail.

"What do you think the surprise is?" he asks me as we pull open the door to our corridor.

"I hope it's some alcohol?" I laugh. "But I don't think I have any smart clothes, though from what I can remember I think I had a dress in the bag I left here. Maybe I can steam it out while I have a hot bath."

"The bath is the first thing I'm going to do too," Oliver says, slowing down at his door. "But you go ahead and use the bathroom first."

I look up at my door.

"Won't be quite as exhilarating as open water."

"Won't be quite as fun, either."

We stop and look at each other. So many unspoken words bounce between us, but I don't know how to say them. I'm all depleted. A husk now void of emotional energy; actually any energy.

"So," Oliver says, shifting his weight. "I guess I'll see you for dinner later?"

"Yes," I nod. "I guess you will."

I smile weakly and push open my door. Not turning back, I know Oliver will be watching, I don't need to see that to make it true.

# Chapter Forty-One

The corridor is dark and feels empty as I make my way down to dinner. My feet make no sound on the thick carpet, despite the heels and the fact my toes seem to be screaming in pain at being squashed into a shoe that's not a walking boot. Though as I looked at my poor feet in the bath they seemed to have shrunk a few sizes because the skin was all puckered and white. But perhaps, more likely, my skin had soaked up so much rain and ocean that it had started to hang off my skeleton like an old battered coat.

The bath I'd wallowed in had been so deep I was worried if I breathed too hard the water would cascade over the edges and soak the wood beneath. But it had been the most wonderful bath I've ever had. It got me thinking that maybe I need to trek more often as it makes me appreciate the luxuries I'm used to.

I didn't really need persuading though, I'd already

decided to make my holidays less relaxing. Spa holidays are still going to feature, of course, but there's so much more that nature can offer that a spa simply can't.

As my skin had turned wrinkly, and my eyes had started to droop, I'd dragged myself out of the bath and wrapped my aching body in a huge fluffy white dressing gown. There was no way I was going to lay on the bed, though it was calling me with its ciderdown and fluffy pillows. I'd miss dinner if I so much as *looked* at my bed, so instead I'd sat at the desk at the window of my room and torn a piece of paper from the pad supplied. The window overlooked the clifftop and the ocean below. A tug at my heart strings had pulled me towards the dark expanse of water. I'm now drawn to it like a drug, knowing it won't always hurt me. But if that's now going to be my addiction of choice, then I'm happy with that. It's healthy and makes me feel alive.

I'd scratched a letter out with a plastic pen that I had found hidden at the bottom of my bag, before I had spotted an ink fountain pen in a marble stand right next to the pad I'd torn the paper from. My brain had taken a while to realise what it was, as I'm not used to my pens needing filling. But I had already finished writing by the time I had noticed it. The letter is to my parents, I'm not sure if I'm going to post it, but it felt good to get all of the words I want to say to them out of my head and down on to paper.

A woman sits behind the reception desk, her name badge pinned to her white shirt reads, Anna. She looks up at me and smiles as she hears me approaching.

"Good evening, miss," she says in her sing-song highlands accent. "You look beautiful. The dining room is just along the corridor."

"Am I late for dinner?" I ask, wondering why it's so quiet.

"Not at, no," she smiles again. "You're just in time."

I wobble down the corridor to the room we'd all eaten in before the trek. The haggis and trifle and deep fried offerings seem like a million years ago now, not just ten days. The Felicity walking up to the door is certainly a different person. I chew my bottom lip as I think back over how reserved I had been, projecting a sunny persona to hide away years of sadness. It's not going to be easy to shift my thinking from negative to positive, but at least I've started. I take a deep breath and push open the door.

At first I think I've come to the wrong room. It's dark, and from the sounds of it, empty. I lean back and peer round at the signage just outside. Definitely the dining room, but maybe there are more than one. Then I hear a shuffle and I look back inside, my eyes adjusting to the gloom. Someone sniffs. Someone giggles under their breath. Then a loud voice shouts *now* and makes me jump out of my skin.

"SURPRISE!"

A cheer rises up in the room as someone flicks a switch and the light illuminates my fellow trekkers, dressed to the nines, holding what look deliciously like champagne glasses.

"Oh my," I say, staggered, taking a glass that is handed to me discreetly by a staff member.

I sip it, using the time to scan my eyes around at the others in the room. Bri looks so luminous in a gorgeous midi dress that Maya fades into the background in her bodycon. James and Sam have scrubbed up and suited up and Sam's hair looks like it's been washed for the first time in a while as it's grown in body enough to surround his head like a fluffy halo. And Oliver? I look around, my heart in my mouth at the idea he hasn't come to my surprise party. But he's here, standing behind two wing-back chairs, in a dark suit that makes his eyes look like coal. I feel a raw stab of wanting right in the depths of my belly, swiftly followed by a cool trickle of shock. For sitting in the wingback chairs, right in front of Oliver, are my parents.

"Mum? Dad?" I say, my feet walking towards them before my brain has really processed that they're here. "What? How?"

They get up. Mum in her best dress that she only ever gets out at friends' daughters' weddings. Dad in what he calls his Sunday best, but seeing as we never went to church it's basically some dark green cords and a paisley shirt that Mum will have ironed.

"Oh Felicity," Mum says, her arms outstretched to gather me up, her eyes glistening. "Look at you."

I feel self-conscious in my navy blue, ankle length dress that I'd only packed for what I assumed would be late-night dinners overlooking the Ganges but had actually stayed scrunched up in the bottom of my bag and had to be steamed in the bathroom with the heat of my bath. I slip out of my heels and loose two inches of height, and all at once feel much better now I can scrunch my toes up in the thick carpet.

"I've had ten days away in the wilderness," I say by means of excuse, running my hands over my huge hair.

"You can tell," Dad says, misty eyed himself. "You look wonderful."

He steps closer and they both take me in their arms. Muffled talk of happy belated birthday spill from my parents as easily as their tears. Someone takes my glass from my hand, freeing me up to squeeze Mum and Dad as hard as I can, my own tears flowing too. I hug them for all the hurt I've caused them over the last nineteen years, for the tears they've held back and the words they couldn't say. But most of all I hug them because I love them and without them I would not still be here.

"I'm sorry," I whisper into Mum's hair.

They pull away, red streaked faces and puffy eyes. Mum leaves her hands on my shoulders, looking at me the way she does with her kind face that used to make me wince because I didn't think I deserved it.

"I'm sorry," I say again, looking between them. "I'm so, so sorry."

Mum doesn't even try to stop her tears now and Dad sniffs his back but it's a small gesture against a tidal wave.

"We're sorry too," Mum sniffs. "There are things we wish we could have done differently. But we have the rest of our lives to talk about that."

"And talk about Frank," Dad adds, his forehead

creasing with what I can only imagine is the expectation of me batting talk of my brother away.

I nod frantically, words are stuck in my throat, held back by the emotion, but I want them to know that it's okay to say his name in front of me.

"But for tonight," Mum adds, opening up her arms and reminding me that we're not alone here in this opulent dining room in the middle of Scotland. "We're here to celebrate you and your birthday."

I wipe at my face with my hands, all of a sudden aware that everyone is looking at me, but my tears are so heavy that I just end up spreading them further. I turn to the rest of my fellow trekkers.

"You've all seen me looking much worse," I say, laughing through the mistiness at their blurred faces.

Oliver steps forwards and hands me back my drink which I gulp down in two great mouthfuls and a nod to the waiter for another. I'm allowed. Though without alcohol for the trek I can feel my head start to swim already. Oliver moves away to allow James and Sam to get close to me, over their heads I can see the staff beginning to bring out the starter platters and lay them on the huge table. I'm not sure if I can think about eating now, so I sip my fresh glass and turn my attention back to the tour guides.

"How did you get them here?" I ask, nodding to my parents who are getting rather cosy with Oliver by the fire.

Sam looks at his feet and shuffles a bit. "We, well *I*, have a bit of a confession to make."

## Wild Swimming

"What?" I ask, looking between him and James, though James' attention is drawn away from me to where Bri is hovering by the food.

"Your parents got in touch with me," Sam says, shrugging awkwardly.

"*What?*" I say again.

Sam puts a warm arm around my shoulders and James takes this as his opportunity to sidle off and talk to Bri, their body language sensual and warm as he slides up to her, tucking a strand of her hair behind her ear. I turn my attention back to Sam.

"Seems your parents are better at navigating our website than you are," he says, teasing. "Your dad emailed us a day or so after you booked. They recognised the name of the guy who owns the business. He'd seen my picture on the site you'd shown him and recognised me from back in the day, recognised the name of the guy who owns *Hidden Holidays* too. So they contacted him, who, in turn, contacted me. Your Dad and your mum asked me to keep an eye on you, told me they were worried. They never mentioned Frank, I don't think they wanted to drop that on me over email."

I can't believe it. Sam looks at me and must see something in my face that makes him speed up his words.

"It wasn't a long email," he continues anxiously. "Barely a few lines. Just letting them know it was you, and that they wanted to make sure you were okay. They *knew*, Felicity. They knew all along that you weren't okay, and I think this was the only way they felt they could look after you this birthday. I radioed them after you told us about

Frank, flew them out here for our return. They were so excited."

"Oh." I breathe out the word, feeling pain flutter in my chest at the kindness of my parents.

It kind of makes sense now, the way Sam gathered me up into the folds of the group, the way he watched over me, the number of times he tried to talk to me about my parents and I steered the conversation away.

"They did state their surprise at you picking a wilderness trek over a wellness spa, though," Sam says, his nostrils flaring in amusement.

"Ha bloody ha," I joke. Behind Sam I see Oliver pick a breadstick up and dunk it in taramasalata. "But I'm glad I did. For so many different reasons."

Sam follows my line of sight.

"What's happening between you two?" he asks.

"Nothing." I shake my head, feeling sad and happy and confused. "It's probably for the best isn't it, holiday romance and all that."

From the corner of the room Maya glances up from her plate, looking past her ex and directly at me.

"Will you excuse me for a minute, Sam?" I say, as he squeezes my shoulder and slides his arm away.

Maya eyes widen as I approach her. I think she thought I was heading for Oliver.

"May I?" I ask, indicating the empty chair next to her.

She nods and I sit.

"If I had known about you and Oliver," I start, thinking there's no point in beating around the bush anymore. "I wouldn't have done what I did. But that's not on me. You two should have been open and honest from the start. Wasn't that the whole point of this trip?"

Maya nods again. "I'm sorry."

"Thank you." I'm taken aback by the smallness of her voice and the way she's hidden in the corner.

"I wasn't thinking," she says. "I was so obsessed with the idea of winning him back that I didn't care who I hurt. Him and me included. I don't really think I *want* him back though."

"Right." I don't really know how to answer that. Not after everything she's done.

"Not because of Oliver," she adds quickly. "He's perfect. But I'm not ready to settle down yet. I want more, I just don't know how to get it."

She looks down at her sad plate of half a cracker and a small bunch of grapes and I'm overwhelmed with sorrow for her. At the beginning I thought she was the great explorer, but she was hiding more than most of us. I reach out my hand and touch her arm.

"You'll get there, Maya," I say. "You just need to start living for yourself and not worry about what others think."

She snorts. "I'm not sure you are allowed to dish out that kind of advice after one day of following it yourself. But thank you, Fliss."

I get up and walk away, I don't feel the need to stay and placate her anymore.

"Oh, and Fliss," she says as I'm walking away. "I'm really sorry you fell down that hole."

I stop abruptly and spin on my heels.

"What?"

"The sea cave? I only meant to scare you, to make you retreat back into your shell. I didn't mean for you to fall in. I'm so sorry."

"Apology accepted." I walk away. Towards the man who gave me the courage to be myself and then whisked it all out from under me.

"Oliver," I say, looking up at him as he stands beside the roaring fire.

"Felicity." He puts his plate on the mantel piece and takes my hands. "You're amazing. Don't ever forget that."

"Thanks," I smile, lifting one shoulder in a small shrug.

We stay for a moment, hand in hand, but I pull away before I sink into his eyes and the taste of his lips that I can imagine if I think too hard.

"I need to go be with my parents," I say, watching his face fall for just a fraction of a second before he pulls a smile back up.

"Of course," he says, gathering me in a quick embrace. "You go and spend time with them."

I lean up on tiptoes and kiss his freshly shaven cheek, the scent of his aftershave forever ingrained in my memory. And before I can think about it, I grab a biro from the pen pot on the mantel piece next to Oliver's half-eaten crab pate amuse bouche and scribble my number on the curve of his palm.

"If you're ever in Camberwell," I say, folding his

hand closed moments too late to think about the possibility of sweat disintegrating my scrawl.

"If I'm ever in Camberwell," he replies, the corner of his lips twitching into a smile.

And I leave him to his platter and his fire and I go and join Mum and Dad and Sam by the food before they steal all the trifle.

# Chapter Forty-Two
## Three weeks later

London is glistening with rain as I run from the bus stop and dash towards my house. The smell is fresh, clean, ripe with possibility. I'm still used to the damp and cold now, even though I've been home from Scotland for nearly three weeks. But my paperwork isn't as hardy as I am, especially in an M&S carrier bag that I had to borrow from one of the receptionists as my own handbag wasn't fit for A4 purpose. So, I duck my head and run the two roads over.

"Hello Skye," I say as I shut the door behind me, shaking my coat out. "Have you had a good day."

Skye doesn't reply, she just wraps herself around my ankles and purrs loudly. It's nice having someone to come home to, she makes the house feel lived in and loved. I step over a puddle that she's left by the front door and drop my bag and coat safely away from the smell. She's a rescue cat and was the first thing I did when I got back, I like to think we'll rescue each other but no doubt she'll have me wrapped around her little paw beans quicker than I can say Whiskas. Fully housetrained according to her bio, but I guess she was allowed to embellish her sales pitch as much as the rest of us.

It's been a weird few weeks. Work is like I never left, though *I* feel like a totally different person. As though old Felicity has been left up in the Highlands, reborn and returned to London with a little less baggage and a lot of impetus to redeem myself. Even my neighbours have started to say hi when they see me over the hedge in the front garden.

My new therapist has called it my breakthrough, but I think it's more than that. It's my *life*. My grief. My trek. The fact I can enjoy all of the above and not feel guilt looming over me like a black cloud. I have had the thought on a number of occasions, as I settled back into my routine and my nice coffee, that maybe someone stronger than me wouldn't have needed to throw themselves into the wilderness to have that sort of epiphany. That maybe regular therapy and a good set of friends would have done the same over time. But I've only just started out with both of those so I'm not being too hard on myself.

My phone shrills at me from my coat pocket. It's Bri. She's wondering if she should wear her trainers for a night out tonight, casually dropping in that she's meeting James before he heads back to London to pick up another motley crew of trekkers. I grin at my phone and reply with trainers are a great way to run home quickly if they want to make the most of his time left in Wales. She's quick with a wink emoji. I put my phone down and go and flick the kettle on. Bri is in regular contact, she's setting up her own dental practice in her home village and is the only dentist I know whose clients will get their own Insta snap at each check-up. Dentinsta Bri. She's living the dream and finding her feet and has dropped James' name into our daily texts on more occasions to just be general chit chat! I'm glad things are working out for Bri and James, but it makes me a little sadder that I've heard nothing from Oliver. Not even a text to say hi. Nothing. Nada. Zip. Zilch.

Why didn't I write my home address or even my email address? Or why didn't I write my number on a napkin or an actual piece of paper? I like to think that he was simply too sweaty to read the digits and they ran off his hand before he had the chance to memorise them. My heart wrenches whenever I think about the opportunity we missed. No doubt he's moved on from the trek and Maya and me already. Back to oncology and the children who really need him, back to caring for others the way he cared for me the whole bloody trek. I hadn't realised while I was in it just how much Oliver made me feel the bravery I needed to feel to just live amongst a group of strangers. He did it with such poise and grace and subtlety that I was unaware of how much of a cheerleader he had been. The tent drinking, making me run down the hill, walking with me, the looks we shared that buoyed me, giving me the strength to carry on when all around me was falling apart. Maybe he feels his job was done there in the Highlands. Clean break and all that.

Sam *has* made the effort. He found me on my socials, which were gathering dust but are now there as a reminder to me that there is a world beyond my four walls. Also, I wanted a sneaky stalk through them to try and find Oliver, but either that's not his real name, or he is so private because of his job that no one can find him. Sam came to visit my parents on his time off between treks, he helped them sort out their borders because Dad's back isn't what it was. Mum and Dad both appreciated the chance to talk to Sam about Frank, they'd nudged me when he left their living room and Mum made some weird gesture that could have been a cross between her snogging thin air and choking on the sausage rolls she'd made for the occasion. I'd told her about Morag and she'd shrugged sadly, probably wracking her brains to think of my next suitor.

I pour some food for the cat while I'm waiting for the kettle to boil. Mum and Dad have been great with me—matchmaking aside—treading carefully and allowing me to take things at my own pace. I may have ripped the plaster clean off up in Scotland, but the rest of the healing needs to be slow and steady. Having them nearby, once again feels like an auspicious, reassuring joy that I am allowed to revel in. Rather than hiding away when I see them through the glass at the front door, I open it up and usher them in with hugs and tea and more hugs.

I thank my organised morning self for cooking bourguignon in the slow cooker, as the whole house smells like beef and red wine. My stomach lets out a gurgle which I hush with a Garibaldi as I traipse back through the house. I grab my work on the way up the stairs and throw it into the office to look at tomorrow. It may well be a Saturday, but I have a big takeover next week and I'm going to boss it. I smile at the thought, but pull the door closed on it for this evening as it's Friday night and I have to get ready for a date with my sofa, some beouf, and the cat.

A couple of hours later, as the sun disappears behind the world for the night, I emerge from my bedroom bathed, no-make up, and dressed comfortably in a pair of slouchy jeans and a Breton top. I throw my wet hair up in a messy bun and head down to butter some of the crispy French loaf I picked up from the supermarket on my way home. Skye is pawing at the kitchen door, but she has a cat flap so I ignore her with the hope that she will find it before she makes another puddle. She's lazy and wants to get to the garden without having to go the long way around. She skulks off and I hear the clatter of the flap a moment later.

Checking the timer on the slow cooker, I pour myself a glass of wine, ignoring the recently boiled kettle. It's cool and refreshing and goes down very easily as I relax into my evening. I stir the dinner, dipping the torn off crust from the loaf in the sauce and eating it all in one go. My phone pings again. Smiling to myself at what mischief Bri is planning now, I go and retrieve it from the table. The lock screen illuminates the new message and my whole world stumbles forwards.

## Chapter Forty-Three

*Do you remember lying under the stars looking up at the Big Dipper?*

The number is unknown, but the way the world is spinning around without me is a sure sign it's from the man I thought had forgotten me. I stare at the screen for a moment, as I'm flung back to the first night under the stars. Inverleck River. The sloping, mossy hill behind the water. The smell of the air so clean, the crackle of the fire so loud I could almost be back there now. I would enjoy it this time around, instead of the heavy weight of guilt that had made me shut my eyes and miss the constellations.

*I remember you saying that you could look up at the sky and feel close to someone even though they were a thousand miles away.*

I type frantically, wanting to read more. To feel more. I have no idea if it definitely is Oliver, but if it's not then whoever has just texted will be as confused as I am right now. When I think back to how Oliver had made the distance between him and his family seem small, his words now seem laced with possibility, with romance, with adventure. My skin is rippling with excitement.

*Are you somewhere you can look up at the sky, right now, Felicity Taylor?*

My head rushes with the sweet feeling of one too many G&Ts on a warm summer's day. I close my eyes to stop the swaying. To feel the feelings triple fold as they turn around in my chest.

*I've opened my curtains* I reply, lifting the blinds at the kitchen sink, but all I can see is my pink cheeked smile staring back at me.

Just holding the phone in my hand and seeing the scrolling dots of a reply makes me feel like Oliver is here with me in my kitchen. I look again out the window, leaning over the sink, with a hand blocking out the recessed lights behind me. It's not enough, the glare is blocking out most of the stars, and the street lights are doing the rest.

*I can see Orion's Belt. Tell me you can see it too.*

I don't bother with shoes as I rush to the front door and try to wrack my brains as to what the belt looks like.

*Look south for three stars in a vertical row.* Oliver adds, reading my thoughts.

A cold blast of wet air hits me as I step into my front garden, my feet are immediately damp with the grass, but I don't care. I search the sky, but all I can see are clouds as the rain hits my eyeballs.

*Too many clouds.* I type.

*Walk a bit further out,* he replies.

I do as he says. Walking back across the lawn to the

tiled path and the lavender bushes that line all the way to the gate, my eyes firmly fixed on the cloudy sky. I turn and walk backwards, looking over the roof as I get further away from the house. I can't remember which way due south is. Still too cloudy to see anything remotely starry. My backside hits the closed gate and I crane my neck as far as I can to see over the chimney pots.

It's no use. I go to reply but there's a message already waiting for me.

*Try looking in the other direction.*

So, I turn, and am blinded by a bright light shining right in my eyes.

"Oh, sorry," a familiar voice says, and I hear three small clicks and the night vanishes behind the lights still burned into my retina.

I don't breathe. As though my breath will blow away this moment that I'm not sure is real.

"Oliver?" I say, as my eyes start adjusting back to the dark.

He's there, his silhouette as broad and tall as I remember, and the breath expels from my lungs as I realise just how achingly familiar a man Oliver actually is. Though different too; cleaner all round, neater around the edges, no beard to hide his jawline and his lips. And three headlamps around his forehead in a vertical line of silvery bulbs.

"Hi Felicity," he says, dropping his chin and looking up at me through his thick lashes.

"You're Orion's belt?" I ask, the lamps making more sense now.

"I forgot how powerful these are," he says, one shoulder shrugging, his eyes not leaving mine.

My nose tickles as my eyes start to prick. There's a little wooden gate between us but Oliver takes a step towards me, tentative, and then he's reaching out his hands and they're around me pulling me closer to him. I lean into his chest, breathing in the scent of him through his damp jumper, listening to his racing heart as it thumps against my ear.

"Oh, Felicity," he says, filling his chest with air. "Every time I picked up my phone I wanted to message you. To tell you how sorry I was for not being truthful. But I didn't know what to say, and the longer I left it the harder it was to write."

I don't move. I can't. I curl my eyes closed and focus on the movement of Oliver's chest as he breathes. I'm in the Highlands again, up the hill at Malfar Caves. The moment before we were interrupted by Sam and my heart races at the memory and the feel of the man beside me.

"And turning up here was easier?" I ask, my face still buried in Oliver's jumper.

"Yes," he sighs, his breath tickling my hair and sending ripples down my neck. "Because I can see you. I spent two whole weeks being right there beside you and this felt more natural."

He leans down and kisses my forehead, his lips warm and soft. I move back so I can look at him. His eyes are wide, dark pools, searching my face, my body, landing on my bare feet and his lips curl into a smile.

"Ever prepared," he says, smiling.

"Over prepared," I return, nodding to his forehead.

He reaches over the gate and takes my hands in his. The rain is heavier now, pelting down on our heads, but I can hardly feel it. Oliver's hair is plastered to his head, a small curl falls over the top torch, dripping with water onto our fingers.

"I know we've only known each other a short while," he says, linking his fingers through mine and holding our hands up in front of our bodies, thumbs stroking mine. "But you've totally taken my breath away. It's no excuse, I know, but that's what flummoxed me back in Scotland. The way you looked at me made all rational thoughts flop right out of my brain. But I'm so sorry for not telling you about my past with Maya. And if you'll let me, I'd love to get to know you a little bit more now you're home."

"I think that sounds like a perfect idea," I whisper.

I look at our hands, soaking wet and cold. I look up at Oliver's face, the face that got me through every single day on our trek. And the man behind the face. The kind, caring, man who puts the needs of others above his own when it actually comes down to it. I swallow. Not quite believing. Oliver slips a hand from mine and with a thumb strokes away a tear I didn't even know was falling, my face is so wet with rain. He moves the thumb down to my lips and I part them slightly, my intake of breath loud enough to hear over the storm that is brewing overhead.

Though the sky around us is huge, the stars infinite, it is just Oliver and me in this moment. As though we are the only two in the world right now. I lift a hand to his and trace his fingers with my own, linking them, drawing them away from my face. Tilting my face upwards, Oliver's eyes look heavy, his own breath ragged, he leans down and bashes my head with his lamps.

We laugh, pulling back from each other. Oliver tugs at the rubbery band holding them tightly to his head.

"Not again," he whispers, throwing them to the floor. "Not again."

With an urgency Oliver pushes the gate open and steps inside the garden, careful to avoid my toes. He lifts my chin with his right hand, his thumb moving gently up my jawbone and I think my legs are going to fail me as he brings his other arm around my waist. A thunderclap cracks up above us and as the lightning flashes, illuminating Oliver for that split second, I count my lucky stars that our paths crossed in the way that they did.

"Will we ever kiss when we're not soaking wet?" I ask, my lips a fraction away from Oliver's.

"We have forever to find out," he says, moving his body so I can feel it next to mine. "But let's not wait."

And he kisses me under the night sky and the millions of stars that have followed us home.

# Acknowledgments

Wild Swimming wouldn't exist without the incredible support and encouragement of so many people, and I am beyond grateful to each and every one of you.

Firstly, a huge thank you to my brilliant agent, Tanera Simons, and the wonderful Laura Heathfield at Greenstone Literary Agency, for believing in this book and guiding it every step of the way. Your enthusiasm and dedication mean the world to me.

A heartfelt thanks to Mary Darby, who sold the first rights to Lexa, my fabulous editor in Germany. You got the ball rolling, and I couldn't have asked for a better champion of this story. Lexa, I'm so grateful for your insight, patience, and encouragement with the German edition.

To Spotify, thank you for transforming Wild Swimming into an audiobook so beautifully. Hearing the story come to life in such a brilliant way has been an absolute joy.

My deepest thanks goes to my mum and dad, whose unwavering love and support have been my constant anchor. I couldn't have done this without you. To my brothers, your belief in me have meant everything, and to my daughter, whose light and boundless spirit inspire me daily—you're the reason that I'm chasing my dreams.

A special shout-out to my old team in Social Care, who put up with me living a double life as I juggled writing and work. I miss you all more than you know.

Finally, to everyone who has supported me, read my work, and shared in this adventure—thank you. Wild Swimming is for you.

# About the Author

Kate is the best-selling author of uplifting book-club fiction. Short-listed for the Romantic Novelists' Association award for New Writers, Kate started writing as a child and never stopped. With a degree and master's in psychology and therapy, it's the humanity of the characters that lead Kate's plots.

Kate is successfully both traditionally and self-published. WILD SWIMMING is her third book, and it has been translated into other languages and audio.

Kate loves Irn-Bru and macarons and can often be found with both, as she ferries her daughter back and forth to the local stables.

## PLAIN SAILING

### One week, one yacht, one fake boyfriend—and a boatload of secrets.

Wren, Quinn, and Verity have been inseparable since their school days, and now, nearly twenty years after Wren first stepped into the enchanting world of Chez Vincent—Verity's idyllic family home—they're back on the stunning south coast for Mama & Papa Vincent's vow renewal. A week on a luxurious yacht, sailing the Dorset coast with friends, family, and endless champagne—what could possibly go wrong?

Plenty, it turns out.

Wren has been keeping secrets. Big ones. Like the fact all's not well at her prestigious architectural firm. And Noah—the so-called 'boyfriend' the Vincents have sweetly invited as a surprise? He's actually her work rival, the insufferable thorn in her side... and very much *not* her boyfriend.

Trapped together on the yacht, Wren scrambles to keep up the charade. But as the sea air works its magic and Noah starts acting less like an enemy and more like the perfect plus-one, Wren begins to wonder—what if the biggest lie of all is the one she's been telling herself?

Also by Kate Galloway

**Sailing, secrets, and unexpected sparks collide in this irresistible tale of second chances and self-discovery.**

Printed in Dunstable, United Kingdom